★★★
BLACKTHORN
THUNDER ON MARS

BLACKTHORN
THUNDER ON MARS

Created and Edited by
VAN ALLEN PLEXICO

Illustrations by Chris Kohler

WHITE ROCKET BOOKS

David –
Lords of
Light!!
Demon
Dogs!!

Van

BLACKTHORN: THUNDER ON MARS

Copyright © 2011 by Van Allen Plexico

Interior illustrations copyright © 2011 by Chris Kohler

Cover art, design and logo copyright © 2011 by James Burns

"Bastion of the Black Sorcerer" copyright © 2011 by Van Allen Plexico
"Cradle of Atlantis" copyright © 2011 by Mark Bousquet
"The Minefields of Malador" copyright © 2011 by Bobby Nash
"Indistinguishable from Magic" copyright © 2011 by James Palmer
"City of Relics" copyright © 2011 by Sean Taylor
"Quest for the Eye" copyright © 2011 by Joe Crowe
"The Ghosts of Acheron" copyright © 2011 by I. A. Watson
"Epilogue: Red Planet Blues" copyright © 2011 by Van Allen Plexico

A White Rocket Book
www.whiterocketbooks.com

ISBN-13: 978-0-9841392-6-2
ISBN-10: 0-9841392-6-5

First printing: December 2011

0 9 8 7 6 5 4 3 2 1

CONTENTS

INTRODUCTION

VAN ALLEN PLEXICO

A warrior brandishing a sword of energy. A princess hurling bolts of magic. A monstrous fighter roaring his rage.

If the trio on the cover of this book looks somehow familiar to you, that's not entirely surprising. Part of the inspiration for this project came from the early 1980s Saturday morning cartoon, *Thundarr the Barbarian*. (Heck, even the "Thunder" in this book's subtitle is an appreciative nod to that show.) Ahead of its time in many respects, it was a post-apocalyptic adventure that boasted art and character designs by none other than Jack "King" Kirby himself, during his "move to Hollywood and earn actual money" period. In brief, as the show's voice-over intro went, in the then-distant year 1994 a "runaway planet" brought about global disaster and led many centuries later to the rise of a new civilization dominated by wizards and warriors, who used the remnants of lost technology to dominate their strange new world.

For a number of years I considered doing a novel or anthology that would touch on similar themes, but the whole thing never quite clicked.

Meanwhile, I had the opportunity in 2009 to edit new paperback and hardcover editions of Edgar Rice Burroughs' John Carter of Mars trilogy of novels. Plunging into Burroughs' world of Barsoom, with its wonderful action and adventure and romance, provided another layer of inspiration for a science fiction storyline—but, again, the entire picture simply would not flesh itself out in my head.

Another element entered the equation the following year, when I happened to pick up the two trade paperback volumes of Kirby's *Eternals* comics reprints from Marvel. Jack had been into the whole "ancient astronauts" and "Aztec space gods" thing when he wrote and drew those comics back in the mid-1970s, and they're just as fun as they sound.

The missing and final piece of the puzzle fell into place when I was recently given—of all things—a new copy of Carl Sagan's classic *Cosmos* hardcover, the book that accompanied his wonderful, inspirational television show from the early 1980s about science and astronomy that had meant so much to me as a kid.

Experiencing Sagan's imminently-readable style was enjoyable enough, but the real revelation came when I happened upon a quote he included from the Popul Vuh of the Maya. In only a brief few lines, it talked about "first men" and sorcerers and gods on Earth, and it evoked all sorts of imagery in my mind that seemed straight out of Kirby and the *Eternals* comics and—of course—*Thundarr*.

At that moment it all came together.

Well, except for one more thing: I didn't want this story to happen on Earth.

Post-apocalyptic Earth has been done and re-done *ad infinitum*. Why couldn't this story—the story of heroes fighting for justice and freedom in a world in ruins—happen someplace else?

Thinking of John Carter and Barsoom, I had my answer. It didn't hurt that I'd recently enjoyed Dan Simmons's excellent *Ilium* and *Olympos* novels, set on a far-future Red Planet. Throw in a little of Jack Vance's *Dying Earth* and Niven and Pournelle's *Lucifer's Hammer*, and swap the brave-but-dense Thundarr character out for someone who was a bit more intelligent, resourceful, contemporary, and interesting—more of a "Nick Fury," in short—and the package was set.

All that remained was a name, and while I favored "Blackstar," Joe Crowe pointed out that such a character already existed in another animated series from the *Thundarr* era—to my vast surprise. (I'd never heard of that cartoon, and had actually borrowed the name from a Lin Carter novel title!) Cover artist extraordinaire James Burns tossed out "Blackthorne," and after I trimmed off the Clavellian final "e," I was happy with it.

The stories you will find in this volume came flooding in quite rapidly from a talented group of writers all seemingly very excited to work in this universe—and their enthusiasm shows in every single one. Each was written in the unique style of its author, and no effort

INTRODUCTION

was made on my part as editor to homogenize them. Part of the fun is seeing the different take that each writer brings to these characters and this world.

And speaking of "seeing" this world—how lucky we were to secure the talents of Chris Kohler for the six interior illustrations. The regular artist on my Sentinels superhero novels (a fact for which I am continuously grateful), Chris relished the opportunity to get to do something a little different here, with this setting and these characters. I think his enjoyment radiates from every picture he created, and he has done his finest work to date on this book.

So there you are—a brief glimpse into the origins of John Blackthorn and his intrepid companions, and how they came to be where you will find them as the first story opens. My thanks go out to those who helped make this book a reality: James Burns for the awesome and radiant cover art and design; all the writers who contributed stories and/or ideas, including Mark Beaulieu, Mark Bousquet, Joe Crowe, Bobby Nash, James Palmer, Sean Taylor, Danny Wall, and Ian Watson; and the New Pulp community in general, who have greeted this project from the very start with nothing but enthusiasm and anticipation. I hope it meets (and maybe exceeds!) their expectations.

And of course as always I thank my wife Ami and my two daughters, Maddie and Mira, for their continued love and support—and for enduring my watching and re-watching of the *Thundarr* series in preparation for this work.

Now—let's get going! The servants of the First Men are on the move, and only bold heroes such as John Blackthorn and his two companions can save us...!

"The first men to be created and formed were called the Sorcerer of Fatal Laughter, the Sorcerer of Night, Unkempt, and the Black Sorcerer...They were endowed with intelligence, they succeeded in knowing all there was in the world. When they looked, instantly they saw all that is around them, and they contemplated in turn the arc of the heaven and the round face of the earth... [Then the Creator said]: "They know all...what shall we do with them now? Let their sight reach only to that which is near; let them see only a little face of the earth! ... Are they not by nature simple creatures of our own making? Must they also be gods?"

--From The Popol Vuh of the Quiche Maya

"Any sufficiently advanced technology is indistinguishable from magic."

--Arthur C. Clarke

BASTION OF THE BLACK SORCERER

VAN ALLEN PLEXICO

John Blackthorn stood in the saddle of his madly galloping stallion and crouched, waiting to leap. In his right hand, the Sword of Light flared to brilliant life. All around him, chaos reigned.

Blinding bolts of lightning flared down from the top of the massive, spider-legged mechanoid that bore his enemy. Screams of dying lizard-men and squawks of incapacitated robots resounded in his ears as his two companions, Oglok the Mock-Man and the Princess Aria, slashed their way through the ranks of attackers like scythes through wheat.

The previously bright sun of mid-afternoon Mars lay entirely obscured and a twilight-like gloom hung over the tiny village that had, in the last few moments, become a battlefield. Backed into a corner, the three companions had found they had no choice but to fight. Now they looked to be overwhelmed, their all-too-brief campaign to free the land from the oppression of the Black Sorcerer already at its end.

"No!" Blackthorn shouted, as if to defy whatever gods there might be in this bizarre, far-future world into which he—a simple American military man—had awoken only months earlier. "No—not yet! It won't end here!" He risked a glance back at his companions, seeing them surrounded on all sides now by their vicious and horrific foes. "Aria!" he cried. "Oglok! *Fight!*"

The gun that extended from beneath the forward section of the big crawler blazed as it fired into the cottages of the village.

13

Avoiding the murderous spray, Blackthorn guided his stallion expertly alongside the vehicle, moving in close. With a mighty leap, he crossed the distance and slammed against the cold metal hide of the gigantic machine. His black leather-like uniform absorbed most of the impact as he frantically scrambled for a handhold. Grasping a knoblike protuberance, he reversed his momentum and swung himself upward, landing on the behemoth's back. Just ahead of him, the open cockpit loomed. He stalked forward, the Sword of Light humming as it pierced the gloom and illuminated the rusted and pitted metal plates on which he strode.

Once more Blackthorn risked diverting his attention from his own actions to those of his friends. In only a second's glance, he could see Oglok in action, his mighty, fur-covered arms a blur as he grasped mutated creatures and death-dealing robots left and right and smashed one against the other, all the while roaring his fury in his own nigh-unintelligible language. Next to him, Princess Aria stood still as stone, her color-changing dress now a radiant, blazing red as she grasped the glowing crystals of her necklace with one hand and flung spells of destruction at the enemy horde with the other.

"Yes!" Blackthorn crowed. "That's it, my friends! *Fight them!"*

As if in response, out of the cockpit sprang a tall, gaunt figure all in black. A deathly pale face, filled with hate, glared out at Blackthorn from beneath a low-hanging hood. One gnarled hand clutched a snake-headed staff and directed it his way. Bolts of electricity flared out, striking the deck all around where Blackthorn stood.

Gritting his teeth as he felt his very short hair standing on end, Blackthorn raised the Sword of Light defensively and advanced a step.

"The Black Sorcerer," he growled, peering at his foe. "I should have known it was you."

"Human fool! You have eluded me for too long! Now I shall take back what is rightfully mine—*you!"*

Brandishing the snake-staff, the Black Sorcerer screamed wordlessly and rushed forward. Blackthorn leapt to meet him, swinging the Sword of Light in a broad arc, its powerful energies crashing into the wizard's staff.

The resulting explosion temporarily blinded and deafened everyone who happened to look their way, and flung both men, rag-doll-like, from the top of the spider-machine, hurling them into the crowd of mutants and robots below.

14

Blackthorn's head struck the ground and his vision blurred. His last sight was of slavering lizard-men rushing towards him, fangs dripping. Then darkness took him.

His thoughts swam, and the bizarre events of the last three months—the events that had led him to this place and time—flashed through his mind in an instant.

He screamed.

Two months earlier...

Awareness returned to Blackthorn with a suddenness almost as disorienting as the sights he beheld once he'd fully opened his eyes.

What seemed like mere moments earlier, he had been caught in an ambush by insurgent forces as his US Army caravan had moved near enemy-held territory. Pinned down outside their vehicles, he and his men had put up the strongest resistance they could manage, but the number of attackers was vast. Someone had betrayed their position to the enemy—it was the only possible answer. And he was sure he knew who.

Morningstar! Colonel David Morningstar, my second-in-command. It had to be you. You recommended that route for our caravan against all other advice, and when the enemy struck, you were nowhere to be found. Blast you!

The battle had been going badly. It had been painfully clear that the American forces were not going to hold out much longer. The insurgents had closed in, guns blazing...

...and then darkness. Blackthorn's vision had gone black, his consciousness had fled. He assumed he had been shot, or perhaps hit with shrapnel from some grenade or bomb. Waking up, his first coherent thought was that he had been carried to a hospital facility, or perhaps was inside an enemy encampment.

This looked like neither. In fact, it looked like nothing he had ever seen before.

He was inside a room—a particularly large room, in fact, towering some hundred feet or more above him, and twice as broad. Banks of machinery lined the walls and covered the floor, leaving only narrow aisles for movement. And, he realized then, everything looked hazy, somehow slightly out of focus. Rubbing at his eyes didn't seem to help. Seeking to move, he found he was fastened securely to the wall behind him.

Then came a loud *pop*, followed by movement just ahead of him. He saw then that he was standing inside a small capsule, and the front half was sliding open. That was why he'd had trouble seeing; he'd been looking through the odd, dark-tinted, slightly distorted glass of the capsule's front. Smells rushed in, some of them strong and even acrid; he thought he could identify an animal scent, some kind of blood, and what might have been the smoke from burning electronic circuitry. As the panel in front of him finished moving aside with a low whirring noise, a shadow fell across him. He looked up—and that's when he became certain he was no longer in the Middle East, and possibly no longer on the Earth itself.

"So—you are awake now, eh, barbarian?"

Blackthorn sought to lean out, to see who had spoken, but the rubbery restraints holding him by the wrists and ankles and around his waist were too strong.

"Long have I awaited this moment," the voice continued. It was high and nasally and did not sound entirely human, somehow. "The moment when my newest servants become animated, arise from their life-crypts, and join my hordes!"

"Who are you?" Blackthorn called, still unable to see the person who was speaking. "Where am I? How did I get here?" He reacted with shock then; his voice sounded utterly strange, as though a different person was speaking his words. The effect was both startling and terrifying.

"So many questions, my new servant," the other voice said; it came now from somewhere above and behind him. Still he struggled in vain to see. "That is to be expected, I suppose, for you have been reborn into a world surely very different from the primitive one you remember."

"Reborn?" Blackthorn frowned. He didn't like the sound of that. "I was in the middle of a firefight with insurgents," he called out. "Are you working with them?"

Now the other simply laughed. It was a classically evil laugh, almost a parody of itself, yet sounded utterly sincere coming from this strange and unseen person.

"What's so funny, friend?" Blackthorn growled, growing impatient. His visibility was extremely limited; not only could he not see the person he was talking with, but only a very small portion of the room around him was visible on either side of the capsule's front. "Why don't you step out here where I can see you? And how about unfastening me from this contraption?"

The other was silent for a moment. Then, "I am not your friend—I am your master," the voice said, and it was low and harsh now. It swelled in strength and intensity as he went on, "I am known as the Black Sorcerer—greatest of the First Men." A pause, and then, "I will free you when I am quite ready to do so. But if you wish so badly to see me, I will be happy to fulfill that request."

From out of the shadows to Blackthorn's left emerged a hooded figure in dark robes. It carried a slender wooden staff in one gnarled hand; the staff ended in the shape of a coiled snake.

"Who are you supposed to be?" Blackthorn asked, almost laughing.

From beneath the hood, the lower portion of a face could now be seen; the skin was deathly pale and the teeth gritted in a horrific grimace of rage. The snake-headed staff came up and lightning flared out, several smaller bolts striking Blackthorn as he remained trapped in the open capsule. He cried out in pain for several seconds before the torture ended.

When his vision cleared, Blackthorn gazed out at his captor. The hood had been pulled back to reveal an entirely bald head and a cold, cadaverous face that glared at him.

"You will remain silent! You will speak only when I command it!"

Blackthorn started to bark back a retort, but restrained himself at the last instant. Shoving his churning rage aside, he forced himself to consider the facts: This lunatic, whoever he might be, controlled Blackthorn's fate—at least for the moment. Nothing could be done until the strange man released him from his bonds. *Go along for now*, he told himself. So he swallowed his anger and forced himself to nod once.

The pale figure appeared to be somewhat mollified by this. He stood upright, his features relaxing a bit, and looked over Blackthorn from head to toe.

"You will find this new body a great improvement over your previous one," he chortled.

New body? Blackthorn's mind reeled at this. What was this crazy man talking about? But then, he considered how different his voice had sounded, and how much stronger and healthier he felt now...

"You're saying you have put me into a new body?" he asked, hoping the question would not provoke another violent response from his captor.

Fortunately, the man who called himself the Black Sorcerer seemed to almost relish the opportunity to brag on his own abilities.

"Yes, quite so," he answered in that high-pitched voice. "My machinery showed me that you were lying wounded and dying on

17

some battlefield of the ancient past, on old Earth," he explained. "So I took your mind—your spirit—and brought it here, to my city and my sanctum, to animate this body."

"Why?"

"Because," the Black Sorcerer said, leaning in close and staring at him with wild, bloodshot eyes, "ancient barbarian though you might be, you surely understand more about warfare and about leading armies than does virtually anyone in this fallen world of the present. It is in that capacity that you will serve me—as captain of my forces, general of my armies, sweeping forth to conquer this land and destroy my foes!"

Blackthorn considered this for a moment, gazing down in thought. Then he looked back up at his pale captor, meeting his eyes. "And I will do this for you—why?"

The Black Sorcerer's featured darkened. His eyes narrowed and his nostrils flared.

"You will do this—and anything else that I order—because I command it!"

"I suspect it's going to take more than that," Blackthorn responded quietly. "I don't really *serve* anyone or anything—aside from my country."

The Black Sorcerer flared with anger. His staff came up, electricity flooding from the snake head, striking Blackthorn in multiple spots on his body.

No, the captive general reminded himself, in the midst of the nearly-overwhelming pain, *not* my *body. Some* other *body, in some other place, that this crazy man has supposedly put my mind into.*

As the agony slowly receded, Blackthorn's vision cleared once again. Now he could see the Black Sorcerer looming over him, his face a leering grin. The man held an object about the size of a small coin in one hand.

"There is also *this*, of course," the lunatic barked at him. "An ancient device—an object of power. It will compel you to obey me, barbarian." His grin widened. "Once I have implanted it within your skull."

Blackthorn recoiled. Much as he wasn't thrilled about being inside some other body, he certainly didn't want anyone drilling holes in its head—in *his* new head!

The Black Sorcerer opened his mouth to speak again, but before he could, a shuddering ran through the floor of the room, followed by a low *boom*. The pale man frowned, eyes widening, and whirled about. "No—not now," he muttered. "Not before my defenses are entirely ready." Then he pocketed the tiny device and quickly stalked away.

"Something wrong?" Blackthorn called to the eerie man.

"Silence, fool! I will return to attend to you in a few moments. But it would appear I have others to attend to first."

Another sound—clearly an explosion, Blackthorn could tell for certain now—rocked the chamber. The Black Sorcerer hurried away, vanishing through an arched doorway on the far side of the room.

Blackthorn stood there, the restraints holding him firmly in place, and wondered exactly what kind of strangeness he had somehow gotten involved in. It all seemed so absurd on the surface. He was still himself; his memories, his thoughts, his emotions all felt exactly the same as they ever had. And yet he had but to look down at what he could see of his own body to recognize that it was not the late-middle-aged form he had inhabited as a general in the US Army. Somehow, some way, his mind—his soul, perhaps—had been stolen away from that lonely battlefield in Southwestern Asia and brought here, to this body.

But—where on Earth was he? Who was this strange man who held him captive? And, perhaps most importantly, just how long had he been asleep before waking up here?

A hissing sound came to him from a short distance to his right. Straining mightily against his bonds, he was able to lean out just far enough to see another glass capsule like the one he currently occupied, and perhaps another beyond it. The nearer one had snapped open and the front portion was sliding out of the way.

"Hey," he called in that direction. "Somebody in there?"

A low moan, followed by several sharp coughs. Then, in a ragged voice, "Yeah, I hear you. Where—where am I?"

"Trying to figure that out, presently," Blackthorn replied. "It sounds absolutely crazy, but we're being held here by a lunatic in a black robe, who wants to make zombie slaves out of us." Quickly he ran through a brief summary of what had happened since he had awakened.

"Okay," the other voice—male, somewhat young-sounding—said. "You were right—it does sound absolutely crazy." A pause, and then, "But I guess I have to believe you, given what I can see of our surroundings here. So what are we going to do about it?"

Blackthorn had been in the middle of thinking about that very topic even as the other man asked. "I'm working on that," he said.

The straps that held his wrists, ankles, and waist secure against the interior of the pod were soft and rubbery, with a slight amount of "give" to them, but not enough for him to actually work a limb free. In fact, the harder he pulled against the restraints, the tighter they seemed to grip him.

"Doesn't sound like it's working out very well," came the voice of the other man.

Blackthorn didn't answer for a few seconds. He was too busy straining with all his might—more might than his original body had ever possessed, even in his youth—against the restraints. All to no avail. Finally he gasped and fell limp. Sweat ran down the side of his face as he breathed heavily.

"Not very well at all," the other man added. "Well. There's probably no use in my trying that, I suppose."

Another explosion, this one even closer, shook the chamber.

"If you can think of another way to get free, by all means, share it," Blackthorn grunted, his strength returning.

No reply. The other man was silent, perhaps testing the strength of his own bonds.

Blackthorn frowned, looking around for any possible answer. He was certain that whatever had distracted their captor wouldn't keep him away forever; surely they had limited time to escape before he returned.

And sticks that thing in my head, he thought. *Whatever it was.*

As his eyes moved about the portion of the chamber nearby, he focused on an odd device resting atop a large bank of machinery. A cylinder made of silvery metal, it looked like a flashlight as much as anything else. Could it be a weapon of some kind? Or just a flashlight?

It didn't matter, as long as it lay well beyond his reach.

"No ideas yet?" he called to the other man.

"Not so far. You'll be the first to know, though, if I think of something."

Blackthorn cursed under his breath. Bad enough to be trapped here—wherever *here* was—by some crazed lunatic. Having a smart-mouthed cell mate only made it worse.

He frowned then. The man to his right sounded oddly familiar, he realized. Not the voice, so much, but his way of speaking…

A bright blue flash filled the chamber. Blackthorn squeezed his eyes closed, but too late—his vision was filled with exploding suns. The man to his right cried out in surprise.

20

Even as Blackthorn furiously blinked his eyes to clear them, a snapping sound came to his ears. An instant later, he felt the restraints that held him inside the capsule slacken and then retract entirely.

He fell forward against the partially-open front panel. Shoving himself back upright, he brought up his booted foot and kicked outward. The semi-transparent panel sheared off, shattered and fell away. He leapt clear, landing on the hard floor of the chamber.

He was free.

But—how? Had it been the flash of light?

No time to worry about such things now, he knew. That was a mystery for later—for when he was out of this place, this whatever-it was...

He looked around quickly, now that he could actually see most of the chamber he occupied. It was a hemispherical room, like a dome of some sort, with arching metal struts holding up the roof. The struts were rusted in places and a couple of them were actually bent, as though something large and heavy had, at one time or another, impacted the roof of the dome from above and driven down into it. The room itself was filled to overflowing with banks of machinery, none of which looked remotely familiar to Blackthorn. Some of it looked so futuristic he couldn't even begin to imagine what it was, even though many of those same machines carried the air of great age, of being worn down over a very long period of time.

He found he didn't like to contemplate what that might mean.

Then he gazed down at himself, now that he could actually move and bend, and was surprised anew by this strange body that was not his and yet now apparently was. He was dressed in a thin, black, leather-like suit with silver metal trim; his boots were black as well, as was the broad belt at his waist, with various small pouches and a holster affixed to it. He could find nothing whatsoever that resembled a weapon.

Then he remembered the flashlight-thing. Shrugging to himself, he grabbed it and held it up, studying its surface markings. He noticed as he handled it that it felt slightly warm in his grasp; not warm like a piece of electronics that has been left on too long, but almost alive.

"Too heavy for just a flashlight, I think," he muttered.

One end was closed metal while the other had a sort of clear crystal piece covering it. There were no raised buttons on its surface, but five squares of different colors circled it about two-thirds of the way up. Cautiously, he touched the green one.

A beam of bright yellow light extended out from the crystal end of the device. Strangely, the beam ended in mid-air, after about eight inches. It shimmered and hummed, looking for all the world like a knife blade—a blade composed of light.

Blackthorn stared at it, eyes wide. His first thought: *What is this?* His second thought, almost immediately: *What do the other squares cause it to do?*

Before trying to discover the answer to that second question, however, he moved to stand before the other capsule. Raising his boot again, he lashed out with a powerful kick which took the front panel completely off its hinges and sent it tumbling away down the aisle. Then he leaned in and used the yellow blade of light to slash at the restraints that held the occupant inside. They parted cleanly and easily.

A dark-haired man stumbled out, one hand held up to block the light from sensitive eyes. He wore a suit similar to Blackthorn's but, instead of black, it was red with gold trim.

"Thanks," the man said, standing on unsteady feet. "Sorry—I think my legs are asleep."

"Wake them up fast," Blackthorn said. "We're getting out of here now."

A popping sound came from further down the aisle. Both men turned to look. A third capsule was sliding open.

The two exchanged glances. The other man offered an expression that seemed to say, "Maybe we should just ignore it and leave." Blackthorn frowned and hurried to the third capsule, easily snapping the front off of it as he had done to the others. Leaning in, he freed the person he found there, then helped him out of the capsule.

This was another man, his hair a dark red in color. He said nothing at first, merely gazing at his rescuers. Then, as they helped him hobble down the aisle, he started to ask the questions expected of someone who hadn't heard the Black Sorcerer's spiel earlier.

Blackthorn stopped him abruptly. "It's a long story," he told the man, "or at least a very strange one—and one we don't really know much of, so far."

"He claims a lunatic in a black cloak brought us here, put us into these bodies, and is holding us prisoners," the other man stated succinctly.

The redhead blinked at this. Surely, Blackthorn thought, if their experiences had been in any way similar, the man must be terribly disoriented. All that was driving *him*, at the moment, was adrenalin—something this big new body seemed to possess in abundance—along with a fierce determination to escape the captivity of the bizarre hooded man. Anything beyond that, he had yet to consider.

"Okay... well..." The redhead looked more confused than ever. " At least tell me your name," he said after a few seconds. "So I'll know who to thank."

Blackthorn met the man's eyes. "John Blackthorn."

The reactions he received, both from the redhead and from the other man, was not quite what he had expected. They gawked at him; their reactions could not have been stronger if he had announced that he was the President of the United States.

"Yes?" he asked, curious at their shocked expressions. He was growing antsy just standing here, vulnerable, though he had no clear idea as to where else they should go—or even how they could get out of this room.

"*General* Blackthorn," the dark-haired man said. He spoke it as a statement rather than a question, but his tone made clear that he was not convinced it was true.

"You know me, then?" Blackthorn said, turning to the other man.

The man didn't reply at first, but his dark eyes narrowed.

"*I* know General Blackthorn, yes," the redhead was saying, his voice rising and growing strident. "But *you* are certainly not him."

Blackthorn glanced down at his bulky, powerful form, and couldn't help but snort a laugh.

"This isn't my old body, no," he told the redhead. "This is how I woke up here." He frowned then. "So—you know me. The old me. So, who are you, then?"

"Major Yuei," the redhead replied, almost timidly. "Anton Yuei."

Now Blackthorn did laugh. Yuei actually managed to look hurt, while the third man merely stood back, watching the conversation unfold.

"What's so funny?"

Blackthorn gestured his way. "Have you looked down at yourself since you woke up?"

Yuei frowned, then looked down at himself. His body was younger and more muscular than it had ever been in his life, though not so ruggedly-built as the new Blackthorn. "Dear lord," he muttered. "What is happening here?"

"I plan on finding out, Major," Blackthorn said. Then he turned to the other man. "Okay—spill it. Who did *you* used to be?"

"I...think I'll withhold that information for the moment," the dark-haired man answered, eyeing both of the others warily.

Blackthorn's expression grew puzzled. "You know who you are, in that new body—and clearly you know us, too—but you're actually not going to *tell* us who you are?" he asked, astonished.

The dark-haired man chewed his lower lip for a moment, then nodded. "For the time being, yes. I think that would be best."

Blackthorn started to say something sharp to the man, but Yuei intervened.

"General—" He hesitated, shaking his head, still not fully believing that this young, blond man was his old commanding officer. "General, if what you said is true, don't you think we should save any arguments for *after* we escape from this place? Sir."

Blackthorn had reddened, his eyes almost seeming to drill through the dark-haired man. Then, slowly, he turned back to Yuei. He nodded.

"You're right, Major. We need to vacate the premises immediately." He looked around, searching for a door. All that could be seen was bulky machinery in every direction. It looked as if the man who called himself the Black Sorcerer had dragged every old, broken-down machine he could find to this room and left it here, turning the place into a scrap yard for computers and...whatever the other machines were. They didn't look like anything Blackthorn had ever seen. As with most of the other things he'd observed here thus far, they somehow combined "futuristic" with "old and worn out." It made for a very strange effect—though not one they had the time to study at the moment.

"Over here," called the dark-haired man. He had jogged to the end of the long aisle that ran perpendicular to the one where their capsules were located. "A door."

Making their way over, Blackthorn and Yuei found the man facing a high, broad double-door set into this portion of the dome wall. There were no visible knobs or handles. They all stared up at it, then looked about for some sort of way to open it. Nothing presented itself.

Blackthorn looked down at the device he carried. Touching the green square again had caused the short yellow blade to vanish; he wondered if it was capable of cutting through the doors—and how long that might take. Or perhaps one of the other squares would yield a larger or more powerful light-blade?

Seeing no other options, he stood at the spot where the two doors met in the center and held the device up. Of the various colored squares that circled it, he could see that one of them was red; surely that one must do something powerful and/or dangerous. His finger hovered over it—

—and the doors slid soundlessly open on their own.

Blackthorn blinked. He looked ahead and found himself standing face to face with… *something*. Whatever it was, it would have seemed incredibly odd to him, if not for the fact that *everything else* he had seen in the brief moments since he had awakened in this room seemed extremely odd.

It was a lizard. No, he corrected himself—it was a man. With his third guess he got it right: it was a *lizard-man*. Some kind of mutated creature with green scales covering its body and dark, slitted eyes that peered up at him from its roughly four-foot height. Had it begun life as a lizard, or as a man? He idly wondered this even as it pounced at him, razor-sharp teeth snapping, and he dodged to one side, then grasped it by the head and twisted, hard. The neck snapped and the thing fell dead at his feet.

"Nice work," Yuei noted appreciatively.

"This body has certain advantages," Blackthorn noted, gazing down at the remains.

Leaning through the doorway and seeing beyond the dead creature to the room beyond, Yuei groaned. "It looks like just another room like this one," he said. "Is there a way out?"

"More of those *things* are coming," the other man said, pointing through the now-open doorway. Indeed, what looked like an entire squad of the lizard-men was charging down the center aisle at them. Blackthorn made ready to charge into battle, and considered touching a different square on the silver device, to see what might result.

Before he could do so, there came another bright blue flash, not quite as blinding as the previous one—the one that had seemingly freed Blackthorn from the capsule. It appeared to disorient the lizard-men, all of whom stopped in their tracks and stumbled about, rubbing at their eyes. Meanwhile, a lingering sphere of blue light hovered in the air above them, then floated upwards along a narrow metal stairway they hadn't yet noticed, to float before a partially-hidden door.

"That's it—the way out," Blackthorn stated, pointing. "I'm sure of it."

"Why is that?" asked the dark-haired man, as he looked about for more danger.

"Because somebody here is helping us. That's the second time they've intervened." With that, he sprinted for the stairs, the other two men following close behind.

The stairs were as rusty and rickety as nearly everything else they had encountered in this strange building. It felt as if, at any moment, the creaking, teetering things could collapse and hurl them all down to the floor. Nevertheless, they made it halfway up the stairs, the army of lizard-men clambering up after them, when the Black Sorcerer returned. The robed and hooded man cried out in fury as he saw them free. In response the lizard-men, clearly terrified of him, redoubled their efforts to catch the three fugitives.

Blackthorn took the remaining steps three at a time and arrived at the hidden doorway first. It was a heavy, wrought iron slab, streaked with rust and grime. He grasped the handle but the door wouldn't budge. As before, no other obvious way to open it presented itself.

The Black Sorcerer continued to shout his anger and outrage. Raising his snake-headed staff high, he caused lightning to flare all about himself. In response, clouds billowed up, surrounding him.

Blackthorn spared a moment's glance down at the bizarre figure, seeing him now rising slowly into the air atop those billowing black clouds. From this vantage point, he could also see another cluster of big glass capsules like the one he had awoken inside. *More innocent people?* he wondered. *People pulled here from...wherever they were before, and plugged into bodies not their own? Madness!* He vowed then and there to end the tyrannical reign of the madman who had brought him and the others here. *Somehow.*

Now the Black Sorcerer was rising up into the air; it appeared as if he were actually floating atop the billowing clouds. He was halfway to the top of the stairs already, his eyes burning with an eerie fire as he closed in on the escapees.

The nameless man continued to wrestle with the long metal door handle, all to no avail. He looked up at Blackthorn, then at the silver cylinder he carried. "Try the weapon. Quickly!"

Stepping between the other two men, Blackthorn held the cylinder up and chose a colored square at random, first making sure the crystal end was pointed away from any of them, just in case. He pressed the yellow square.

A blade of vibrant, shimmering golden light sprang out, extending to the length of a rapier blade and at least an inch thick.

Blackthorn gasped. He held the blade carefully before him, hearing its low hum and watching as what looked like some kind of tiny, sparkling particles moved up and down its length. He felt an instant affinity for it; he could have stood there and stared at it for hours, at least, despite its near-blinding brightness. But lighting flashing all around him—and the cries of his two comrades—brought him back to reality. The crazed man in the black cloak and hood had floated nearly level with them and was closing in.

Blackthorn turned his back on their enemy. He raised the glowing blade high over his head and brought it down along the seam between the door and the doorframe. Sparks flew madly and all three men cringed. When they looked up again, the door stood partly open.

Blackthorn looked down at the weapon he had discovered and grinned.

Out into darkness they ran. Blackthorn reached back and slammed the heavy iron door closed with a resounding clang, then touched the shimmering yellow blade of his new weapon to the seam between door and wall. It fizzed and popped and appeared to be welding together.

"Nice work," the nameless man said, nodding appreciatively. "Maybe that will provide us with a few extra seconds."

They all turned and looked about. They stood high up on a narrow walkway that projected out from a smooth, severely weathered wall. The wall and the walkway curved around and away gradually, revealing the building to be a massive dome. The only illumination came from weak stars overhead—no moon at all—and a few sporadically flickering electric lights positioned along the wall ahead. Two big columns, seemingly carved from solid marble, stood just ahead; between and through them ran a stairway curving down toward the ground. The landscape outside the dome lay shrouded in obscurity.

"Where now?" Yuei asked, panic rising in his voice.

"Down—where else?" the other man said, gesturing toward the stairs.

The door behind them clanged as though a giant were smashing his fist into it. Then it clanged again. It began to shudder, the weld Blackthorn had created already looking as though it could snap at any moment.

Yuei and the other man took one look at this and then turned and ran for the stairs, passing between the columns and disappearing down the stairs. They passed under one of the flickering lights and then disappeared into the inky blackness. Blackthorn brandished his exotic weapon and, facing the door, backed slowly toward the stairs, covering the others' retreat.

The weld gave way. The door swung outward and back around, crashing into the wall to its left. Clouds of smoke billowed through the doorway, and then a snake-headed staff protruded out, electricity dancing across its surface.

Blackthorn whirled and leapt between the columns as forks of deadly lightning streaked past. The electrical blasts burned his legs where they struck and momentarily stood all the hairs on his body on end.

"You cannot hope to escape, mortal!" crowed a shrill voice from the other side of the doorway. "You will serve me—or you will die!"

Blackthorn landed hard, tumbling down a half-dozen steps while just managing to avoid a lethal blast. The suit he wore seemed to be providing a tiny bit of protection from impact and from the burning blasts. He hadn't really had a chance to study it yet; it seemed made of leather, but didn't feel that way; it was very light and extremely soft to the touch, and its surface revealed only the finest texture.

Scrambling back up the steps, he could see that the Black Sorcerer had backed off in order to allow his army of lizard-men to advance. They were topping the inside stairs even now, and the first few of them rushed toward the doorway. Pivoting about, he hacked at the nearest column with his weapon—what he had already begun to think of as his "sword." Then, with a mighty kick, he sent the column crashing down, blocking the doorway. He barely avoided being crushed by it as it fell.

Down the long, curving stairs he ran. The night was so dark he could scarcely see what lay ahead. Something occurred to him and he concluded it might be worth giving it a try: He halted on the steps and held his still-blazing sword before him. First he touched the yellow square again, and the shimmering blade vanished. Then he considered the remaining squares—green had produced a knife-like blade and yellow the long rapier. Red seemed likely to create something even more dangerous, so he avoided that one for now and instead touched the white square. The result was exactly what he'd hoped for. Bright white light shone out in a steady beam. It now really was a flashlight.

Able to move much more rapidly now that he could see where he was going, he quickly caught up to Major Yuei and the other man as they all reached the bottom of the stairs. Both men observed this new use for his device but neither commented.

"We still don't know where we are," Yuei groaned, turning slowly and peering into the night all around. Only the lights on the side of the dome they'd just evacuated provided any real light, aside from Blackthorn's flashlight. "But that guy didn't seem to work for any government I know of. So I would imagine that all we have to do is get off his property and find the nearest American embassy."

Blackthorn had a strong feeling that they were a long way from any American embassies, but he kept this thought to himself for the moment.

A neighing sound came from a short distance away. He brought the flashlight up, shining it in that direction.

"Horses! Hey!"

Yuei ran over, the other two following quickly. Indeed, three tall horses stood in a little group, saddled and ready. Their reins were lashed to a tree.

"This is handy," Yuei grinned, freeing a dark brown one.

"Too handy," the other man said, frowning.

"I agree," Blackthorn said, "but—seeing as these literally *are* 'gift horses,' I don't think we're in a position to refuse them. Especially considering that loon and his lizard-men are going to be on us any second now."

As if on cue, the cry of the lizard-men echoed from the base of the dome some fifty yards to their right. The main bulk of them had apparently come back down the interior stairs and were now emerging from a ground-floor exit, and scurrying their way.

Blackthorn leapt into the saddle of the white stallion and grasped the reins. "Alright, gentlemen," he called, "let's ride!"

The third man climbed onto a gray stallion and the three of them galloped away into the night, the furious curses of the lizard-men receding behind them as they rode.

Behind them, a short distance around the base of the dome from the lizard-man army, a slender individual stood in the deepest, darkest shadows and watched the three men ride away. Then, nodding in satisfaction, the figure leapt onto a brown mare and started out after them.

They rode for a bit more than two hours through what turned out to be a very large, thick forest. The trees were old and gnarled, and the well-worn path they followed wound back and forth among them.

They crossed three shallow creeks along the way, providing water for the horses. The air was cool, though not uncomfortably so, and the strange outfits they had awakened wearing proved extremely effective at regulating temperature. Blackthorn's device provided them light to help them find their way, at least until the sun came up and filtered pale light down through the trees. They all wondered where they were and, after Blackthorn filled the other two in on everything the "sorcerer" had told him, *when* they were. No one spoke of it, though. They just rode on in silence, hoping that somehow it would all turn out to be an elaborate joke, or a dream, or...*something*.

The sun, Blackthorn noted, now that it had risen at last, seemed unusually small and distant. As he squinted at it, another surprising sight came to him through a break in the trees. Quickly he halted his horse and stared, and the others did likewise as they drew up beside him.

"What is that?" asked Yuei, unwilling to take his eyes off of it.

"It's a mountain, obviously," the third man stated—but he, too, continued to stare.

"It's no mountain I've ever seen," Yuei said, shaking his head.

Blackthorn was busy studying every detail that could be made out from their rather poor vantage point. It was definitely a mountain and, judging by the shape, definitely not one he'd ever encountered before, either. It was huge—it went up and up and up— something that was obvious even from this far away. And yet it was part of no broader range; it stood there as a solitary titan, dominating the entire landscape in that direction. He could just make out what looked like tremendous castles or fortresses here and there along its slopes, or at least on the lower portions. And something like a gigantic antenna extended up from the summit.

"I'm getting a really funny feeling about this—this—" Yuei looked around, his face contorted with confusion. "This *everything*. Nothing makes sense!"

"Hold it together, Major," Blackthorn barked at him. "We'll find answers soon enough."

"We may not like them when we do," the third man commented in a quiet voice.

Blackthorn turned on him, frowning. "Speaking of answers," he said, "I'd like at least one from you."

The other man took this in, seemed to think about it for a moment, then nodded.

"You're right," he said. "I apologize for not giving you my name earlier. But you have to agree, this has all been disorienting in the extreme. I haven't been sure either of you actually was who you claim to be."

"You know us, then?" Yuei asked.

"I know *of* you. I was a civilian contractor assigned in a supporting role to one of your units. The name's O'Fallon. Tony O'Fallon."

Blackthorn ran that name through his mind quickly. It seemed somewhat familiar, but he couldn't be certain. A lot of things seemed hazy now; in truth, he was having increasing difficulty in remembering a great deal of his former life, and it felt as though more was slipping away every moment.

He put such thoughts aside and nodded to the third man. "Very well, Mr. O'Fallon." Then he pointed to the trail ahead. "Shall we, gentlemen?"

They rode on. About an hour later, the forest slowly gave way to an open meadow, and as they crossed it, Blackthorn became aware of a strange feeling creeping over him. He glanced at the others, and saw that they, too, were experiencing it. Both men were frowning and Yuei was scratching at his arms.

"What *is* that?" Yuei asked, looking around, agitated. Now a soft hum or buzz could be heard, drifting across the grassland.

The third man, O'Fallon, pointed off to the right. "I think it's coming from there."

Sure enough, they could just see some sort of tower protruding up from among the tall grass. By silent consent, they all began to make their way towards it.

Blackthorn quickly came to believe that doing so was a mistake. The closer they drew to the tower, the louder the sound became, and the more creepy the feeling it was producing.

"Like ants crawling all over me," Yuei growled.

O'Fallon nodded. Now he was scratching, too.

Blackthorn scowled.

The tower was still some distance away; it looked to be around three hundred feet tall, slender and made of gleaming metal. It reminded Blackthorn of a cell phone tower, and he said so. "And it's beaming out a signal of some kind. A pretty strong one."

O'Fallon nodded, while Yuei scoffed.

"If that's what it is, it's got a serious malfunction happening," he said. "Or *something*."

They remained there a bit longer, staring at the thing and feeling their skin crawl. Again by unspoken mutual consent, they didn't draw any closer. Instead, a few minutes later, they returned to the path they had been following and continued on.

As morning gave way to midday, they were all growing weary and the horses desperately needed a break. It was then that they emerged from the thickest part of the woods and came upon a village. Now Blackthorn was sure they were still in Asia or the Middle East, for he had never seen a town like this in America or Europe. It looked like something out of the *Middle Ages*; primitive mud huts and shacks made from rough-cut timber, arranged along the banks of a broad but shallow stream. As they rode in among the dwellings, they spied a central building that was a good deal larger. It appeared to be made of stone and metal, but was clearly very ancient, crumbling around the edges. Some sort of bright paint had covered most of it in days long gone by, but had now faded to only the slightest hint of color. Each of the three riders noted this and sought to reconcile it with the modern Earth, failed, and did not comment upon it aloud.

A small group of men and women had emerged from their cottages and Blackthorn brought his little procession to a halt. He studied them casually; they were practically in rags, their clothes stitched together from various mismatched pieces and patterns. No weapons were in evidence but he could sense a sort of low-level hostility; he suspected others were watching, perhaps from places of concealment, likely armed and ready to attack at a moment's notice.

"Greetings." he called out to them. "Anyone here speak English?"

"We understand your words, stranger," an older man near the front of the group replied, "but I don't know what 'English' is."

Blackthorn frowned. He glanced back at the other two riders; Yuei shook his head in bewilderment and O'Fallon simply frowned.

"It's what you're speaking now," Blackthorn informed the man.

Now looks of bewilderment came his way from the villagers, too. Blackthorn shook his head, growing annoyed already, and decided to move on to more pressing matters.

"Can you tell us where we are?" he asked. "And who you folks are?"

The older man—seemingly some sort of village elder—stepped closer. "My name is Ardin." He gestured toward the small group behind him, which had swelled in size as more villagers approached, eyes wide, to see the strangers. "These are my people. Our town is called Domrik," he said. "Are you new to this area?"

"You could say that, yes, Ardin," Blackthorn replied with a smile. "My name is John Blackthorn. I'm a general in the United States Army."

The elder frowned. "I am not familiar with that army," he said. "Does it serve one of the First Men? Or oppose them?"

Blackthorn had been about to introduce the other two. Now he stopped and stared down at the old man.

"You've never heard of the United States Army? How is that possible?"

"America," Yuei added, smiling at the elder and trying to be helpful. "USA."

The old man looked back at his fellow villagers, but all he received from them was blank stares and shrugs. "I fear," he said, turning back to the riders and smiling apologetically, "that none of us have heard of your kingdom. We apologize if this gives offense."

"It's not a kingdom," Major Yuei said, anger growing in his voice. "It's the United States of—"

Blackthorn shushed him with a quick gesture. "Easy, Major. I'm starting to think we're a lot farther from home than we originally thought." Then he hopped down from his horse, took the elder's hand and clasped it firmly. "We're very tired and hungry, and are indeed strangers here. Could we perhaps—"

"Say no more," Ardin replied. "Guests are welcome." He pointed toward the old stone and metal building. "Come to the village hall. You will have food and drink, and places will be prepared for you to rest." He smiled. "And we can discuss your kingdom further. Perhaps I have heard of it, but under a different name."

The other two dismounted and together they followed the elder along the narrow dirt street, while villagers led their horses away to be tended. After a short distance they arrived at the doorway to the ancient, crumbling building. Blackthorn paused and took one last quick look about before going inside. Something felt wrong—very wrong—to him. Not so much about the villagers as about the entire world in general, though he couldn't quite put his finger on it. He wasn't thrilled to place himself practically at the mercy of a strange group of peasants straight out of Medieval times—peasants who had apparently never even heard of the United States!—but he desperately needed more information, not to mention food and sleep. And so, reluctantly, he followed his two companions inside.

An hour had passed and they had eaten as much as they could manage. The trio sat on one side of a long, wooden table that crossed most of one end of the old building. Other tables ran perpendicular to it, filling that half of the room, and most of the spaces were occupied by people eating lunch. The villagers were all exceptionally polite and very generous, supplying a seemingly endless procession of food and drink. It seemed as though they all spoke English, though none of them called it that, and Blackthorn was starting to suspect things were far more complicated than he'd first imagined.

Time to start getting some answers, he decided. He looked across at Ardin, who sat opposite them, and bowed his head respectfully. "We thank you for your great generosity," he said. "But now, if you're willing, I have a few questions."

"Of course," the older man replied with a polite smile. "And I have a few questions for you, as well."

"Such as?"

"You say you are a general. Do you serve one of the First Men? And is your army nearby?"

Blackthorn remembered the elder asking about these 'First Men' earlier. Meeting Ardin's gaze, he asked who they were.

Now it was the elder's turn to be amazed.

"You do not know of the First Men?" He pursed his lips and stroked his straggly gray beard. "Truly you must be from some distant kingdom—though I have never heard of any that had avoided *all* dealings with those great sorcerers."

"Sorcerers?" This perked up Blackthorn's ears. "As in, the *Black* Sorcerer?"

"Ah!" Now Ardin smiled. "So you *do* know of the First Men. Yes. The Black Sorcerer is one—the one who rules much of this area. There are three others, and each dominates some portion of the world."

"The world?" Yuei asked, leaning forward to stare at Ardin. "You mean this area, right? Pakistan, or Afghanistan, or wherever we are."

The old man shrugged. "Again you name kingdoms that are unfamiliar to me. You must have traveled a great distance."

"Greater than I thought," Blackthorn muttered.

"As I asked earlier," Ardin said, "is your army nearby?"

Before Blackthorn or Yuei could reply, O'Fallon leaned forward. "Let's just leave that an open question for now, eh, General?"

Blackthorn glanced over at the man, frowning. He could see the logic, though. Better to keep a few cards hidden, at least for now. And probably better not to freely admit that they were all alone. He nodded, then turned back to Ardin.

"Okay—let's go over this. You don't know of America, or Pakistan, or Afghanistan," he said to the elder. "But you and everyone in your village speaks perfect English. So—where on Earth are we?"

The elder frowned at this for a moment, then brightened. His blue eyes twinkled and he smiled broadly. "Ah! I think I see the confusion now," he said. "You're referring to ancient kingdoms on *old Earth*."

"I am?"

"Yes—quite so. But you see, that's not where you are now."

The three glanced at one another, truly alarmed.

"What exactly are you saying?" Blackthorn demanded, his voice rising. "This isn't '*old* Earth?'" He thought about how he and the others had awoken in glass capsules, in entirely new bodies. "How long did we sleep in those capsules? How far in the future are we?"

"Where on *any* Earth are we?" Yuei added, almost frantic.

The elder laughed. "This isn't Earth *at all*, my friend."

Blackthorn simply stared back at the man. "What? What are you saying?"

"This world—the world you're standing on—it's the planet Mars."

It took more than an hour for the three strangers to settle down and begin to accept what the elder was telling them: they were not on Earth, but on the Red Planet, and clearly far in the future from the time they knew. From what the old man said, they gathered that the Mars they now stood upon had been terraformed many, many years earlier, complete with Earth-like gravity and atmosphere. Legends told of how the great civilization that had engineered this transformation had eventually collapsed, hurling the world into savagery and barbarism. The unfathomably advanced technology they had used to perform such feats had long since been lost, with only a few functioning artifacts surviving to the present day. Blackthorn gathered that at least one more advanced civilization had

35

arisen here in the time since then, contributing their own super-technology, only to be hurled back down again by various disasters.

He did not like to contemplate just how much time must have passed since his own era.

"What of the Earth?" he had asked Ardin. "Civilization must have collapsed there, too, or else someone would have come to restore order...?"

"There are stories of visitors from the planet Earth, far back in the ancient past," the elder replied, "but nothing at all in modern times. We have no way of discovering the truth, of course."

"This can't be," Yuei moaned, rubbing his face with both hands. Fatigue and all the shocks of the past few hours were taking their toll; the man sounded as if he were about to cry. "It can't."

"I would agree, Major," Blackthorn said, squeezing his eyes closed as a headache blossomed fiercely, "except—look around. We've all been in denial, but it's obvious we're not on the Earth any longer." He rubbed his fists into his eyes. "That mountain we saw, for example."

"Olympos Mons," O'Fallon said. "Yes. Mount Olympus. Biggest mountain in the entire solar system. And it's on Mars."

"But," Yuei said, his voice growing even more desperate, "that would mean that even if we *could* get back to Earth... We're far in the future. Everyone we know is dead."

"Long dead, from the look of things," O'Fallon said, nodding. "We have to be talking a thousand years, at least. Probably more than that."

Blackthorn tried to accept the entire idea, and found that he simply could not—not yet. It was just too much. He needed some rest, but doubted he would be able to fall asleep any time soon, given all the troubling thoughts now running through his head. He rubbed at his eyes a bit more, his head really pounding now, then looked out at the dining hall. He frowned, seeing two newcomers entering the building. They were both quite large—at least seven feet tall—with stooped shoulders. They wore long cloaks and hoods that concealed everything about them save their stature. This made Blackthorn think of the Black Sorcerer, and he tensed, his fingers brushing the perpetually warm surface of his silver weapon where it hung at his belt.

"Maybe if we went back," Yuei was saying, "we could find a way to make that Sorcerer guy send us home—back to our own bodies, to our own time."

36

"Somehow I don't think so," O'Fallon said. "He brought us here for a reason—so we could be his slaves. Remember?"

"No one can 'make' the First Men do anything they do not wish to do," the elder interjected. "The First Men hold supreme power on this world."

"So this 'Black Sorcerer' is one of what you're calling the 'First Men?'" asked O'Fallon. "Who are they, exactly?"

"They are mighty wizards, four in all, each ruling a portion of the world."

"Wizards?" Yuei scoffed. "They claim to have magical powers or something?"

"They do," Ardin answered. "As all learn, to their regret, when they oppose the First Men."

"I can see why it would seem that way," O'Fallon said. He looked at Yuei. "From what Ardin here has told us, there have been at least two periods when technology grew extremely advanced. If these four wizards—the 'First Men'—have control of whatever's left of it, they would certainly be able to set themselves up as whatever they wanted to appear to be."

Blackthorn was only half-listening to the conversation. He continued to stare at the two newcomers, who had for the past minute or so been in quiet discussion with a younger man of the village. Now they approached.

Blackthorn snapped his weapon free of his belt, still keeping it beneath the table. Yuei and O'Fallon broke off their conversation as they realized what was happening.

The two big figures drew near, halting just behind Ardin on the opposite side of the table. If the older man was aware they were there, he didn't appear troubled by that fact.

Without taking his eyes from the new arrivals, Blackthorn ran his fingers along the silver device he held in his lap, seeking the yellow button that would trigger the sword blade. He became painfully aware that hadn't yet learned the feel of the weapon well enough to choose a setting without *looking* at it, and promised to rectify that situation immediately—if he lived past the next few seconds.

The two both simultaneously drew back their hoods.

Blackthorn and the other two men with him gasped. The two cloaked individuals were like nothing he had ever seen before.

"What—what in the name of all that's holy *are* they?" Yuei managed to choke out.

The two creatures—and Blackthorn could think of no description better for them, at least for the moment—were extremely muscular and covered entirely in fur; the taller one's coat was darker brown, while the shorter one's was a lighter sandy color. In both cases, dark, piercing eyes stared out over a sort of pug nose and broad mouth—a mouth that featured two frightening fangs protruding down over the edge of the lower lip from above. Both wore a sort of crude tunic and shorts that appeared to have been cobbled together from different brightly-colored scraps of heavy fabric.

The taller of the two leaned over the table, looking intently at Blackthorn.

"This is Ungus," the village elder said calmly, indicating the shorter, blonder creature. "And his nephew, Oglok."

"You didn't answer the question," O'Fallon pointed out, his voice very calm and flat, his muscles tensed to fight or, more likely, flee.

"What are they?" Yuei repeated, still staring almost mesmerized at the savage visages before him.

"They are Mock-Men, of course," Ardin replied, his tone indicating his surprise that anyone would not know such a thing. "They have a settlement in the hills to the south."

Yuei glanced at Ardin, puzzled. "Mock-Men?"

The taller was pointing at Blackthorn now, and at the table—or rather, the general realized then, pointing at the fact that Blackthorn's hands were hidden under the table. *He's pretty sharp, whatever he is,* Blackthorn saw then. *He doesn't like that he can't see my hands. And he doesn't know me. He's suspicious by nature—or just very careful. Interesting.*

The shorter creature—Ungus—emitted a sound that was something of a cross between a long growl and a bark. Yuei and O'Fallon jumped as if they were startled by it but, to Blackthorn's amazement, he found he could understand what the Mock-Man was saying. He was asking, *Who are these strangers? Are they dangerous.*

Blackthorn clipped his weapon back to his belt and slowly brought his hands up to where they were visible, setting them on the table before him. The taller one—Oglok—watched this motion carefully, then seemed satisfied and leaned back, taking a position just behind his uncle.

"They are here to discuss trade among our local villages," the elder explained.

"Trade?" blurted Yuei. "I thought they must be here to kill us all—to eat us!"

Ardin laughed hoarsely at this. "The Mock-Men? Hardly."

Blackthorn was intrigued by this. "What do you mean?"

The elder shrugged. "The Mock-Men are pacifists, for the most part."

"Pacifists?" Yuei exclaimed. "These guys? Are you serious?"

Elder Ardin gave the Major a puzzled look.

"Truly you have never encountered a Mock-Man before?" He shook his grizzled head in wonder. "I keep forgetting that you three are from very far away." He gestured towards the two fur-covered beings. "There are many legends about the Mock-Men, many of them contradictory. The one thing the old stories have in common, however, is that they were created from normal humans, many ages ago, by a powerful wizard, to serve as a monstrous army for him. But he didn't cast the proper spell; or perhaps a rival wizard interfered. In any case, the Mock-Men turned out as simple farmers and artisans, for all their strength and fierceness of visage. They fight only when absolutely necessary—and never with relish."

"Mock-Men," O'Fallon whispered. "Mockery of men."

Ungus, the elder of the two beings, emitted a series of barks and grunts. Before Ardin could answer, Blackthorn stated, "Yes—we do come from far away. Very far away."

Ungus looked surprised. He faced Blackthorn and rattled off another string of sounds.

"No, we have no allegiance to any wizard," the general said.

The others were all staring in amazement at Blackthorn.

"You can understand them?" Yuei asked, astonished.

"Obviously he can," O'Fallon stated. "The question is, how? Why?"

"If you have never met nor even heard of the Mock-Men," Elder Ardin added, "how can you know their language? Only through many years of study with them was I able to master it."

Blackthorn shook his head. "I'm not sure," he said, "but I have a guess." He wouldn't say more.

After a few more minutes of conversation, and with no obvious threats in evidence, the adrenalin that had been driving the trio of escapees started to wear off. They wished good evening to the Mock-Men and then Elder Ardin graciously showed them to small cabins where they could sleep.

Their first day on Mars was over, and they were still alive. Blackthorn considered that a remarkable success. Stripping off the black leather-like uniform he'd been wearing since he awoke in this bizarre new world, he lay down on his primitive bunk and closed his eyes. Ten seconds later, he was asleep.

His dreams were strange and disturbing, but nowhere near as strange as his new reality.

Two more days and nights passed with Blackthorn and his two companions enjoying the village's hospitality. They contributed where they could, cutting logs and tending to the horses, among other jobs. In the evenings, they engaged in long discussions with Ardin and the other elders, trying to learn as much as could be learned about this strange new world. O'Fallon in particular read through all of the village's ancient records and pressed the older inhabitants for any shreds of knowledge about the world that they might possess. Blackthorn, meanwhile, absorbed what information he could and kept his remarkable silver device hidden, for a number of reasons.

Ungus and Oglok, the two Mock-Men, remained in the village as well, working out details of their trade agreement with Ardin and awaiting the arrival of elders from nearby towns for a larger meeting. On two occasions, Blackthorn was able to enjoy a brief conversation with Oglok over a meal and the local brew. Oglok explained that he found conversations with the human enjoyable mainly because the others tended to treat him as only a sort of bodyguard for his uncle. Blackthorn, to the contrary, found the creature to be a fascinating individual, full of humor and interesting insights, and warmed to him quickly.

Life in the village was so calm, so serene—particularly after the harrowing first few hours they had experienced in the Black Sorcerer's lair—that the three men out of time nearly grew accustomed to living there. And then, as the sun was setting on the third day after their arrival, an incident occurred which set off a chain of events that brought everything they had learned thus far into question and set them all on a collision course with the Black Sorcerer once more.

It began when the village's guards came marching down the main street, a beautiful young woman in their custody. Blackthorn first learned of her arrival when one of the guards entered the main hall, where he was working, and told him that she had specifically asked to meet him.

"What?" Blackthorn had frowned at the man. "I don't know anyone else here. Certainly no young women!"

The guard had merely shrugged. "She asked to see John Blackthorn."

Puzzled and more than a little intrigued, the general had walked out into the street. The little procession of guards was waiting, the young woman at the center. O'Fallon was already standing nearby, and Yuei emerged from one of the huts. They all approached.

"She was camped in the forest nearby," the leader of the guards reported. "We think she'd been there for at least a day."

"Three days," the young woman corrected. Her remarkably elegant dress shimmered a greenish color in the light of the setting sun. She glared at the leader. "There was no need to arrest me, or whatever you're doing. I was on my way here anyway. I need to talk to General Blackthorn."

Everyone looked at Blackthorn, surprised.

"No, I don't know her," he stated firmly. "Never met her before."

"That's true," the young woman said, nodding. "But I know *you*."

"How?"

"I was there," she said, "when you... *arrived*."

Blackthorn tensed. That could only mean a connection to the Black Sorcerer. He started to reach for his hidden weapon.

"Settle down," the woman said, motioning for calm with her hands. "I'm not with *him*. I escaped, too. In fact, if not for me, you three probably wouldn't still be alive."

Blackthorn considered that, glanced around at the others, and then looked directly back at the woman.

"I see," he said. Then he turned to the chief of the guards. "Take her to the jail. She and I need to talk."

"The pub would be better," she said with a smile. "Assuming that these..." She glanced around at the villagers, her distaste for them obvious. "...*people* have a place here where we can get a drink and a private table."

Blackthorn considered this, then nodded.

The guards, most of whom had already come to like and respect Blackthorn, moved aside and the woman followed him into the dining hall. O'Fallon and Yuei glanced at one another quizzically, then followed along.

41

"Not exactly what I had in mind, but I suppose it will do," the woman said as they sat at a table in the rear corner of the stone and metal building.

Blackthorn studied her. She appeared to be in her mid-twenties, just over five feet tall, and slender. Her features were vaguely south Asian, her skin a medium-tan. A rich shade of eyeliner framed her dark eyes, and her sleek dress, which in the light outside had appeared green, now took on an almost golden hue.

"You seem to know who I am," Blackthorn said, ignoring her comments. "Who are you?"

She straightened up and smiled at him, her teeth dazzling. "I am the Princess Aria," she stated, as if that answered any and every possible question he could have.

He shook his head. "Princess of what?" he asked.

She looked offended by this at first, but then shrugged. "You wouldn't know, would you? You're not from this place—or this time."

This startled him. "How did you know that?"

"I saw you and your friends wake up in your capsules."

He slid a hand down under the table, reaching for the energy sword.

"I was a prisoner of the Black Sorcerer, too," she continued. "How do you think you escaped?"

"How? We fought our way out," Blackthorn replied testily.

"Ah, yes—but how did you get loose from your bonds in the first place? How did you find the door that led out? Why did you just happen to find three horses waiting for you?" She laughed. "And for that matter, who snuck word out to the local warlords to stage a rebellion at the very moment you and your friends were waking up, so that the Sorcerer would be distracted and leave you alone for a time?"

Blackthorn absorbed this, frowning. "You're saying that—all of that—was *you*."

Smiling again now, she nodded. "All me."

He continued to consider what she was saying. "Okay. Assuming I believe any of that—you have my thanks."

She smiled again. "You're welcome."

He glanced over at his two companions, who were seated a couple of tables away, pretending to eat and trying their best to overhear. He chuckled, then returned his attention to the young woman.

"You were a prisoner? Why?"

"I'm a princess," she pointed out again. "From one of the Black Sorcerer's subordinate kingdoms. Occasionally he takes tribute from his subjects. On one recent occasion, I was the price he demanded from my kingdom."

"For what reason?"

"How should I know?" She shuddered. "I wanted to get out of there before I had to find out the hard way, if you know what I mean."

His mouth a tight line, Blackthorn nodded. "Probably wise."

"You think?"

He ignored this. "And how did you escape?"

"I made friends with a couple of his lieutenants. I think they were actually created the same way he created you."

Blackthorn frowned at this. "Created? He didn't *create* me."

"Oh, really?" She laughed. "Have you looked at yourself lately? As in, since you woke up in his laboratory? How much of the 'you' I can see *now* was the 'you' *before* you came to be here?"

Blackthorn couldn't help it: He did look down at his fit young body, clad not in an American general's uniform but in a futuristic black suit that looked like black leather and moved like spandex.

"I get your point," he told her, "but the person *inside* here—" He tapped his head. "—the real John Blackthorn—is no different than the one that used to exist on the Earth."

"Oh, is that so?" she asked, her expression clearly revealing her skepticism. "And how much of your previous life do you remember?"

He didn't hesitate. "All of it."

She laughed. "Really?"

Anger swelled through him. "Yes."

"Describe it for me, then. Any of it. Your home. Your family. Your friends."

He frowned deeply. He tried to summon up those memories, but found his head pounding again. The same thing had happened the night before, when upon lying down to go to sleep, he had tried to recall his wife's face and found that he could not. He couldn't even remember the name of the town he had lived in when not traveling with the Army.

The princess could see him struggling and she reached out, placing a hand on his arm. He opened his eyes and looked up at her.

"You see? I'm telling you the truth," she said. "And this is after only, what? Three days?" Her expression now was one of sympathy. "It will get worse, I'm afraid. You'll forget everything that didn't happen here, on Mars. They always do."

Blackthorn pulled away from her touch and set his jaw firmly.

"Why did you come here?" he asked, emotion filling his voice, causing it to quaver slightly. "Why not run back to your family, your home?"

She shrugged. "I don't really want to go home."

"What do you want? What did you want from *me*?"

She pursed her lips and turned away, staring through an open window at the village outside. Several seconds passed, and Blackthorn thought for a moment that she wasn't going to answer, but then she looked back at him, and the smile had returned.

"I want to go with you. You and your friends. I want to join you."

"Go with us where? Join us in what? We're not *doing* anything."

"You will," she said.

Blackthorn frowned at this. The young woman—the princess, supposedly—seemed to have all the answers, including answers for questions he hadn't even thought of yet, much less asked.

"We will *what*?" he asked, growing frustrated at her responses.

"You'll go. You'll do. And I want to be a part of it."

Blackthorn shook his head, not in reply but simply in confusion and annoyance.

"Why?"

"For fun," she said, simply. "And because, sooner or later, you'll come into conflict with the Black Sorcerer. And I want to be there when you do."

At last she had said something that made sense to Blackthorn.

"You want revenge on him for taking you away from your homeland," he stated.

"Of course." She shrugged. "And for other things." Her eyes met his again. "The Black Sorcerer needs to go. To be taken down—crushed—utterly defeated. Nobody in all the centuries has been able to do it."

"But you think I can."

"No," she said, appearing surprised. "I think *we* can. We. Us. Together. You need me just as much as I need you." She hesitated. "Well—not like that. You know what I mean."

Now it was Blackthorn's turn to laugh. He felt as if he were finally starting to understand the young woman. Clearly there was a lot more that she *wasn't* saying—she was far more complicated even than she first appeared—but, if what she had told him thus far was even remotely true, then her motivations made a degree of sense. Somewhere along the line, she'd concluded that Blackthorn represented her best chance at getting back at the Black Sorcerer, and maybe at experiencing some excitement, too, and she had therefore helped him and his comrades to escape, and then followed them here.

"Okay," he said. "Assuming we do make some move against the Black Sorcerer—and I'm not saying we will, at least not immediately—what do you have to offer? Why would it benefit us to bring you along?"

She snorted at this. "I would think it obvious."

Eyes wide, Blackthorn waited.

"Knowledge, for one thing," Aria pointed out. "My years of education by the finest tutors available. Or were you planning on pumping these farmers and goat herders for their secret, inside knowledge of Mars, sorcery, and the First Men?"

"That's a fair point," he conceded. "What else?"

"Power."

He waited patiently.

She sighed. "Power, abilities, magic. *Sorcery*," she whispered.

"You can do magic?" he asked.

"Sorcery," she repeated. "Sure. I was taught all sorts of things, growing up. And I'm wired. It's part of the reason the Black Sorcerer was so interested in me. And it's the kind of ability you'll need on your side." She grinned. "Or did you expect that fancy light you're carrying around to do everything?"

He wasn't sure what she meant by some of that, and he wasn't happy that she knew about the energy sword device—though hardly surprised that she did, at this point—but he ignored it all and asked, "How about a demonstration?"

She frowned. "What—do something here? Now?" She shook her head. "These simpletons would go nuts. They don't much care for sorcery—or even *talk* of sorcery, in case you haven't noticed I've been keeping my voice down about it."

"I would stand up for you," he told her. "I would say you were a friend of mine, and didn't represent a threat to the village."

"Oh, and you've been here so long, they'd just instantly take your word for it, huh?"

Blackthorn brought one hand up to his forehead and pressed, his headache back and booming now. The woman was remarkably annoying, but he had to admit that she did seem very useful— assuming anything she was saying turned out to be true.

"One demonstration," he said. "Here. Now."

She gave him a sour expression but then shrugged. "Okay, fine. But when the authorities come running, just remember that I told you so."

She nodded towards a table about a dozen yards away. It was rough-hewn and heavy, and no one was sitting at it.

"Here we go," she said. "I'll make it fly. A little, anyway. Hopefully not enough to attract too much attention." She raised her right hand above her head. A faint blue light surrounded it.

From out of nowhere came a big, dark shape that rushed out at them. Blackthorn saw a discarded cloak fluttering to the ground and fur flashing past. Something grasped Aria by the wrist and pulled her hand back down. She started to scream, then cut the sound off as she stared up, wide-eyed, into the scowling face of Oglok. His brow was furrowed and he growled beastly sounds at her.

"Hey, what's this?" Aria demanded, struggling to pull her arm free from the big creature's grip. "What's he doing?"

As before, Blackthorn had no trouble interpreting the Mock-Man's language. "He says he doesn't like sorcery. Apparently none of the Mock-Men do."

"I know that," Aria sniped. "But it's none of his business—"

"He seems to think it *is* his business," Blackthorn explained, continuing to listen to the creature's barks and snorts. "He doesn't want any sorcery practiced in the village, at least while he and his uncle are present here."

"I don't really care what he wants," Aria snapped—but then she cried out as the big creature tightened his grip.

"She wont' do it, Oglok," Blackthorn told the Mock-Man soothingly. "That's right, isn't it, Princess? You won't do any more sorcery."

"What? But it was you that asked me to—" She groaned at the strength of his grip. "Okay, fine, yeah—no sorcery. Fine."

Oglok appeared to consider this for a moment, then released her hand.

Aria whirled on him, her expression almost savage, her hands coming up.

"Remember," Blackthorn told her quickly. "No sorcery."

She glared at Oglok for a moment, then slowly settled herself down, though she kept one eye on the Mock-Man.

"How am I supposed to prove anything to you now," she asked, "if I can't use my powers here?"

"You've already proven plenty," Blackthorn said.

46

"What?"

"For Oglok to react that strongly," he replied, "I'm confident that you have the potential to be *plenty* dangerous."

The Mock-Man had seated himself at the next table over and continued to watch her carefully. She gave him a sardonic smile and he grunted affably back at her.

"But we don't really know anything about her, General," Major Yuei was saying as O'Fallon looked on. "She could be in league with that lunatic."

"If that were true," Blackthorn replied, "she could have long-since revealed our location to him. She helped us to escape, and followed us here afterward. She just wants to be in on whatever we decide to do about the Black Sorcerer."

Across the table, Yuei pursed his lips at this and sat back on the bench, looking away. Next to him, O'Fallon had his arms folded across his chest, appearing pensive and somewhat agitated. They had waited off to one side as Blackthorn and the princess had their conversation, and had wasted no time in coming over once she had taken her leave and departed for her quarters. Neither man seemed particularly taken with her.

"*Are* we planning to 'do something' about the Black Sorcerer?" Yuei asked. "Is that the plan now? And, if so, exactly *how*—sir?"

Blackthorn glanced at O'Fallon; the man shrugged. "I for one am open to suggestions," he said.

The general stroked his jaw, now sporting a day's worth of beard since his last shave. "If we do," he said, "she can be a great deal of help. She knows things—at this point, she probably knows more about our lives on Earth than we can even remember."

O'Fallon looked up in alarm at this. They had already discussed the fact that the details of their past lives were fading rapidly from their minds. It was a sickening feeling, but there seemed to be nothing they could do about it. It was as if this new world, this terraformed Mars, was asserting itself upon them as the only reality they could know—the only reality they had ever known.

"How could she know anything about our lives on Earth?" O'Fallon asked. He appeared more agitated now than either of the other men could remember seeing him before.

"She was there, in the Black Sorcerer's headquarters, when he captured us—our souls, or whatever—and plugged us into these new bodies. She says his choices weren't random—his machine was able to let him view everything that was going on, back in our time, and then he selected people who were most likely to provide the psychological traits he desired."

Yuei nodded at this, but O'Fallon only grew more agitated.

"But now he's going to regret bringing this particular trio of soldiers through," Blackthorn said. "Well—soldiers and support personnel," he added, nodding toward O'Fallon. "Because I'm starting to think that the princess is right. We have a duty to take that loon down. From what Elder Ardin has said, these 'First Men' are just overgrown warlords, thugs who use their monopoly on high-tech machinery to dominate the countryside." He smiled at the other two men, chuckling softly. "Maybe we're here for a reason, huh?"

"More combat?" Yuei asked, growing pale. "Everywhere we go—more fighting, more killing." He frowned, appearing shaken.

"What's the matter with you, Major?" Blackthorn asked, leaning forward. "You're a soldier. You should understand—it comes with the job."

Yuei shook his head. "I'm not a soldier anymore," he said quietly. "In case you haven't noticed, there is no US Army anymore—and no United States!"

Blackthorn took this in, darkening.

"We *are* the United States Army here, Major," he said in a low but powerful tone. "We have certain responsibilities—"

"Not anymore!"

Yuei's outburst startled Blackthorn. He opened his mouth, closed it again, and shifted his gaze from Yuei to the other man. O'Fallon didn't return the look; he was staring off to the side, seemingly lost in his own thoughts.

"I should be dead," Yuei whispered after a few seconds of grim silence. "The ambush. Somebody sold us out. I should be *dead*."

"But you're not."

"No—I mean it," the Major said more forcefully. "I *should* be. I can remember being hit. More than once. I was bleeding—pretty badly."

"Yeah—I was, too," O'Fallon added hurriedly. "I was sure I was dead."

"I have a feeling we were all pretty much done for, back in the real world," Blackthorn agreed, trying to calm himself. "One way or another, our old bodies are long gone. But we're here now—alive and kicking—and just like I told that lunatic when he woke me up in this asylum of a world a couple of days ago, I'm not serving *anyone*. And if that means beating down and overthrowing all the wizards

48

and sorcerers and crazed maniacs this world can throw at us, I'm perfectly happy to do it."

Yuei listened to Blackthorn's diatribe and, after a few seconds, slowly nodded. "Maybe you're right, General," he said. "I don't know. Maybe…"

Blackthorn looked from Yuei to the other man. "What about you, Tony? Thoughts?"

O'Fallon barely seemed to be present with them anymore. He blinked, then glanced over at the other two. "Yeah," he replied, his mind still far away. "Sure. You can count on me."

It was an assassination attempt, Blackthorn realized before the night was over. An assassination attempt, pure and simple.

The alarm went up shortly after midnight. Village guards rushed toward the guest huts even as Blackthorn stumbled out of his own accommodations, his black pants in place but his top still back in the shack. Yuei emerged from his own hut and looked around; he had managed to pull his entire uniform on but nothing was properly fastened.

Yuei saw Blackthorn stalking toward the guards who were gathering around the entrance to Princess Aria's hut and hurried over after him. "What's going on, General?" he asked.

"About to find out, Major."

"He ran that way," one of the guards called, pointing down a darkened side road that passed narrowly between dwellings.

Blackthorn took one step in that direction, then halted and instead hurried to the princess's hut. He pushed through the congregation of guards and leaned in the doorway. There he saw the young woman lying on her cot, a guard kneeling beside her. Her eyes fluttered open; when she saw Blackthorn there, she tried to sit up, but instead started to cough violently.

"What happened?" he demanded, looking all around for signs of trouble.

"Your *friend* happened," she managed to say at last, between coughs. "He tried to kill me—first with a knife, and then by simply strangling me. Fortunately, I really *can* do sorcery—as I told you!" She grinned savagely. "After I zapped the knife away from him, I levitated it and poked him with it a few times, until he gave up on choking me and ran away." She rubbed at her neck. "Not easy to do while somebody is trying to strangle the life out of you, by the way."

Blackthorn was utterly puzzled. "My *friend*?" He turned about, seeing Major Yuei entering behind him. Then he looked back at the princess. "What friend?"

"The Colonel," she said, as if it were obvious.

Now Blackthorn was utterly bewildered.

"What colonel? Yuei here is a major, and O'Fallon's not even a soldier—he's a contractor."

Aria laughed—a harsh, raspy thing, what with her throat having nearly been crushed. "'O'Fallon?' That man's name isn't O'Fallon. And, seriously—a contractor? You think the Black Sorcerer had any interest in bringing a contractor into this world?"

Blackthorn was still confused, but now a sick, sinking feeling was forming in the bottom of his stomach. "What are you saying?"

"You really don't know!" Aria laughed again, even harder. "He's been fooling you! Well." She rubbed at her sore neck. "I saw it, you know—I was able to see, on the Black Sorcerer's machinery, as he studied all of you and made his selections. I watched as he chose you, and Yuei, and the Colonel."

Blackthorn stomped forward. "What are you talking about?" he demanded—though he really did know the truth now, in his heart, full well. "What colonel?" He leaned down closer. "Who *is* Tony O'Fallon?"

"He's the man who betrayed you into the ambush, back on your world and time," the princess replied. "I was wondering why you would associate in such a friendly fashion with him. I really did think you knew. Huh." She shrugged. "He's Colonel David Morningstar."

They searched all through the night, but O'Fallon—David Morningstar—was nowhere to be found. He had fled deep into the forest.

"I can see it now," Blackthorn told Yuei and Oglok as the three of them sat in the dining hall, sipping drinks the next evening. They'd gotten very little sleep. "He got really agitated when I mentioned that the princess knew more about our past lives than we remembered ourselves. He must have been afraid she would reveal who he actually was. So he tried to kill her."

"I can't believe that guy was right here with us, all that time," Yuei growled. "No wonder he was so reluctant to give us a name. It probably just took him a while to think of one that sounded plausible, but that neither of us could really challenge."

Oglok grunted menacingly and shook his great, furry head.

Blackthorn nodded. "He's gone now, and it's done. He's been exposed before he could do us any real damage. And yeah, Oglok—nobody got killed. So, aside from the princess having a sore throat, it worked out okay, I suppose."

At that moment, the princess herself strode up to their table. Her dress had changed in color again and now radiated a brilliant emerald green, the same color as the crystals strung along her necklace. Her long, thick, black hair was piled atop her head and held by various pins. She didn't look tired or injured at all—quite the opposite—as she stood directly before Blackthorn and smiled. Her dark eyes sparkled.

"When do we leave?" she asked.

Blackthorn frowned and glanced at the others. "Leave?"

"To begin preparing for the rebellion," she said, matter-of-factly.

"Rebellion? What rebellion is that?"

"The one you're going to lead, of course. The rebellion against the Black Sorcerer and the other First Men."

"Hold on, now," Blackthorn began, but Aria shushed him.

"No, no," she said, "we all know you're going to do it. It's just a matter of getting started. And so I say the sooner the better."

Blackthorn opened his mouth to object, then closed it. He was rapidly coming to learn that, with this princess, there was almost no point in arguing. She always seemed to be at least one step ahead of everyone else.

Across the table, Oglok let loose a string of barks and grunts.

Blackthorn turned to him, eyes wide. "You, too? Are you sure?"

The big furry creature nodded firmly.

Aria's eyes flicked from Blackthorn to the Mock-Man and back. "Oh—wait." She visibly deflated a bit. "*He* wants to come?"

"That's right," the General said. "He says he's tired of being just a bodyguard, and wants to contribute to the welfare of this world." He started to smile. "And—if we really are doing this—I think it's not a bad idea." He looked to Yuei. "Wouldn't you agree, Major?"

Yuei was staring resolutely down at the rough tabletop. He said nothing for a few seconds, then slowly looked up at Blackthorn. "O'Fallon—Morningstar, I mean—was right about one thing," he said, his voice very weak. "It seems as if our old ranks are now defunct, along with the entire US Army—and, I guess, the United States itself. And, if that's true, then I would just as soon sever any connections I have remaining to it."

Blackthorn scowled. "But, Major—"

"I'm not a major anymore," Yuei said quickly. "That man is dead. He died a long time ago, shot by insurgents in an ambush." He held his hands up and looked at them. "I don't know who this new person you're talking to is, but he's not Anton Yuei." He ran his hands through his hair. "Anton Yuei didn't have red hair and freckles, for God's sake!" He stared ahead wildly for a moment, then sighed. "I'd like to take some time to figure out who this new man is, that I've become—and what he should be doing in this new life."

Blackthorn considered several different answers, then finally just nodded. "Alright, Anton. I'm not going to force you to help us. Do what you have to do."

Yuei nodded. Then he stood, nodded his head to Blackthorn and the others, turned, and walked out.

Princess Aria watched him go, then smiled a flat smile. "We're better off without him," she said. When Blackthorn turned to say something back to her, the smile only widened, her teeth dazzling him. "So," she said cheerfully, "when do we leave?"

Blackthorn lay on the hard ground, his head pounding. He tried to pull himself up to his hands and knees, but found the process very difficult at first. Then, as his vision cleared, he saw the deactivated Sword of Light—he remembered that Princess Aria had told him that was its proper name—lying nearby, deactivated. Quickly he snatched it up and managed to regain his feet, though he swayed from side to side somewhat. He looked around; lizard-men and enemy robots were congregated here and there, fighting Aria, Oglok, or the village guards, but there was no sign of their main adversary. The explosion that had resulted when his energy blade had touched the Black Sorcerer's staff had thrown him clear of the huge, spider-legged assault vehicle, and he idly wondered if perhaps it has actually destroyed the Sorcerer himself. Somehow, he doubted it.

Two months had passed since his arrival on this far-future Mars, and during most of that time he and Oglok and Aria had traveled from village to village along the fringe of the massive forest, sowing the seeds of revolt against the First Men. In most cases they had been welcomed into the towns, given food and shelter, and allowed to address the population. No one seemed anxious to rush out, take up arms, and start a war against the mighty wizards of Mars,

however. Some small progress had been made, but there was much work yet to be done.

And then the Black Sorcerer's scouts at last found him. The wizard, desperate to recover his escaped pawn and furious that the man had fallen through his fingers once already, decided to accompany his army in their efforts to recapture him, to make certain they succeeded.

It was just before dawn when the leading edge of the Black Sorcerer's army assaulted the village where Blackthorn and company were staying. The General and his companions awoke to the sounds of screams and explosions and rushed out of the primitive cottages they had been loaned by kindly and generous townspeople. There they saw, in the gloom of early morning, a horde of lizard-men and battle robots arrayed along the outskirts of the town, doing battle with the night guardsmen. Beyond them, the massive, spider-legged vehicle fired its underbelly cannon at anyone and anything in the village that moved.

Blackthorn had ridden to the attack as his friends defended the village. He had met the Black Sorcerer in battle atop the crawler, and the explosion when their weapons touched one another had hurled him down to the ground.

And now the evil wizard had vanished.

A still-shaky Blackthorn ignited his blade and turned in a slow circle, his every sense alert despite his pounding headache. The man—if man he was—had to be nearby.

Then the crawler's engine revved up again and Blackthorn whirled about, stumbling back a few steps.

"He's gotten back into the cockpit somehow," he growled as he raced forward, leaping out of the way of one of the massive legs as it swung out and down at him.

Three big robots clanked towards him from the other side of the crawler, their arms coming up and directing weapons at him. He leapt into the air, the blasts of their weapons just missing below his booted feet, then deflected himself off the next big metal leg as it swept forward. Tumbling in a somersault, he lashed out with the Sword of Light and lopped the heads off two of the robots in one slice.

Landing behind the third, he brought the blade up just as the robot reversed the angle of its elbow joint in a manner impossible to a human and aimed the gun directly at him. The shimmering yellow blade easily deflected three quick energy blasts, and then it slashed through the arm-gun itself. Blackthorn continued the swing, taking off the upper portion of the robot's head. What remained of the mortally wounded mechanical man staggered around for several more seconds before collapsing in a sparking, blazing heap.

Blackthorn didn't slow down. He slashed at two lizard-men as they rushed towards him; seeing the deadly glowing blade passing only inches before their noses, the two scaly monster-men whirled and ran headlong into the trees, never to be seen again.

Passing out from under the spider-tank, Blackthorn gazed upward, attempting to spot his adversary. Before he could move further, however, the swiveling gun underneath the monstrous vehicle's nose swung around and fired directly at him. Instantly he was covered from neck to feet in a tight cocoon of exotic webbing, pinning his arms to his side and his legs together. He teetered and fell over, the still-ignited Sword of Light tumbling from his grasp and rolling to a stop a few feet away.

"I told you, human," came the high, nasally voice of the Black Sorcerer from atop the crawling behemoth. "You are mine!"

The gun whirled about then and fired a rapid series of shots in the direction of Blackthorn's companions. In a matter of seconds, both Aria and Oglok were similarly ensnared.

Black smoke billowed out from somewhere atop the crawler, and down through the miasma slowly descended the cloaked and hooded form of the Black Sorcerer, riding on the clouds, his snake-headed staff gripped tightly in his right hand.

Blackthorn tried to reach the Sword of Light where it lay nearby, but his arms would not move at all.

"You have led me a merry chase, human," the wizard growled as his feet gently touched the soil. "But, as I told you at the start, you are here to serve me—and serve me you will!"

Blackthorn cursed softly and attempted again to reach the sword hilt. He found he could barely even move his fingers, much less stretch out his arms.

The surviving few lizard-men were dragging the other two captives over and the Black Sorcerer regarded them with interest.

"So—a Mock-Man," he muttered, studying Oglok's face. "But not one I am familiar with." He snorted. "No matter. You shall serve me well in the mines, my furry friend."

Oglok said nothing, but his stare was patently murderous.

Then the wizard gazed upon the third captive as his minions dragged her forward and lay her before him. His dark eyes widened in surprise.

"Well, well. Aria. So. Here you are."

"Here I am," she agreed, frowning up at the hooded figure.

He darkened. "Your insolence has never gained you any special favors in my court," he said, glaring down at her. "And if ever you *needed* my favor, it is now—for I am most unhappy with you."

The princess didn't reply. After a moment, the Black Sorcerer started to turn back to Blackthorn, but Aria saw something at the limits of her vision and cried out, "You're an idiot!"

The wizard froze and turned back to her, facing her in full.

"Such foolishness, Aria," he said in a low voice filled with menace. "Such foolishness to speak to me so. Can you imagine the punishments I shall inflict upon you, once we have returned to my sanctum?"

"Not foolish at all, actually," she replied. "I needed you to keep looking over here a little longer. But now you can turn around."

The Black Sorcerer frowned. Perhaps he had quickly understood what Aria meant, or perhaps he heard a noise as his attacker approached. Either way, his eyes widened dramatically and he whirled about—but not quite quickly enough. Blackthorn, now free, advanced on him, the remains of the webbing hanging in tatters from his torso, the glowing blade of the Sword of Light flashing out. Frantically the wizard brought his snake-head staff up to block, but the shimmering blade struck it hard, like a piece of forged metal, and smashed it from his grip.

"What?" the wizard cried, stumbling back, gazing down at his staff in shock and surprise.

Blackthorn swung again, and this time the tip of the energy blade sliced through the fabric of the sorcerer's robe across his chest. Sparks sprayed out as some hidden electronic component shorted out. The Black Sorcerer shrieked in agony and dismay. He started to lunge for the staff, but Blackthorn stepped over it and jabbed the Sword of Light down, making contact with the snake-headed end.

"NO!" screamed the sorcerer, torn now between attacking an armed and angry Blackthorn while he himself was unarmed, or retreating and leaving his primary weapon behind.

The sword still touched the staff where it lay on the ground, more and more energy pumping into it. The staff glowed orange, then white—and then it shattered, coming apart in a powerful but very contained blast. Blackthorn tried to leap out of the way as he

56

saw what was happening, but was still hurled several yards away, tumbling across the rocky soil.

The Black Sorcerer gawked at the remains of his staff in silence, seemingly unable to speak at all now. He stared for a moment at the rapidly blackening shards that were all that was left of it now, scattered across the ground. Then he turned tail and ran back towards his crawler machine.

Blackthorn gathered himself up and switched the setting on his sword to the smaller utility blade, then hurried over to where Oglok and Aria lay trapped in netting.

"Nice work, Aria, in distracting the Black Sorcerer while I freed myself," Blackthorn said as he sliced at her restraints.

"Wasn't hard," the dark-haired woman replied with a smile. "I could see what you were up to—how you'd figured out the way to cut the webbing."

Oglok grumbled something. Blackthorn nodded as he moved to the big creature and cut through his bonds.

"That's right, my friend," he answered the Mock-Man. "I couldn't reach the Sword of Light. But I could move my entire body, almost like an earthworm, by squirming around. All I had to do was crawl over to the sword, where it lay, and touch the restraint webbing to the blade. Without cutting my own hands or arms off in the process, of course." He smiled. "The webbing cut easily and came right off."

By this time, the wizard had scaled the side of his big crawler and was back in the cockpit, cranking it up. Blackthorn and the others braced for a renewed battle, though they had higher hopes now that the wizard's staff had been shattered.

Alas, such a conflict was not to be. Just as the crawler began to lurch forward again under the Black Sorcerer's direction, its rusty metal legs moving and its belly-cannon swiveling around to aim at the three companions, an explosion erupted from its left side. Scarcely a second later, another blast sounded from further back in the central section. A third explosion and the crawler's movements ceased entirely.

With that, the few robots that had managed to repair themselves and regain their feet promptly fell over, their indicator lights going dark.

Blackthorn and the others gazed upward in surprise. A small flying vehicle, triangular in shape and bright red in color, hovered over the crawler. The guns attached to its undercarriage swiveled down and made ready to blast the wizard's war machine again. Such an action proved unnecessary; the crawler was well and truly dead.

The Black Sorcerer stood atop his crawler and shouted furiously but unintelligibly at the flyer for several seconds. Another blast from the flyer's guns, only narrowly missing, abruptly cut off the wizard's diatribe; scrambling along the length of the big vehicle, he leapt down through an opening in the hull. A metal hatch sealed closed over him. A moment later, an entire section of the big machine separated away and launched itself into the air, rockets underneath flaring to life and carrying its lone occupant away. The flyer's guns attempted to track the escape pod and fired several shots at it, but the Black Sorcerer's little vehicle accelerated with such rapidity that the blasts never came close. An instant later, it had vanished into the pale sky.

"There he goes," Blackthorn growled to his two comrades as they watched the small flying pod zooming away. Then he turned his attention to the red flying vehicle, which was descending toward them. "I wonder who our mysterious benefactor was?"

The flyer hovered about twenty feet above the Martian soil. The cockpit hatch slid open and a lone figure emerged. He had dark hair and wore a leather-like suit similar to Blackthorn's, but all of red. He smiled a flat smile down at the others, surveying them from on high.

"Colonel Morningstar," Blackthorn greeted him warily. He had switched off the Sword of Light, but his finger hovered over the red square. In the weeks since he had acquired the weapon, he'd taken the time to discover what each of the buttons on its surface did, and the red one seemed particularly useful in the current circumstance. "Your timing was excellent. We appreciate the assist."

"General Blackthorn," the man stated coldly.

"Why don't you come down here and let us thank you personally?" asked Princess Aria, her voice level and innocent-sounding, her dark eyes narrowing to slits. Sorcerous blue energies swirled about her hands. Beside her, Oglok growled menacingly.

"I believe I'll stay where I am," Morningstar—the erstwhile Tony O'Fallon—replied. "I merely wished to deliver a message."

"Oh?" Blackthorn kept his finger near the red square. "And what might that be?"

"Simply this: It's every one of us for himself now. Our old world is dead and gone, Blackthorn. Our military is ancient history. Our ranks are defunct. We have no further links to that world, that society. This new one is all that matters. And I intend to carve out

58

my own place in it. A particularly large place, as it happens," he added.

Blackthorn took this in, then nodded. "You've become quite ambitious."

Morningstar shrugged. "The opportunity presents itself. The man meets the moment. And all that."

Blackthorn laughed. "Right. You're the man to rule this entire planet. *You*."

Morningstar appeared to take no offense at this. "These are strange times," he replied after a second. "And strange places." He paused, looking off into the distance. "Think of how Napoleon came to power in France. It could never have happened but for the Revolution, the turmoil, the chaos—he stepped in at the perfect moment with a firm, guiding hand, and a genius for leadership. And he swept all of his rivals away."

"So you're the Martian Napoleon, then?" Blackthorn couldn't help but chuckle.

"Perhaps I am," Morningstar answered. "We'll see."

"I suppose we will."

The two men gazed at one another in silence for several seconds, the others watching and waiting, unsure of what was about to happen. They could see that the Sword of Light was ready in the General's hand.

"David," Blackthorn called up to the other man at last, his voice even.

"Yes?"

"Why did you do this? Why help us?"

Morningstar stared down at him, appearing unsure—as if he himself didn't know the answer. Then, "I suppose it's because I feel bad about how things went, back on Earth," he said. "I owed you something, for the betrayal. It wasn't supposed to go that way. You and Major Yuei and the rest of the command team—you weren't supposed to be involved." He shrugged, looking away at the dim and distant sun for a moment. "But that's war for you. Things happen that nobody intends."

Blackthorn nodded.

Morningstar shifted his gaze back down to the General again. "We're even now. Square."

"You think so?"

Morningstar shrugged again. "As far as I'm concerned, yes. As I said, all old relationships are null and void. The past is gone." He smiled. "I fully intend to take the place of the First Men. Just one at first, maybe, but eventually all four. They won't stand in my way." His smile vanished. "And neither will you."

He climbed back into the cockpit of his flyer and revved the engines.

"All bets are off, Blackthorn," he called out as the flyer curved slowly around overhead. "The next time we meet, may the best man win."

"Understood."

"The Black Sorcerer will be back before long. You three had better make yourselves scarce." The cockpit bubble snapped closed. The flyer zoomed off into the Martian sky.

Blackthorn watched the vehicle until it vanished over the horizon. Then he relaxed his grip on his sword and turned to Oglok and Princess Aria.

"Why didn't you blast him?" Aria demanded, visibly angry. Oglok echoed her question with a low grumble.

"He helped us. He drove away the Sorcerer."

"So?"

"It was my decision," the General stated with finality.

Aria folded her arms and sulked but reluctantly nodded. "But— if he pops up again," she said, "we are taking him down."

"Hard," Blackthorn agreed.

While bandaging their wounds, they were approached by the village's elders. Blackthorn feared at first that the townspeople would be hostile, blaming the trio for bringing the wrath of the Black Sorcerer down upon them. Far from blaming the visitors for the attack, however, the villagers had only grown more resolute in their opposition to the First Men.

"Build your army of revolution," the chief elder told Blackthorn, clasping his hand firmly, "and our people will rush to your banners when you call."

Blackthorn met the older man's eyes and nodded solemnly. "The day is coming," he replied. "Be ready."

He and the others helped carry the dead and wounded away from the battlefield and into places of shelter. Afterward, several young villagers brought the trio's horses to them. Blackthorn thanked them and the three companions mounted.

"So Colonel Morningstar fancies himself a wizard—a First Man—now, eh? Well, four dangerous lunatics or four hundred, nothing has changed, my friends," he told the sorceress and the Mock-Man as they slowly trotted their horses out of the village and back onto the trail. "Our mission has only begun. And nothing will sway us from it. We will see this strange new world *free*."

Aria grinned and Oglok roared his approval.

With that, Blackthorn pointed toward the path ahead—the path that led to the next village along the forest's edge, and to the next group of humans they would tell of the coming revolt. He spurred his powerful white stallion and the beast reared up, braying loudly.

"Aria," Blackthorn called, his voice clear and booming in the still morning air. "Oglok! *Ride!*"

Together the horses surged forward and the three companions galloped off in the direction of the rising sun, as the moons of Mars hurtled overhead.

CRADLE OF ATLANTIS

MARK BOUSQUET

The Sword of Light blazed and hummed in the diminishing night, and John Blackthorn wielded the long blade with a natural ability that surprised him when he bothered to think about it. So he didn't. He was a soldier, cultivated at West Point and steeled in the Afghanistan theater, and there wasn't a weapon in existence that he didn't know how to use, and use well.

Why should an energy sword be any different?

A voice someplace deep in his head told him a sword was different because he'd never picked one up before a few months ago, and yet here he was cutting down automatons in the dying light of an alien planet with the practiced skill of a man born with the weapon in his hand.

"Four. Score. And. Seven!!!! Four. Score. And. Seven!!!!"

Blackthorn dropped to one knee and shot his sword out in a long arc with his left hand, killing President Abraham Lincoln. It was the fifth or sixth Abraham Lincoln that he'd cut down since this battle began over an hour ago, along with ten John Kennedys, six Bill Clintons, four Nixons, three Washingtons, and about 26 Franklin Pierces.

Blackthorn grinned as three more Pierces stumbled towards him. They weren't all actually Franklin Pierce, of course, but if Blackthorn didn't know which President the robot was supposed to be, he labeled him a Pierce and kept taking them apart with the Sword of Light. Truth was, he barely knew any of them, and for all he knew, Clinton might have been Bush and Nixon might have been Adams. Memories of his previous life came and went and he was thankful that Aria had suggested this retro-Earth amusement park as a way to try and keep his memories alive.

"Fkkkkkkoursssssskkkkkkoorrrrr-!" the broken Lincoln at his feet shouted.

Blackthorn jammed his sword through Lincoln's jaw, causing the robot to spark wildly before dying. The automatons moved slowly but there were hundreds of them. Blackthorn gave a quick look around at the decrepit amusement park, his eyes finding his two companions. Oglok the Mock-Man was halfway up the roller coaster, wildly challenging a horde of robot spiders in his own grunting language, while Princess Aria must be in the Big Top, given the magical bursts of energy that ripped through the tent. Alongside them were a band of dirty, half-emaciated men and women who lived in the shadow of the park. Blackthorn felt an acute pang of homesickness that he hadn't felt since his first days in boot camp at the sight of the park – twisted and horrific as it was, it was the most Earthly thing he'd seen since he closed his eyes on that battlefield back in Iraq. So much had happened since then. He was on Mars. He was in a new body. He was thousands of years in the future. He'd fought lizard men and robots and magical maniacs. It was all so new and strange and he had never been further away from home than he was right now... and yet the simple sight of this amusement park stuck three miles outside of a broken city of glass somehow made what had happened to him seem impossibly real, and brought memories of Earth flooding back into his mind.

"Give. Me. Liberty. Or. Give. Me. Death!"

Blackthorn was a soldier. He'd spent his entire professional life learning to control and suppress and channel his emotions, and the need to do that hadn't changed even if everything else in his life had.

"Give. Me. Liberty. Or. G-kkkkkkkkkk!"

Blackthorn killed "Franklin Pierce" for the twenty-seventh, twenty-eighth, and twenty-ninth times, and then lost himself in violence.

"To Oglok!"

"Huzzah!"

Clay mugs containing berry wine were raised in celebration to Oglok. Not an hour ago the tan fur-covered Mock-Man had stood at the very top of the roller coaster and tossed the Sorcerer of Fatal

Laughter to the concrete a thousand feet below. The body of one of the four most powerful men of Mars, one of the four men that fought for control of this planet and spent their days fostering gear and hate amongst the people of this crippled world, had hit the ground with a fabulous crash, his body breaking in several points and scattering parts in every direction.

Like the Presidents, the Sorcerer was an automaton and his death signified no real victory. Blackthorn, still feeling his way on Mars, was disappointed in the revelation, but none of the proud, dirty people who called themselves "Nots" were either surprised or dismayed, and instead took the opportunity to celebrate as if the actual Sorcerer of Fatal Laughter now lay in hundreds of parts at the foot of Thunder Mountain. Apparently, this was not an uncommon occurrence, as the Sorcerer would bring the automatons to life under his control every few months as a means of keeping the unrest. The news made sense to Blackthorn, who thought these Nots fought much better than their emaciated, dirty bodies would have led one to believe.

A basket of bread made its way to Blackthorn's hands and he dutifully took a small, round loaf and passed the bounty to the Not next to him.

"Thank you, hero," Sihla, the female Not, said with sparkling eyes and what would have been a dazzling smile if her teeth weren't encrusted with plaque and grime.

Blackthorn ignored the invitation and instead turned to his right to wait for the next bowl of food to come his way. He felt Sihla's hands on his back through his black leather armor and heard her mumble something about how the jacket was ripped, and something more about how she could repair it if he'd just take it off, and on and on. The transplanted Earthman did his best to ignore Sihla. Even through the grime that caked her tawny skin and black hair, the raggedy brown dress that every female Not wore, the nicks of blood from the battle just fought on a body that was caught somewhere between being thin and emaciated, and the yellow teeth that created such a heartache in Blackthorn for toothpaste that it shamed him, it was obvious that Sihla was an attractive young woman. Though she looked to be in her late twenties, John guessed she was closer to twenty than thirty due to the hard life on Mars, and if she had been born in Virginia or Dublin or Sydney it was easy to guess that catching her eye would have made any man stand a bit taller in his boots.

"Why are you called Nots?" he asked, shrugging off her touch.

"Because we're nothing," Sihla replied in a low voice. "To the First Men, to the people from the finer cities," she glanced to Aria, "people like us are nothing, naughts, zeroes, beneath their grander designs. We are simply meat to be used whenever one of their mad schemes calls for a human sacrifice."

A bowl of large, white, hardboiled eggs was next to come down the line and as Blackthorn's hands took the dented metal bowl from the hands of a young male Not, his eyes caught Princess Aria's from the other side of the picnic table. Her beauty was unmatched, but as they sat here in the midst of such poverty, the flawlessness of Aria's skin, the smell of her perfume that he would occasionally catch while they rode on horseback across the planet, and the toned shapeliness of her body made Sihla, with all of her hard work and sacrifice, the more attractive woman. Aria was hard to figure and Blackthorn knew there was more to her than she was letting on. He wondered what the Nots could tell him about her; these people were polite to her but there was a coolness that was unmistakable.

Blackthorn grunted. Questions for another time, he reasoned, taking one of the softball-sized eggs and handing the bowl to Sihla.

"You do not want to talk?" Sihla asked, a small hurt evident in her voice. Blackthorn wondered if any man had ever *not* shown an interest in her, because beauty in a community was always relative. Sihla might not have looked appealing standing alongside the NFL cheerleaders the USO would send to the Middle East to give the boys a little American cheesecake, but compared to the rest of the women in this community that was scraping out an existence in the shadow of an amusement park, she was centerfold material.

"Sorry," Blackthorn grunted to her, apologies always coming hard to him. He motioned towards the Thunder Mountain roller coaster that dominated the park, then towards the Big Top off to their far right and back to the Funhouse on their far left. "This reminds me so much of home," he explained to her with what he hoped was kindness. "I didn't expect to see it."

Sihla brightened immediately, and John felt something stir inside of him as her brown eyes widened along with her smile. "Our elders tell us that this place was built for the human colonists that came to Mars. If this place could talk it would be pleased to see it could still fulfill its original purpose."

Blackthorn offered a smile and turned to his egg. He had remembered that he loved eggs, especially when they were hard-boiled. How could he forget something like this? While other men in his unit would bribe the men who delivered supplies for extra cases of alcohol or cigarettes, Blackthorn always bribed the mess staff in order to ensure an extra scoop of scrambled or an extra drop of over easy. With the sudden longing for home, and the largeness of the egg in front of him, John looked forward to this next bite of food more than he'd ever looked forward to a meal.

The Nots had no silverware, so he broke the egg in his hands and felt his mouth water at the sight of the yellow gold in the egg's center. Giving Sihla a smile, Blackthorn put a handful of yolk in his mouth and bit down, expecting deliciousness.

It was disgusting.

If Blackthorn was a lesser man he would have cried.

"You do not like it?" Sihla asked, placing a hand on his left arm.

"It's horrible!" Blackthorn spat, not realizing or caring that his comment was an insult to his guests. What did a soldier care of being polite company?

"You do not have this food on Earth?" Sihla asked. "It is called-"

"We have them," Blackthorn grumbled, his eyes unable to leave the sight of what still looked like heaven on his plate. "Our eggs are smaller, but the ones we eat most look just like this, smell just like this, cook just like this, even taste like this ..." He let the thought sputter and die and without thinking grabbed his mug of berry wine and took a big gulp. When the others had toasted Oglok, the Earthman had only pretended to sip from his mug because he'd always hated wine. He hated the fruitiness of the taste and how soft it made him look to others. Appearances weren't just appearances in the military and he couldn't be seen drinking anything other than beer and whiskey in front of his men – hard drinks for hard times and all that.

The berry wine tasted like fruit punch and John Blackthorn of Earth hated fruit punch.

It was delicious.

And as he stared dumbly at the food that should be delicious yet wasn't, and the drink that should be terrible but was refreshing, Blackthorn knew that it was the fault of the body that was currently his, yet wasn't his own. It was the body that lay gasping for breath back in the sand that loved eggs and hated wine, and the body on Mars that felt the opposite. Maybe it would be better to forget his memories of home. *No*, his mind insisted. *No! If I forget, then I will lose who I am!*

He wanted to find something to punch and so rose from the table and left the Nots to their celebration without looking back.

If he had, John would have seen a smile break wide across the face of Princess Aria, a smile that told anyone who saw it that a plan was very much coming together.

Wandering aimlessly down Mythical Lands Boulevard, John was determined to ignore the legendary exhibits on his left. To the right of this wide walkway were a series of shops and game stations—he wanted to experience authentic Earth, not mythic legends that hardly anyone believed in anymore. Though the years had taken their toll on the buildings, he could make out their intent. No matter his own desire, eventually the mundane repetitiveness of the right side of the walkway gave way to the exhibits on the left, as large building after large building offered visitors chances to experience Earth's myths. Blackthorn passed the Parthenon, promising a view of the gods, and a pyramid that offered an internal maze. Their presence made Blackthorn feel more homesick but calmed his anger, sending him into a slow spiral of dull depression.

John was never one for myths, but a sudden image of a set of twins from Boise burst into his brain, the memory nearly dropping him to a knee. The twins had kept telling everyone they were only in the Army to get experience using equipment they'd need when they became treasure hunters after their tour.

"Aliens built Tenochtitlan, you know," Lukas Magnusson had told his general one day. "Same as the pyramids. Oh sure, they used human slaves to do the work but they gave the humans the plans and directives."

"And don't even get us started on Atlantis," his brother Mats had added. "Most advanced civilization in the history of the planet happened a couple thousand years ago? Please. How does that happen?"

"They're not from here," Lukas had answered. "Aliens, man. Aliens."

As if on cue, Blackthorn came upon the Atlantis building. Looking like a futuristic fantasy, "Atlantis" must have once been a shimmering white castle. Now it was just another damaged, rotting hulk. There were holes punctured in the castle, exposing the metallic framework beneath. Its size was immense; John guessed it as equivalent to a five-story office building, highlighted by massive emeralds and sapphires laid onto the towering golden spires. Rags that once must have been glorious, vibrant flags fluttered pathetically in the evening's lazy breeze. What was once a water-filled moat was now empty and partially caved in, a resting place for broken parts and forgotten carnival rides, and the bridge that led from the walkway to the castle looked like it wanted to collapse.

"It is ironic you are drawn to this exhibit," Princess Aria said as she came up behind him.

Blackthorn turned to his companion, not hiding the look on his face that told everyone he wanted to be left alone. "If I had wanted your company, Aria, I would have remained at the table."

"I don't think Sihla would have allowed that," the princess said with a smile.

John grunted. "Why is this building ironic?" he asked, changing the subject.

The Martian princess came to stand beside him, her own blue dress torn, smudged, and burned from the battle. She had fought well today, from what Blackthorn had seen, yet the Nots would not celebrate her victories as they had his and Oglok's. Aria would have had it no other way.

"What else would it be called when the homesick Earthman, standing in an amusement park built to commemorate his home, came to rest before Mars' one, great contribution to Earth?"

Blackthorn blinked. "Could you say that in a more confusing manner?"

Aria smiled, desperately trying to keep the flash of victory out of her eyes, and snaked her right arm inside his left. "The legendary Earth city of Atlantis, John Blackthorn, was built and populated ... by Martians."

John grunted in disgust.

"How else can you explain how the most advanced civilization in the history of your world happened several thousand years prior to the ages of industry and silicone and quantum? They were colonists from another world." Aria gently touched Blackthorn's shoulder and lowered her voice. "I had hoped bringing you to this park would rekindle some of your Earthly memories. I understand that they are important to you."

Blackthorn started to answer and then stopped. He'd felt like Aria had been herding them in this direction, but he didn't realize her intent had—

A massive explosion rocked the amusement park behind them. Before John and Aria could run back to the picnic tables, Sihla led a group of women and children Nots towards them. Rounding the corner that brought them onto Mythical Land Boulevard, they ran wildly, fear in their eyes and actions. Once Sihla made direct eye contact with them, she stopped running forward and instead simply pointed the others towards Atlantis. "Run!" she urged them. "Run and do not look back! Get to the safety of the Great Rocket!"

Blackthorn and Aria were on the run, passing the group of fleeing Nots without acknowledging them. "What is it?" John asked Sihla, but before she could answer another explosion rocked the park. The three of them turned back in the direction of the picnic tables, tucked away behind a mini golf course, broken hot dog stands, and a wild maze of shrubs that had once resembled animals but was now simply overgrown weeds. A fireball rolled up into the sky, and a moment later Oglok's burning body came hurtling in their direction.

The Mock-Man's body slammed into the top of a Ring Toss booth. Lucky for Oglok, the bottles in the booth had long since been re-purposed by the Nots into drinking containers, and so when his blazing, heavy body crashed through the thin roof, all he had to land on was ripped and shredded stuffed animals.

Blackthorn and Aria ran to him. Oglok's entire coating of brown fur was ablaze, and the yellow mane that ringed his face was cut hard across the left cheek. His right eye was swollen and there was a cut deep enough on his stomach that even though the Mock-Man was barely clinging to consciousness, he still found some strength to hold his guts in place.

"They came out of nowhere!" Sihla explained hurriedly as John used the faded, flattened stuffed animals to try and suffocate the oxygen that burned his companion's body. "He's here! He's really here this time! The Sorcerer of Fatal Laughter!"

"How do you know?" Blackthorn asked without turning.

"Come!" Sihla urged, looking back outside the booth to see if the Sorcerer's minions were yet on them. The park began to shake with the heavy thudding from some unseen machine. "I am sorry about your friend, but we must get to the Great Rocket now! We must!"

From his knee, Blackthorn spun hard on her, the Sword of Light appearing in his hand as if by magic. "No man is left behind while he still breathes," he said in a low, commanding voice that told Sihla and Aria not to question him.

"Take Oglok to safety!" Aria ordered Blackthorn, and then ordered Sihla to show him the way.

"And leave you to fight whatever's coming?" Blackthorn grunted. "I don't think so, Princess! I think—!"

Aria called upon her magic to create a small, golf-sized ball of energy in her hand, and shoved her palm directly into Blackthorn's chest, shocking him just enough to remind him of her power. "Don't be so male, Earthman," she grinned. "I can't carry the Mock-Man given his hatred of magic, and you can't fight like a Princess of Mars!"

Blackthorn started to protest when a swarm of buzzing metal flies, each as large as a baby kitten, whooshed into the booth. "Go!" Aria ordered, sending a wide arc of yellow energy ripping through the fly-bots. She moved out of the booth to draw the bots' attention, but made certain to keep her back to Blackthorn. Was the Sorcerer of Fatal Laughter actually here? It seemed impossible ... but if he was ... could that possibly mean her calculations were actually correct?

Could it mean that buried somewhere beneath them ... was the lost city of Atlantis?

Blackthorn hated abandoning Aria, but the princess was probably right – it was better if he carried the heavy Oglok to safety while she battled the annoying fly-bots. The Mock-Man hated magic and while he was down, he wasn't out, and he might be more than Aria could handle. Blackthorn still didn't like it, but everyone had a role to play for a mission to be successful, and this was the best option for all of them getting out alive. Sihla led him forward amidst a fleeing group of male Nots, and in moments he was back at the white castle of Atlantis. Moving as gently as he could across the damaged bridge, Sihla led him through the big, open doors and inside the castle, where a wide room of white walls and a magnificent marble fountain awaited him. John could see how this once would have been impressive, even though the ages of dirt and decay robbed the room of anything close to splendor. Now, the building was simply struggling to stay upright. Just like the rest of Mars. Just like the Nots. He watched as the Not women and children ran to their fathers and brothers without comment, having seen this scene play out dozens of times in his years of service.

Across the room, Sihla gave one last look outside the heavy gates. "Close the doors!" she ordered.

Blackthorn heard the order as he carried Oglok to the safety of a far corner, where other injured Nots were undergoing a rough medical treatment. That had to mean everyone was back inside. Blackthorn gave a quick thanks for Aria's safety, though he was surprised that she'd managed to enter Atlantis so quickly after them. Thus it was to his immense anger that when he turned to greet her, the princess was nowhere to be found.

"Where is Aria?" he asked Sihla roughly.

The Not turned up her nose. "With her own kind," she snorted, and other Nots nodded in agreement.

"What is the meaning of this?" Blackthorn demanded. "Aria fought with you against the Sorcerer! Her magic allowed you—" at this, he looked to the emaciated men, "—to escape! Oglok took the brunt of the assault, and you repay him by—"

Sihla slapped Blackthorn in the face, stilling the soldier's tongue. "Do you even know with whom you ride?" the Not woman asked in an accusatory whisper. "Princess Aria," she said the name with absolute disdain, "is—!"

Oglok's roar silenced Sihla. The Mock-Man was on his feet, his fur burned and his flesh scarred, and he was not happy. Speaking in the guttural grunts and shrieks of his kind, Oglok pointed a large, meaty paw at Sihla and back towards the gates as he barked and growled, sending the Nots retreating from the man they were just celebrating.

"Agreed, my friend," Blackthorn nodded grimly to Oglok, clasping his arm, and his hand went back to his sword. "Open the gates so that we may leave. We would rather die in battle protecting one who—"

"Sihla!" a voice from the far staircase called down. "Come to the lookout tower!"

Sihla looked to Blackthorn and Oglok. "Come with me," she offered quickly. "See what can be seen from the tower. Perhaps," she said in a bitter voice, "there is no need for you to exit these walls." Sihla's brown eyes blazed. "Unless you would fight for one already dead."

Turning to leave, Sihla's body was jerked to a halt as Blackthorn grasped her arm. At once, every man, woman, and child in the room who had a weapon had it pointed at the Earthman. "As I expected," he grunted, letting her go. Oglok grunted a question to John, who answered simply, "Not all is as it seems here, my friend."

Sihla made a point to push past Blackthorn so she could be the first up the stairs. "What is it you see, Liget?" she asked the male Not who had called to her.

"It's here, Sihla! After all this time, it's here!"

Sihla reached a hand out to grab Liget's dirty, sand-colored hair. "What is?" she demanded.

Liget's eyes could not hide his fear. "*Fatality!*"

Blackthorn watched carefully as Sihla's face drained of blood.

Princess Aria no longer bothered to hide the smile on her face as she was led in handcuffs inside *Fatality*, the Sorcerer of Fatal Laughter's massive, rolling sanctum. *Fatality* was the largest vehicle on Mars. A towering, lumbering monstrosity nearly five hundred feet tall and half as wide, *Fatality* looked like a nightmarish black tank writ large—which is more or less what it was. Moving on heavy tracks and containing a whole city of servants to do the Sorcerer's bidding, the appearance of *Fatality* on a city or village's doorstep had the effect of turning on the lights in a dark room full of roaches.

Everyone ran.

The swarm of fly-bots took her up the massive ramp to one of the entrance doors at the rear of the moving city, where she was handed off to a pair of Jokers, the Sorcerer of Fatal Laughter's highest ranking officers. The Jokers were cyborgs, but at the earliest stages of their man-to-machine evolution, and they wore bright purple armor adorned with gloves and boots of green. On their chest was painted a smiling green mask, signifying their rank.

"Hello, Princess," one of the Jokers' said. He was an older man, with the top half of the right side of his face replaced with metal and wires. "So nice to see you again."

"Send my greetings to the Sorcerer, Uriah," Aria answered with a smile, holding up her handcuffed arms and disintegrating them with her magic.

Uriah laughed mockingly. "Do you think the Master would spoil his eyes with the sight of you yet again? How many times have you been captured now? No, the Sorcerer can't be bothered with you today."

Aria frowned. She wondered if she'd overplayed her own importance, but she wasn't going to show that to a Joker. "Is the Master still busy building himself," she glanced to Uriah's waist, "some new equipment?"

Uriah grinned, exposing broken teeth. "I'd slap you, Princess, but the Master has given strict orders not to harm his allies."

The last time John Blackthorn was this sickened by the opulent monstrosity of his enemy was when he had stood in Saddam's palace. No sooner had the thought entered his mind than he grunted in agony, every memory of Earth bringing another hammer-shot of pain inside his head.

After a moment the pain faded away, his vision cleared—and he gawked at what he saw. *Fatality* was so large, so imposing, so ridiculous that not even the Neo-Con hawks in the Pentagon would dare dream of submitting a budget for something this large. It was like the Sorcerer of Fatal Laughter had taken the middle third of a Great Pyramid, painted it black, put it on tank tracks, and then loaded it up with as many weapons as he could find. There was no rhyme or reason to the deployment of weapons that Blackthorn could see; but the randomness of their locations did not minimize their threat.

"Aria is in that?" he asked.

Sihla nodded. "One of my men saw them take her inside."

John grunted, wondering if Sihla slipped or didn't care to hide her position anymore. He decided to call her on it and see where it got them. "Your men?"

If Sihla had made a mistake in letting that piece of information out, her placid face didn't reveal it. "I'm in charge of all military matters."

Oglok barked. John translated. "He says you're very clever, cultivating that whole 'Not' angle when you fight like a trained militia. It's a clever ruse."

Sihla made no apologies. "Yes, we are very clever half-starving to death just to keep ourselves safe."

"So noted," John answered with his standard apology. "Now, why don't you tell Oglok and me the best way to get inside that beast?"

Sihla shook her head. "There are other matters that demand your attention, Blackthorn. Come, it is time for you to see the origin of Earth."

Two Jokers led Aria into a circular room. A bead of sweat began to form on her skin; while time spent as a captive of any of the First Men was never pleasant, there was a certain amount of privilege she generally expected and was afforded given the identity of her father. But this treatment ... this was far, far different.

The interior walls were dark grey, with wires wiggling out between cracks at odd angles. *Fatality* was a weapon of war, not a carrier for comfort. As her eyes adjusted to the lighting, she became aware of the person standing across from her and blurted out his name.

"Morningstar!"

"Aria. So glad you remember me," David Morningstar answered with a smile. Tucked inside a red bodysuit, Morningstar was a transplanted Earthman who'd served under Blackthorn on Earth. Now that they were on Mars, however, the former Colonel acknowledged no one as his superior officer, and where Blackthorn wanted to overthrow the First Men and deliver this world back to its people, Morningstar wanted to overthrow the First Men and take their place. "Tell me, Princess, does my good friend John talk about me?"

Aria gritted her teeth as she could see six weeks' worth of plotting and planning falling by the wayside. To be undone by the Sorcerer of Fatal Laughter would be bad enough, but if she'd been undone by this ... this *human*, that would be shameful! She'd spent weeks slowly urging Blackthorn to this amusement park. Carefully, Aria had suggested moving in this way at every opportunity, but she'd never brought up the subject of the park. She was counting on Blackthorn's homesickness at seeing this place to help drive him to retrieve the legendary weapon without ever having to mention that artifact.

She wanted the Voice of God for herself, after all. Blackthorn would probably want to leave it with the Nots.

Morningstar smiled and motioned to a round, wooden table that sat in the center of the room. "Would you like some tea? I met a woman in the prisons here on *Fatality* who knew you when you were a ... *captive*," his eyes twinkled, "of the Black Sorcerer. She let me know that this particular blend of tinoro leaf made your favorite tea."

Aria scoffed. "It's probably drugged."

"Then don't drink it." Morningstar motioned for the Jokers to leave.

Aria grinned. "That was a mistake, Earther. You need the back-up."

Morningstar ignored her and sipped tea.

Infuriated at his ego, Aria called forth her magic and—

Nothing.

She offered an irritated glance at the walls of the room. "The walls are lined with lead?"

Morningstar shook his head, picked up a remote control off the table, and pointed it at a section of wall, bringing an analog television to life. The screen showed only static. "A jamming signal blocks out your access to magic so long as you stay within *Fatality*. A gift from me to the Sorcerer who sits at the top of this craft. In exchange, I have decided I need not tell him of your ... visit."

"Impressive," Aria admitted, slumping her shoulders to feign defeat—and then attacked! She rushed hard at the transported Earthman, and he simply kept smiling his handsome smile at her as she approached and then launched herself forward, her right boot extended.

Morningstar waited until the final moment and swiveled easily to the side, sending her boot hurtling past his chest. Reaching out, he body-blocked her body, knocking her to the metal floor. "Get up and I'll put you down again," he said, and Aria believed it. She cursed herself for her over-reliance on magic; her hand-to-hand combat skills were still good enough to take most common opponents, but clearly the man standing over her was anything but common.

For the first time she allowed herself a long look at Colonel David Morningstar. He was neither as tall nor as muscled as Blackthorn, but he was attractive in a way that John could never be—refined, classy, like he belonged in finely tailored costumes, surrounded by luxury. If he could be controlled, Aria thought he would have made a perfect mate for her; but then, if he could be controlled, he wouldn't be the kind of man she wanted. Deciding to risk the consequences, she rose to her feet and moved across the room to pour herself some timoro tea into a small cup. Acting as if the setting was perfectly normal, she sipped her tea gingerly, ignoring the dryness of her mouth caused by battle. She was pleasantly surprised to find that David had already seasoned it with honey. Nodding her appreciation, she asked, "What now? If you're attempting to keep secrets from the Sorcerer of this craft, you are not long for this world."

Morningstar placed his hands behind his back and smiled at Aria as if he knew she was already his to play with as he pleased.

"We're going to be allies," he instructed her, smiling like a snake about to feast on an unguarded nest.

"Why on Mars would we do that?"

"Because neither of us can find the Voice of God alone."

"It is time you hear the truth about the origin of your world, John Blackthorn of Earth," Sihla said in a low, reasoned voice, as they descended the stairs to head back to the main hallway.

"Is this where you tell me that Atlanteans were the first people to colonize Earth?" John asked.

"It is not I that will tell you," she explained somberly. "It is time for you to hear the Message of the Ancients."

Blackthorn looked to Oglok, who merely shrugged and grunted. His friend looked like hell, all burned tan fur and bleeding wounds, and he gave the Mock-Man the okay to get himself treated. Reluctantly, Oglok agreed, and John accompanied Sihla into a small amphitheater. John guessed the room was originally made for 200 patrons, arranged in stadium-style seating. The seats, walls, and curtain that shrouded the stage were all red and worn, and the room smelled strongly of rot and mildew.

Sihla motioned to someone unseen behind them, and John glanced upwards to see a projectionist give her the thumbs up. He stood with Sihla at the back of the seating area and watched as the stage's red curtain was pulled to one side on automatic tracks. A movie screen was revealed, and John felt another acute pang of home when the picture started playing, complete with scratch marks on the film and pops in the sound. In his mind he could smell and taste some buttered popcorn, but then the memory of the eggs from earlier came back to him and he pushed the nostalgia aside for the job before him.

A title card appeared on the screen, reading:

ATLANTIS: THE LOST CITY OF MARS!

A male voice that reminded John of the old 1950s newsreels he'd seen parodied on TV began speaking.

"Welcome, visitors, to the story of Atlantis, the First City of Mars! In the early days of the red planet, a race of green-skinned people used apes as slaves!" The images on the screen began to match the voice-over. "The apes eventually tricked their overlords by shaving themselves clean of fur and appearing pink-skinned and hairless! They defeated the Green Martians and took Mars to dizzying new heights of technological advancement! Taking a hundred years, they built themselves a huge, sprawling city of technology and they called this city Atlantis! Atlantis ruled Mars for a thousand years of peace and prosperity, but it was not to last! Jealousy erupted on the back side of the planet and Atlantis began to receive reports from the outer colonies that there was an army forming, a Black Army of incredible might that was coming … coming to destroy Atlantis!"

Blackthorn was already bored. This was the origin of Earth? Preposterous. The soldier in him was more interested in why *Fatality* hadn't started bombing this fake castle.

"Fate intervened before the army ever reached the gates of Atlantis, however, as the city's scientists discovered that a passing comet also hid an approaching asteroid … an asteroid that was headed straight for the shining city! Preparations to escape the planet were enacted, but spies within the High Council alerted the Black Army, and now they attacked not to take the city, but to take Atlantis' spacecraft! If they could not escape, they would make certain the hated Atlanteans shared their doom! In the ensuing battle, only one rocket managed to escape Mars! Only one ship managed to escape destruction! Only one Atlantean survived as the rest of his people were buried under tons of asteroid rock, and pushed deep into the heart of Mars!"

A picture of a red rocket ship blasting away from the surface of Mars appeared, literally passing the approaching asteroid like two ships passing in the night.

"The Great Rocket contained only one Martian, a small boy named Hercules, and he journeyed, alone but not afraid, across the vast universe before finally crashing down on Earth! With the lessons taught him by the machines of the Great Rocket, Hercules built his own technological marvel, his own shining city, and he christened it with the only name possible: ATLANTIS! But he would never again see his home! Though his ship was able to access the city's computers and teach him of his people and of their science, Hercules would never again set foot on Mars, and no Martian would ever again set foot in what was now, and forevermore, the LOST CITY OF MARS! For buried somewhere underground, lost to the ravages of time, lay the greatest scientific and technological achievement in the history of Mars! Somewhere beneath the surface of this planet ... lies the Sleeping Army of Atlantis!"

Sihla waved her hand and the projectionist turned off the reel. "What follows from there on is a brief history of the Earth city Atlantis, but I am assuming you know all of this, being from Earth."

"Of course," Blackthorn answered, keeping any sarcasm out of his voice. The whole story sounded to him like a FUBAR report of all kinds of different stories: *Planet of the Apes* meets *Superman* meets whatever that last *Lord of the Rings* movie was called, he thought through a painful grunt. Of course, since he'd never seen *Planet of the Apes* and never read Superman and never seen nor read that Hobbit stuff, and only heard about them from the yapping of his soldiers, he could have been wrong. "Not to be rude, Sihla," he said, changing course, "but Oglok and I must rescue—"

"So like Martian men!" Sihla spat disgustedly. "Always wanting to fight and never wanting to learn! Did you not learn the lesson of this recording?"

"Hercules was a Martian?"

Sihla balled her hands into fists and tried her best to remain calm. "How would you and the Mock-Man ever hope to succeed against *Fatality*? Did you not hear the recording? Atlantis holds the greatest stores of weapons in the history of Mars! Follow," she ordered with a harsh snap of her voice, "it is time for you to see the Great Rocket before the Sorcerer of Fatal Laughter smashes through our front door."

Blackthorn wanted to protest the absurdity of the Atlantis story, but followed dutifully, standard operating procedure for a soldier. Sihla was right about one thing, at least. There was no easy way for Oglok and him to break into the Sorcerer's monstrous machine.

"I thank you for not playing dumb," Colonel David Morningstar said to Princess Aria as they walked through the hallways of *Fatality*. Aria had been in the craft before, but never this section of it. The hallways were sometimes cramped and sometimes wide, and the entire interior had the feeling of pieces being added whenever pieces were at hand. There were metal panels, white panels, grey tunnels... Sometimes the hallways were square, sometimes rectangular, and sometimes round. Clearly, this was a fitting home of the being known as the Sorcerer of Fatal Laughter.

"Playing dumb would not stop you from asking for help," Aria replied, "and revealing that I know of the Voice of God does not guarantee me giving it."

Morningstar's eyes sparkled with such a devilish delight that Aria couldn't tell if the thrill that ran through her as a result was one of fear or excitement. "What do the legends say the Voice of God can do, Princess?"

Shifting slightly on her feet and feeling vulnerable under the Earthman's gaze, Aria answered, "It allows one to communicate across the surface of the planet. Some legends claim it even allows one to communicate across the stars."

Morningstar nodded. "It was how the Atlanteans were able to communicate with the Great Rocket."

Aria raised an eyebrow. "You believe these legends?"

The Earthman reached into the messenger bag slung over his shoulder and removed a book. "Benefits of time travel," Morningstar smiled, and Aria's eyes went momentarily wide as she saw the book's cover: "*Atlantis: The Martian Connection*, by Lukas and Mats Magnusson."

"I nailed their sister."

79

"I've never seen that book—"

"What did I say about playing dumb, Princess?"

He handed her the book. Flipping open the paperback, Aria saw her own name scribbled on the backside of the front cover. "You have me at a disadvantage, Colonel."

He looked at the book in her hands and sighed. "I actually read about half of it. I think that's a record for me. There really should be audio books on Mars," he added.

Stopping in a tight section of the tunnel, he reached toward Aria and grasped her arms. "Help me, Princess. Help me capture the Voice of God and I swear to you we will use it to destroy the First Men."

Aria studied his face and contemplated her options. "You should join with Black—"

Morningstar scoffed as he spun away from her. "Let me put it plainly," he said as he turned into a corridor on his left. Aria followed him down a descending walkway. "The Voice of God is a communication device, and communication devices need someone on both ends—one to send the message and one to receive it. It is a weapon that has to be shared. I can share it with you, or another." He stopped at a solid black door, resting his hand on the handle. "Your father, perhaps."

Aria stopped dead and said nothing.

Morningstar looked at her over his right shoulder, offering her a roguish smile. "Blackthorn wants to give this planet back to the meek. I don't want that, Princess." He opened the door to the garage, revealing a large rock-digging machine. "And neither do you."

"Sihla!" Liget called to her as she and Blackthorn moved through the halls of the amusement park castle. "A Rock Grinder has been released from *Fatality!*"

"We must hurry!" she acknowledged, motioning for Blackthorn to move faster. "The Sorcerer intends to tunnel straight through the rock to Atlantis!"

"How could he know its location?" Liget asked, but Sihla ignored him. The First Men had spent generations attempting to find the Lost City. Eventually, one of them would have found it by luck if not skill.

Oglok rejoined Blackthorn in front of the Great Rocket, his wounds now bandaged. The ship looked to Blackthorn like something out of a Bugs Bunny cartoon—tall and curved, like a football stretched thin to a height of nearly forty feet. The rocket was red, with three white wings at the base, and a glass window at the front. It was placed on the other side of the theater and stood alone in a high-ceilinged room that once undoubtedly held glass but had been covered up with boards and sheets of metal. On the walls of this display room were the painted exploits of Hercules, which Blackthorn saw as a mixture of this new, Martian Atlantis story combined with the mythological Hercules of the ancient Greco-Romans.

Blackthorn wanted to say something, but the reverence the Nots had for this place kept his and Oglok's tongues still in their mouths.

"For generations upon generations we have protected the secret of the Great Rocket," Sihla said, as the Nots all bowed their head in silent prayer. "The Nots have lived in fear of this day, when one of the First Men would come to our door and try to take the secrets we hold dear. The presence of *Fatality* makes this clear." She looked to Blackthorn. "The Sorcerer of Fatal Laughter brings his war machine for one purpose and one purpose only, John Blackthorn. He comes to claim the weapons of Atlantis, and Heaven help us all if he finds them because, if he does, not even the combined might of the other three First Men will be able to stop him."

Blackthorn shook his head. "But there's nothing here that can help him." He took a step towards the Great Rocket, intending to bang on its hull, but the gasps from the Nots stopped him in his tracks. "Does this rocket even fly? Does anything here even still work?"

It was Sihla's turn to move to the rocket. Her dirty fingers danced along the dented metal hull as she walked around and around the ship. Oglok grunted, trying to keep his guttural voice as low as possible. Blackthorn replied, "She's touching the bolts that hold the rocket together. It must be a code."

Sihla finally finished and stepped back, on the opposite side of the Great Rocket from the Earthman and Mock-Man. From someplace beneath the ground, everyone could hear ancient gears begin to grind back to life and slowly, slowly, slowly, the Great Rocket began to descend beneath the floor. When only the top cone remained, Sihla moved to the machine and hit three bolts on the edge of the front window, which caused the entire top cone section to split in half and fall backwards. "Help," Sihla said, and Blackthorn and Oglok moved forward. The Not woman pointed to the white baby's cradle that would have held the young Hercules, and the two men pulled the cradle out of the ship. They could look down into the interior of the Great Rocket now, and what they saw was a ladder that ran straight down the entire middle of the ship.

"We go down?" Blackthorn asked Sihla, knowing the answer.

"We go down," she replied, "because we must reach Atlantis before the Sorcerer of Fatal Laughter."

Blackthorn nodded. He hated leaving Aria behind, but he could see this came first. If Sihla was right, an armory awaited them with enough power to end the threat of the First Men for good.

Oglok wailed.

"Me, too, buddy," Blackthorn said, slapping the Mock-Man on the back. "Let's hope there're some lights at the bottom."

Inside the Rock Grinder, Morningstar chuckled. "My dear Princess, you didn't think I'd travel without a magical dampening shield, did you?"

Aria's face went red and she crossed her arms in the co-pilot's seat, her magic failing her for a second time. Biding her time, the princess sat and watched through the Grinder's monitors as the massive drill at the front of the machine bored them deep into the planet.

One thing was certain in her mind: If the Voice of God was waiting for them, Aria would own it before this day was over.

Blackthorn and Sihla led the way forward through natural tunnels in the rock, with Oglok trailing several steps behind. Every fourth or fifth person in line held a lit torch, offering the only light in the dark. John knew he could use his Sword of Light as a flashlight (there were five squares on the sword's hilt, each with a different power), but given that they were underground he wanted to conserve the weapon's energy—as long as he could avoid using it, he would, because he didn't know what was waiting for them at the end of this journey. The tunnels were winding and wide and always moving down. Something had been gnawing at Blackthorn, and he raised the issue with Sihla. "If you have all of these weapons hidden away down here, why haven't you used them? If you have a Sleeping Army, why not awaken them?"

"A wise question," she answered in a low voice, not wanting her fellow Nots to hear her. "We have waited for a rebellion to arise that could make use of the weapons of Atlantis because we are too few and too weak for them to be of any use. If we used the weapons today, the First Men would be here tomorrow."

"If you had these weapons, you could have raised an army," Blackthorn countered with a heavy dose of skepticism, "or you could have simply awoken the army that's been waiting down here."

"Blasphemy!" Sihla spat at him. "The ancient laws are clear— the Chosen Ones will awake for us only in our darkest hour, only when we are on the verge of complete and total defeat!"

Sihla had no further answers for him, and he let the point sit between them, as the tunnel opened out into a high-ceilinged cavern that held a small underground lake.

"The legends are true!" Sihla gasped at the sight of the water. Behind her, Liget saw the sight as well, and ran past Blackthorn and Sihla to the shore of the water. His feet kicked up dozens of small, grey rocks as he approached several old boats resting on the shore.

"Be careful, Liget!" Sihla called. "We do not know—!"

Blackthorn moved ahead of her and turned to step in her face. As each subsequent Not emerged from the tunnel, praises were raised and dirty men, women, and children ran in Liget's wake. John ignored them and did his best not to put an actual finger into Sihla's chest. "The legends are true? Have you ever been down here?"

Sihla shook her head. "The ancient laws forbade it."

"I'd like to read those laws," Blackthorn grumbled, "but I'm guessing you don't actually have them written down, do you?"

Sihla didn't answer, causing Oglok to snort and growl.

"What did he say?" Sihla asked, turning to glare at the bandaged and burnt Mock-Men.

"Do you really need it translated?" Blackthorn asked, turning away from the Not leader to head towards the water.

"AAAAIIEEEEEEEEEE!!!!"

Blasters, bows, and one shimmering Sword of Light were drawn at once as everyone looked around to find the source of the scream. Yellow tentacles the size of buses burst from the water and darted towards the shore. Blackthorn ordered everyone back as he rushed forward, but Oglok grabbed him by the collar of his leather uniform and hauled him to the ground. Shouting an obscenity at the Mock-Man, Blackthorn scolded himself a moment later as a large bird swooped over his prone body, its massive red talons snapping above him.

Oglok delivered a guttural scolding, his massive paws pointing to the ceiling. As John rose to his feet he could see things moving in the dark above them. The lights from their torches provided only a modicum of light, which was just enough to further scare portions of the Nots. Sihla moved beside them after ordering the non-fighters back into the tunnel that had brought them here.

"What do your legends say of water monsters and bird assailants?" Blackthorn asked roughly.

Sihla had no answer.

Another bird swooped in to attack them. It looked like a scrawny vulture, but one easily three times the size of any bird Blackthorn had ever seen. "Deal with it," he ordered Oglok, who was happy to oblige. As the bird dove at Sihla, picking out the weakest target, Oglok reached up with his powerful paws, grabbed the bird's leg and hauled it to the ground.

The first yellow tentacle slapped the shore a few feet in front of them and now that it was close Blackthorn could see that it wasn't a tentacle at all, but an electric eel. As the large body crashed into the shore, hundreds of small rocks were sent flying. Oglok was busy ripping the guts out of the vulture, so Blackthorn stepped forward alone, slashing at the massive eel with the Sword of Light. The effect was largely the same as if he had sliced through part of a bus—there was a slight recoil from the creature but nothing that stopped a second and then third tentacle from hitting the shore. The head of the eel opened up and snapped at the Earthman, who responded by cutting the beast in the mouth. Blackthorn turned to the Mock-Men. "Oglok, I need your help!"

Oglok howled and rose to his feet, his eyes widening in challenge at the dozen eels that all emerged from the water around the same location, indicating there were but parts of an unseen center. His eyes focused outward, Oglok missed the two vultures that dropped from the ceiling and dug their talons deep into his shoulder. The Mock-Man howled in rage, but the vultures had him and flew his large body off the shore, heading for the darkness above them.

"Oglok!" Blackthorn yelled. An eel knocked him to the ground, and then another eel shot its tongue at the fallen soldier, wrapping him up and hauling him into the air.

On the shore, Sihla called the Nots into action. Both of their allies were held above the underground lake—Oglok carried increasingly higher by the two vultures and Blackthorn being tossed to and fro by a giant, yellow eel. Oglok disappeared into the shadows as the Nots readied their weapons. "Concentrate on the eels!" she ordered, not wanting to hit Oglok with a random blast. "Aim near the water!" she added, pointing to the area of water where eight giant

eels now pushed into the air. The Nots dutifully fired their weak blasters and bows and arrows, but they had no effect.

High above the lake, Blackthorn was wrapped in an eel tongue that had the tensile strength of heavy steel wire. Impossible to grab because of its spongy wetness, the soldier found it impossible to so much as wriggle free. The eel kept him completely off-balance, and Blackthorn's eyes could not focus on anything; he'd see the dark ceiling, the shore, the water below, and the horde of giant yellow eels wriggling around him. "Least it hasn't tried to eat me—yet," he grumbled inwardly, closing his eyes so he could concentrate on the Sword of Light in his hand. The last thing he could afford to do was drop the weapon and so he gripped it as tightly as he could in his powerful hands and began swinging the sword wildly, hoping to hit something that would knock himself free.

It wasn't working. He opened his eyes to see the Nots firing gamely at the center of the eel creature. Their attempts weren't working, either.

"GROWUARRRRAARAA GLARRA!"

Blackthorn craned his neck to see Oglok fall from the sky and drop into water with a slapping thud. Instantly, all of the other eels rushed towards the spot in the water where the Mock-Man had fallen. Knowing he had to do something radical, even if it meant burning through the Sword of Light's energy supply, Blackthorn looked down towards the root of the eels, took aim, waited for his eel to give him a second's pause. Then he depressed the red square on his sword's hilt, launching what he had come to think of as an "energy grenade"—a singular burst of destructive power—at what he hoped was the heart of the creature.

The grenade exploded at the water's surface, blasting huge chunks of flesh off three of the eels. Each of the eight eel heads went rigid, pointing straight at the ceiling as each squealed in pain. Blackthorn fired again. This explosion blew one of the eels free from whatever it was connected to beneath the surface and injured two others. A third grenade took two more eels out of the picture and finally caused the eel that held him fast to drop him.

Blackthorn fell hard into the water, only to be hurled into the air again as the creature's bulbous head emerged from the deep. He landed with a thud on the creature's collection of eight blue eyes, each the size of a beach ball and as squishy in his hands as a bowl of thick Jell-O. Roaring his own challenge in honor of the still-missing

Oglok, Blackthorn clicked off the red square and depressed the orange square, sending a steady orange laser beam into the eyeball at his feet. The eel heads screamed in pain and horror above him. Blackthorn kept firing and the eyeball exploded, coating Blackthorn's boots and pants in a gelatinous muck. The creature began to shake, knocking him off-balance and into the wriggling eels that were connected to something deeper in the water. Switching the Sword of Light back to his preferred energy blade, he began slicing and hacking at the creature's eyeballs.

The giant beast thrashed hard enough now to knock John into the frothing, bloodied water, and as the soldier readied himself for the next attack, he was pleased to see that the creature had had enough and dropped the entirety of its damaged head and eel extensions back into the water.

A momentary sense of pride was all Blackthorn allowed himself. He screamed for Oglok again and again. Dipping his head into the water, he tried to look for his friend, but the water was so dark he couldn't even see the massive, bright yellow eel creature, let alone one Mock-Man. The vultures began to circle and out of anger, Blackthorn blasted at them with his sword's laser. His mind raced, thinking of what he could do, when the water twenty feet in front of him began to bubble.

Oglok's head broke the surface along with a mass of debris. The Mock-Man gasped desperately for air, and then let loose a victorious howl. Spotting Blackthorn he grunted excitedly through big gasps. Blackthorn heard the words and finally turned his attention to the debris that had bobbed to the surface alongside his friend. His eyes widened.

Weapons.

Lots and lots of weapons.

Morningstar watched the computer graphics overlaid on the front window of the Rock Grinder, feeling a desire to make a crack about how it reminded him of Pong, but said nothing. He could feel Aria's excitement growing despite herself and the last thing he wanted to do right now was anything to dull her anticipation of finding Atlantis.

"Almost there," he said instead, altering the steering column to flatten out the Grinder's path. Within moments they could feel the front drill break into open air, and shortly thereafter they were ascending through the roof of the machine to look at where they'd been deposited.

Morningstar exited first and Aria followed. The first thing she saw was the wide grin on his face, and the second was when she turned around and looked forward.

"It's true," she whispered excitedly. "It's all true!"

Before her lay a cavern of such immense proportions that she could not make out the far edge. The Rock Grinder had brought them out onto a massive upper plaza, and before them was a wondrous garden with a large lake off to her left. Light poured into the cavern from various holes in the ceiling and walls, allowing them to see what looked like a forest of green.

Poking out at various points in the cavern's forested floor were tilting spires. "Atlantis!" she said breathlessly. "We have found the Lost City!" Turning to see the Earthman's expression, she was stunned to find him looking somber. "What could possibly be wrong?" she asked. "Look at that giant spire off to the right!" She turned from the man in red to take in the city's largest structure, a giant grey tower that was leaning to the right. Windows dotted its surface and straight down the middle, in script that must have been fifteen feet high apiece, was the letters: A-T-L-A. The tree line hid what came next, but could there be any doubt? Aria burst with joy and the unmistakable tingle of power that would soon be hers. "This is Atlantis, Morningstar! This is—!"

Snapping with a sudden, intense burst of anger, the Earthman took one step forward and jammed both of his hands into Aria's shapely back, knocking the princess off the Rock Grinder and into the dirt twenty feet below.

Stunned and hurt from the fall, she turned and glared up to him, her emotions flaring, her face conveying a look of disbelief and anger. "What is the meaning of this? Come with me! Help me find the Voice of God!" she pleaded, knowing she could use his help in locating the device somewhere in this massive, hidden city. That she'd probably kill him after they found it was no different, she reasoned, than what he surely intended to do with her.

"Go away, Aria," Morningstar groused. "The Voice of God is yours. If you can find it, it will be useless, but you won't find it. This place has been stripped centuries ago."

With that, Morningstar climbed back down into the Rock Grinder. In moments the machine's large drill traveled on its track to re-locate itself at the rear of the machine, and then it drove back into the hole it had already created. It left one very happy princess in its wake.

Morningstar might know of the Voice of God, but he was apparently completely unaware of the Sleeping Army of Atlantis. Aria smiled, thinking that he should have read a book by someone other than the Magnussons.

One quarter turn to Aria's left around the outside of the cavern, Blackthorn was having a similar reaction to Morningstar's. After the Nots had excitedly gathered all of the guns, Blackthorn had wanted to leave. The weapons were waterlogged and he didn't want to be near the Nots when they learned they'd just collected guns that would never fire. He loaded Oglok and Sihla into a boat and headed out across the lake and down a slow-moving stream. The creatures above and below left them alone, having learned their lesson. Within minutes the boat had picked up its pace and soon they could see that the stream was going to deposit them in a second lake. Sihla was almost giddy with excitement and it bothered John to have to tell her that they were not going to find what she thought they were going to find.

Sihla didn't believe him then and she didn't believe him now. Standing in the middle of the small, wooden boat, the three of them looked out and up at what they could tell was an extensive forest that had overgrown a fallen city.

"It is the Lost City, Blackthorn! Can you not see this? Look to the massive tower in the distance! Look at the letters: A-T-L! Is there any doubt that the rest of the letters do not spell out Atlantis?"

Oglok barked semi-excitedly and semi-questioningly at Blackthorn.

"Atlantis, my friend," he said to the bedraggled Mock-Man. "It says Atlantis."

Oglok's reply was clearly a question.

Sihla ignored them both now, not bothering to dampen her excitement.

A burst of magical energy off to their right and halfway up the wall let them know that Aria was here. The princess sent a calm burst of blue, green, and white fireworks in the direction of ATL Tower.

Blackthorn took the Sword of Light off his belt to answer with a burst in kind, but all he could manage was to turn the weapon into a flashlight, its energy reserves having been almost completely depleted.

An hour's march into the forest had not diminished Sihla's delight. While they found no evidence of a once majestic city, they did come across piles and chunks of debris. Sihla saw this as evidence of a city buried in the rock, figuring that what they were seeing was what had been tossed up when the asteroid hit the First City, and John Blackthorn was in no mood to continually disagree with the leader of the Nots ... who were, he now knew, not even Nots.

When they reached the giant, leaning tower, Sihla clapped excitedly, pointing to the large letters that clearly spelled out, "ATLANTIS."

Oglok grunted.

"No," Blackthorn said. "We wait for Ar—"

"Too late," Aria said, climbing out of a window nearest to the ground. "Already here. Already explored," she said, pointing back to the tower. The princess looked to Sihla and shook her head. "I am sorry, Sihla, but the legends were wrong. There's no sleeping army inside this tower, and no weapons. This tower has been completely stripped of anything mechanical or technological. Unless we intend to fight the First Men with tables and chairs, Atlantis is useless." She looked to Blackthorn, and said, "You've got the same look on your face that Morningstar had."

"Morningstar?" John demanded, but Sihla put a hand on his arm to let him know that the floor was hers.

The Not leader looked around at the three of them, wondering why they were all so stubborn as to not see what was so obvious! She tried again. "ATLANTIS!" she yelled, pointing at the letters that moved up and away from them. "The Lost City!"

Blackthorn put a comforting hand on Sihla's shoulder and pointed to a painted logo beneath the "S" on the side of the tower. "Do you know what this symbol is?" he asked, tapping the large painted image. It was a rectangle of blue with a circle of gold stars at its center. He looked to Aria. "Are there other rectangular symbols on this tower?"

Aria nodded. "There are four—one on each side. One is white with a red circle, the second has three bars of red, black, and green, and the third has red and white stripes, and a blue field with white stars. How do you—?"

"Flags." Blackthorn turned to Sihla and said, as gently as he could. "Your legends are wrong, Sihla. Atlantis might well have been the First City of Mars, but it wasn't Atlantis that sent a Great

90

Rocket to Earth. It was Earth," he tapped the tower that was actually the hull of a spaceship, "who sent a great rocket to Mars."

Sihla said nothing. Wracked with despair, she fell to her knees.

"All is not lost," Blackthorn continued somberly. "This vessel must have been stocked with the flora and fauna you see around you. There is food to gather and game to hunt. You can feed your people with what you see here. You can grow strong in body as well as mind."

"The Sleeping Army?" she asked pleadingly. "They were to be our best hope!"

Blackthorn knelt in front of Sihla and made her look into his eyes. "Sihla, you are the Sleeping Army."

"What?"

"Somehow the message has been lost down the ages," he explained. "You are not the 'Nots,' Sihla. At least not as you think. You were not named for being not-human. You were named for the men and women who crewed this vessel. They were called 'nots,' as well. *Astronauts*, to be exact. You must be their descendants. *You* are the army that will rise up and overthrow the First Men and deliver Mars back into the hands of its people."

Sihla felt her world crumble. She wanted to tell him he was wrong. She wanted to scream. She wanted to beat the truth into him. But all she could do was offer up watering eyes as a lifetime of beliefs crashed down upon her half-emaciated body.

"Only us?" She choked down a sob. "If we are the chosen ones... what chance do we have against the power of the First Men?"

"Strength in numbers," Blackthorn said softly, hoping it sounded believable.

THE MINEFIELDS OF MALADOR

BOBBY NASH

It happened all at once.

One moment everything was quiet, peaceful, almost serene, which was in and of itself an uncommon occurrence on Mars' war-torn landscape. The three riders moved at a leisurely pace. None of them spoke as each desired some quiet time to contemplate their next move. They had been riding for days after a speedy exit from one of the Sorcerer of Night's infernal traps.

Now that they were away from the danger, the riders were enjoying this rare moment of peace and quiet.

They should have known it wouldn't last.

John Blackthorn and his companions, faithful Oglok the Mock-Man and the lovely and mysterious Princess Aria, had been minding their own business, riding along the open countryside when chaos erupted all around them.

The first explosion startled them.

"Lord!" Blackthorn shouted as his steed reared up on its hind legs and nearly threw him. It was all he could do to stay in the saddle.

The second blast caused the horses to panic and they tossed both Blackthorn and Princess Aria from the safety of their mounts and slammed them to the ground. The princess flattened against the rocky red earth. Instinctively, the bright green of her outfit morphed to a reddish hue that matched her surroundings. It was not the first time Blackthorn had witnessed Aria's clothes change color to match her mood, although this was more of a survival instinct, he assumed.

At the moment, standing out in the wide-open expanse in his black clothes, he stood out like a sore thumb and made an easy target.

Explosions ripped across the uneven landscape in waves, churning the red Martian soil into mulch. A rain of red dirt fell down atop them. Somehow, Oglok managed to keep hold of the reins of his beast of a horse longer than his companions had, but eventually even he was thrown as the ground bucked and heaved beneath his steed's hooves. Oglok landed hard on the broken soil, but with a quick roll he was back on his haunches, kneeling to keep his balance and make himself a smaller target. Not an easy feat for someone as massively built as he. The Mock-Man let loose with a quick string of epithets that Blackthorn didn't completely understand, although he got the gist of it from context. The big guy wasn't happy and John couldn't blame him.

He had already gotten to his knee when the next blast rumbled through the ground. *That one was close!* John threw himself atop the princess, covering her head with his body while using his own arms to protect his as a cascade of dirt and rock rained down on top of them.

"You okay?" he asked.

"I will be," she said with a hint of strain in her voice. "As soon as you get off of me."

"Right," Blackthorn said as he rolled to the side, dumping a mound of red Martian clay from his back. He got to his feet, eyes scanning the horizon for any sign of their attackers. He had one hand on the hilt of the Sword of Light, ready to ignite it at the first hint of a new assault. After a moment, he let out the breath he'd been holding.

"What was that?" Aria asked as John helped her to her feet.

"I don't know," he whispered, eyes still scanning the horizon. "Oglok, you see anything?"

The big Mock-Man roared an angry reply. He held a piece of broken wood like a club in one hand and a rock in another. In the hands of a lesser man, these might look like an odd choice of weapons, but in Oglok's hands, they could prove lethal.

"Yeah. Me neither, pal," Blackthorn said.

"I think we should ride on as swiftly as our mounts can run," Aria said as she reclaimed her horse and saddled it.

"Wait," Blackthorn said softly at first before shouting a follow up. "Wait!"

"For what?" Aria asked.

A growl from Oglok asked a similar question.

"Just... humor me a minute," Blackthorn said as he reached down and picked up a small rock, roughly the size of a Martian Spiney Apple. He hefted it easily, checked the weight by tossing it a couple of inches in the air and easily catching it. He did this three times while he stared out at the torn up expanse that had probably been a lush Martian landscape once upon a time.

Aria and Oglok stared at their strange human friend. He often displayed odd habits, but they were learning to accept his peculiar nature. Sometimes they even found it entertaining. This was not one of those times.

"What are you—," Aria started impatiently, but fell silent when Blackthorn threw the rock as hard and as far as he could in a high arc. The three of them watched as it sailed through air and landed with a *crack* as it bounced off another rock before coming to rest with a soft *thunk* in the plowed clay.

Their friend had been expecting something—anything—to happen, but nothing did. Oglok looked at Aria, who simply shrugged. She was just as confused as he was, which wasn't unusual. Their human friend often said and did things neither of them understood.

Blackthorn reached down and picked up another rock of similar size and heft. He tossed it in much the same manner as the previous one, only in a different direction, several meters to the right of the first one he had thrown. This one also landed with a soft *thud* in the clay.

Nothing happened.

Oglok growled a question.

"Just testing a theory," Blackthorn answered.

Another growl.

"Sure," Blackthorn said as he tossed a third stone to Oglok, who caught it easily. It looked tiny in his massive furry hands. John pointed toward a barren area off to the left of the first rock he had thrown. "Think you can hit the center of that empty spot out there?"

The Mock-Man grunted playfully as if he couldn't believe his friend had asked such a stupid question. He reared back and let the stone fly. It rocketed from his hand like a missile. Oglok had fantastic aim and the rocky projectile found its mark easily.

The ground exploded on impact.

The shock wave rumbled violently and once again knocked Blackthorn to the ground. Thanks to Oglok's quick reflexes and firm hand, Aria's mount didn't rear up in panic and she remained in the saddle.

"Yeah. That's what I was afraid of," Blackthorn said as he got to his feet and clapped his dusty gloved hands together. "Mines. We've wandered into a minefield."

"What's a mimefield?" Aria asked.

He started to explain the difference between mimes and mines, but decided against it for fear they might ask him to demonstrate miming and he was in no mood to be trapped in a pretend invisible box. "A minefield is where someone plants bombs... uh, explosive devices under the ground." He used his hands to explain, laying one atop the other.

"Why would anyone do such a thing?"

"Because, Princess, it's an effective weapon. The bomb only goes off... explodes... when someone steps on it or if there's a change in temperature or pressure. A good freeze or heat wave can cause them to explode prematurely."

Oglok grunted.

"Well, obviously, we didn't step on one," John said in response to his friend's inquiry even as he scanned the horizon. "Maybe someone else did."

Another grunt.

"I wish I knew, pal. The only thing I know for sure about minefields is that they have only two possible objectives," Blackthorn said. "To keep something out or to keep something in."

"And which one do you think these are meant to do?"

"I wish I knew, Princess. I wish I knew." Blackthorn patted his mount, but did not get back in the saddle. "Come on," he told the group. "We're going to have to walk this slowly. There are certain to be more mines all around us."

"More?"

Blackthorn nodded.

"We must be cautious."

And cautious they were.

"This is taking forever," Aria complained, not for the first time.

John Blackthorn looked up at her with clear annoyance. The princess' impatience was understandable, but her constant complaining was getting on his already frayed nerves. Navigating a minefield, something he'd only had to do once before, a lifetime ago back on Earth, was tricky business. One false move and he could blow them all to kingdom come. It wasn't exactly the way he'd envisioned shuffling off this mortal coil, to be certain.

John was crouched on the ground. Using a large stick he'd found and shaped to a flat point with the Sword of Light, he probed the ground ahead of himself. If he found a mine then they would sidestep it and adjust course. Not an easy feat on its own, but with the horses it was proving downright dangerous. So far Oglok and Aria had been able to keep the beasts calm, but he could feel the animals' discomfort. Not to mention Aria and Oglok's growing impatience, only they were more vocal about it than the horses.

"Would you rather step on a mine and explode?" John asked through gritted teeth, his tone betraying is exasperation.

"No." She blew out a breath. "Of course not."

"Then let me do this and—"

A growl from Oglok brought him up short.

"What did he say?"

"He wanted to know where they came from."

"They who?" Aria asked, scanning the horizon.

"Them," Blackthorn said, pointing toward a large rocky outcropping where two small humanoid men were frantically waving their arms and motioning them over to where they stood. They were not far away and, from the looks of the debris pattern, smack dab in the center of the minefield.

"Come! Come!" one of them shouted and flailed his arms to get their attention. "You must hurry!" He reminded John of his grandfather with his wild unruly hair and slightly hunched shoulders.

Blackthorn turned to his companions. "What do you think?" he asked just as another mine exploded. This one was closer than the others, but not as powerful since only one had detonated this time.

Oglok grunted a response.

"I agree. Getting out of this minefield is probably a good idea. There's no guarantee I'll be able to sidestep all of them and I really have no desire to be blown up today."

"Can we trust them?" Aria asked.

"I don't know," Blackthorn answered. "But at the moment our options seem rather limited, wouldn't you say?"

He took the princess' look of irritation as confirmation.

"Let's go," he told them and led the group, along with the horses, across the worn path that wound its way through the mines toward the entrance to a cave, which from the look of it was a mine of a different sort.

"This way," the man urged, trying to hurry the group along.

They were bipeds, much like Blackthorn and his companions, although they were shorter and far skinnier. Their skin was dark, or at least he thought it was on first impression. Once he got closer he could tell that they were covered in a fine gray powder and black dirt from inside the cave.

"They're miners," Blackthorn whispered.

Oglok snorted in derision.

"No, not the guys planting the landmines," Blackthorn said. "At least I hope not. I guess we'll find out soon enough."

As they reached the two miners, John gave a nod to them. "I'm John Black—" he started, but was cut off when the man who had been shouting at them to hurry grabbed him by the arm and dragged him toward the cave entrance.

"No time for that now," the miner said. "We have to get inside quickly!"

"Why?" Aria demanded.

They crowded into the cave, trying to keep the horses calm. Something in the caves had spooked them and their instincts were telling them to run. Unfortunately, there was nowhere to go except back into the minefield, which would surely end in tragedy if one of the steeds stepped on a mine.

"Hurry! Before they attack again," the second miner said with urgency as he pushed Aria deeper into the cave.

"Before who attacks?" Blackthorn asked, his hand landing on the hilt of the Sword of Light. Before anyone could respond a mine exploded topside and John was thrown to the ground. The last thing he saw was the cave ceiling collapsing on top of them. He covered his head with his arms just an instant before a large rock slammed into him.

Then everything went dark.

And the cave was as silent as the grave.

John Blackthorn woke in a dark, strange place.

It wasn't the first time something like this had happened to him, especially in the time since he'd woken up here on Mars. His life had become one long adventure after another, most of them ending with pain in one part of his body or another. He'd given up hope of understanding what was happening to him long ago. His focus now was on survival.

Blackthorn sat up quickly, which he immediately realized was a major mistake. The world started spinning wildly around him. He felt dizzy, his vision blurred, and there was a ringing in his ears. He also had an incredible urge to throw up, but somehow he managed to hold it together. He assumed it was because he'd sustained a concussion in the cave-in, which made sense. He touched the bandage that had been applied to the cut on the side of his forehead and winced again. It was extremely painful and throbbed.

It hurt too much to fall back on the bed so he decided to sit there unmoving until it passed. Once the dizziness lessened, he slid his legs over the edge of the cushion where he lay. Calling it a bed would have been generous. Basically, a mattress stuffed with some type of feather had been placed atop a flat rock. It was surprisingly comfortable, all things considered.

A familiar rumble called out from the darkness.

"I'll be okay, pal," he answered. "I just hurt all over more than anywhere specific." He gave a small, pained laugh that was more uncomfortable than it was reassuring, which was how he had intended it. "Where are we?"

Oglok snorted a short answer. He leaned forward so his friend could see him in the one shaft of what he assumed to be artificial light that filtered through a crack in the stone ceiling. The Mock-Man had scavenged some new clothes, a pair of mining coveralls. Of course, with his height, they were cut off just above his knees.

"Underground," John repeated softly. "Thanks. That much I remembered."

Oglok's answer sounded like a bark.

"And our new friends?"

Another bark.

"Got it," John said, getting to his feet. The people who had called to them had treated and bandaged his wounds and given Oglok his new clothes. "Let's go check on the princess, okay?"

The Mock-Man put an arm around his friend and helped him cross the room until he was near the door. John straightened and stood on his own. Always the soldier, he had to show his newfound friends that he was a strong warrior. He took a deep breath and pulled open the door. The wood cracked with the exertion, the hinges squeaking from years accumulating rust, a common problem with all metal inside the dank and moist caves beneath the Martian surface.

"You are well?" the grandfatherly man who had ushered him inside earlier asked. He had a big, toothy smile fixed on his scruffy but friendly-looking face. He still appeared grandfatherly, but it took a second look for John to recognize the man. When they had met before, his skin was a deep gray from working the mines, but now that he had washed up, John saw that his skin was pale, except for his cheeks, which burned a bright pink. His hair and beard were silver bordering on white, but with all of the dust in the air there was no way it would ever reach its fully bleached potential. Even Blackthorn felt a coating of the dust on himself. He felt grimy, but kept that to himself. The last thing he wanted to do was complain to those who had opened their homes to him and his friends.

"I'm John Blackthorn," he sad, sticking out his hand to the man, who looked at him strangely. When Blackthorn realized that the Martian man didn't know to shake hands, he let it fall back to his side and instead offered a smile, despite the pain doing so caused.

"D'iurk Crefarn," the little man said, his voice hoarse, no doubt from too many years breathing in the dust of whatever mineral was commonplace in these mines.

"It's a pleasure to meet you, Mr. Crefarn."

"I am curious," Crefarn said as he started walking deeper into the cave's open tunnel. "What brings you to Malador, J'ahn?"

"My friends and I are just passing through, D'iurk," Blackthorn said as he and Oglok fell into step behind the miner. "We didn't even know anyone lived here until you led us out of the minefield. By the way, what's with the mines? You have a strange way of saying 'no trespassing.'"

The look on Crefarn's face could only be described as a mixture of confusion and humor, which caught John off guard. He turned to regard his friend, but the Mock-Man simply snorted. "I feel like I'm missing the joke," John said.

Oglok responded in his own fashion.

"Your friend is correct," Crefarn said with a nod. Obviously he understood the Mock-Man's guttural language. "This... minefield, as you call it, is not of our design."

"Then who put it there?"

Suddenly interested in his dirty shoes, the miner stared at the floor. "That is a rather long story, J'ahn."

Blackthorn smiled. "I'm in no hurry," he said.

"Very well," Crefarn said, his grandfatherly smile once more in place. "I'll take you to your companion and we can talk as we go."

"Lead the way," John said.

The tunnels that made up the mines extended much farther than he had first expected, but John Blackthorn quickly came to realize that there was much more to his new friends than simple cave

101

dwellers. There was an entire civilization beneath what had once been the Republic of Malador. According to his guide, Malador had been a rich and stable area that had thrived under the auspices of a great sorcerer. This powerful wizard had taken Malador and its people under his protection and had sworn they would be kept safe.

The wizard had kept his promise.

Until the Great Burn.

That's when everything changed.

"The only survivors of the Martian apocalypse in Malador were the miners," Crefarn continued as they walked. "The miners, who had been little more than slaves to the Maladorian elite who reaped the rewards of the mines, suddenly found themselves the masters of their own futures. They, and we, take some solace in the knowledge that the caves, which those who lived above ground would not have found themselves, and I quote, 'dead in,' died because they did not have the safety of the caves to protect them."

"Don't you just love irony?" Blackthorn said, returning the smile with one of his own.

The little miner smiled and raised his eyebrows. "There is no iron in these mines, I assure you," he said.

Blackthorn bit his lip to stifle a laugh. This wasn't the first time one of his Earth-born expressions had been misinterpreted. He was about to attempt an explanation of irony, but thankfully, they reached their destination first.

"We have arrived," Crefarn said and motioned John and Oglok to take a look at the place his people lived. They stood on a ledge fed by the tunnel system. The ledge overlooked a great open cavern that was filled with color, light, and jubilant laughter.

"What is this place?" John asked, his eyes wide with excitement.

"This is my home," Crefarn said.

"You live and work underground?" Blackthorn asked.

"Yes. We have all we require here," the miner replied. "Why would I want to go to the upworld where there exists so much strife and turmoil?"

John smiled. "I can't think of a single good reason," he said.

"Nor can I," Crefarn agreed.

"Your home is very beautiful," John said as he looked out over the community the miners had built beneath the Martian soil.

Oglok roared his agreement.

They followed Crefarn down the stairs carved directly out of the rock until they reached the cavern floor. Several small giggling children ran past them, nearly knocking John and Oglok off their feet. The Mock-Man roared a warning at them and shook his fists, but received only a rousing peel of laughter from the youngsters who assumed that the big man's bark was worse than his bite.

"John," a familiar voice called from somewhere behind him. He spun at the sound of his name and saw Aria rushing toward him. She wore a shimmering dress that sparkled blue in the artificial colored light all around them. The dress only heightened her already natural beauty. She looked like she was glowing.

"It's good to see you," he told her as they shared an embrace. "Are you okay?" he whispered in her ear. Even though they had only ridden together a short time, there had been no end to the seemingly harmless peoples they'd run across that turned out to be anything but. It never hurt to err on the side of caution.

"I'm fine," she whispered back.

"I'm glad," he said and smiled before turning back to face Crefarn. "So, about the minefield?" he asked their host.

"Ah, yes. That," Crefarn said as if discussing the weather. "I'm afraid that's not so easy to explain."

"Why not?"

"The great magic that makes the ground tremble and rupture has surrounded our home for generations," Crefarn said, suddenly somber. He sat down on a rock and slumped forward.

"Interesting."

"How so?" Aria asked.

"Minefields are very dangerous," John stated. "However, if you systematically destroy the ground where they're buried then you can eventually detonate all of them. There were an awful lot of explosions upstairs earlier."

Oglok growled.

"I'm not sure how it's possible," John answered. "Unless the mines had some kind of regeneration technology. Blow one up and another takes its place."

"I've heard rumors of such things," Aria said. "It is whispered that some of the dark sorcerers has found a way to make the earth explode on command. I had always believed this to be a falsehood conceived by the sorcerers themselves. Perhaps I was mistaken in my belief."

"In the forests outside of Malador lives a race of beings, monstrous in appearance and vile in their attitude of others, called the Norval. Their War Dogs want nothing more than to wipe us off the face of Mars and take what is ours for their own use."

"So the mines are there to..." John prodded.

"We assume the great magic was put in place to keep the War Dogs from reaching the Light. When we heard the terrible rumbling of the magical barrier we assumed that the War Dogs had once again tried to enter Malador and had been destroyed. You can imagine our surprise to find you there instead."

"I can imagine," John said. "But we weren't the ones who triggered the mines."

"It was not you? You did not awaken the magical barrier?" Crefarn grew nervous at this realization.

"I'm afraid not," John said.

Oglok sniffed the air.

"Come. We must make sure the Light is protected," Crefarn said, quickening his pace. "If the War Dogs are once again on the move, we must protect the Light."

"The Light?"

"We are the children of the Light, J'ahn," Crefarn said as he turned a corner into a new cave, this one sloping slightly downward. "My people are natural explorers, J'ahn," the old miner said, relating the tale of his forebears. "When my ancestors first arrived in these caves so many years ago, they scoured every inch of this place and in doing so made a fantastic discovery."

"What kind of discovery?" Aria asked.

"Life-changing." Crefarn said. Off of the blank stares of his guests, the miner added, "Come. I'll show you."

John, Aria, and Oglok fell in step behind Crefarn as he led them to a cave that was away from the main complex.

"That great sorcerer he mentioned," John said softly to his companions. "Does that sound like anyone we know?"

"Aside from the benevolent part, his story does ring true of Lord Ruin," Aria said. "As one of the *First Men*, he would certainly have taken territory as his own and it is rumored that he is a student of the metallurgical arts."

"As I recall, he also had a thing for blowing stuff up," Blackthorn added, which prompted a laugh from Oglok.

"Do you think this is one of his experiments?"

"I don't know, Princess," John said. "Just keep your eyes open, okay?"

"Always," she replied, once again not grasping the joke.

D'iurk Crefarn had gotten several steps ahead of them so they picked up the pace to catch up, which didn't take long thanks to the old miner's short legs. When they got closer they realized that he was still talking up a storm, telling the rich history of his home as if he hadn't noticed that they had fallen behind.

A short time later he broke off his story. "We have arrived," he said, bringing them to a halt.

"It's another tunnel," John said.

"Not just any tunnel," Crefarn corrected.

A barricade had been erected at the entrance, but it was a simple one and easily circumvented. John assumed it was there to keep the kids he had seen running around the community area out. The tunnel entrance was smaller than the other, more spacious ones they had seen thus far. Although Crefarn, as short as he was, had no trouble walking inside, Blackthorn and his companions had to stoop to fit inside. It was especially difficult for Oglok with his height, but the Mock-Man managed with only a few snorts of complaint.

"This one seems older than the rest," John commented.

"Very observant, J'ahn," Crefarn said as he lit a torch and handed it to Blackthorn, who in turn handed it to Aria before accepting a second one from the miner. The fur-covered Oglok, not surprisingly, declined the offer of a torch. There were lights in the ceiling, but they did little to quell the darkness.

Blackthorn left the Sword of Light attached to his belt, even though it could have easily lit the tunnel for them. He did not want to disclose the sword's power unless he had to. It wasn't a matter of trust. He liked Crefarn, and believed him trustworthy, but they had been fooled before so he decided to err on the side of caution, especially if Lord Ruin or one of his cronies was lurking about.

"This was the first tunnel ever dug by my people," Crefarn continued. "We keep it preserved as a reminder of how far we've come and as a monument to the sacrifice of our ancestors."

"An honorable consideration," Aria admitted.

"Thank you, Princess," Crefarn said with a slight bow.

"You mentioned a fantastic discovery?"

"Yes, J'ahn, I did," Crefarn said. He motioned through the darkness toward a bend in the tunnel ahead where a faint blue glow pushed back the gloom. "And there it is."

They walked ahead, careful to keep pace with the miner. When they rounded the bend, all three of them stopped dead in their tracks. Whatever he had been expecting, nothing in his imagination could have prepared John Blackthorn for the sight he beheld.

Thick veins of glowing blue pulsed through the rocks, filling the cavern with an icy blue haze that made John think of colder climates and days spent hanging from an ice floe, held aloft by a piece of nylon cord scarcely a half inch in diameter. Those were good days. Despite the memory of colder times, the pulses were actually warm and filled the cavern with soothing comfortable warmth.

"What is that?" he asked.

"That," Crefarn said reverently, "is the Light."

Aria took a step forward. "That's the Light?" She sounded almost disappointed.

"Yes, Princess," Crefarn said, smiling proudly. "It is great and powerful magic."

"How does it work?" Aria asked, taking a step closer to the pulsing blue vein.

"I do not know."

"Your very survival depends on this gift you've discovered. How could you not understand it?" Aria asked, her voice rising slightly.

The miner shrugged.

"Aria..." John warned, drawing out the syllables of her name. It was not the first time he'd seen her get lost in some mystical doohickey. He figured he needed to rein her in before she got lost in the magic of the light.

"Can you not hear it, John?" Aria asked, a smile stretching her face as she held out a hand toward the pulsing blue energy. "It sings. The Light sings to me!"

"What are you—" Blackthorn would have continued with "—talking about?" but before he could get the words out a violent rumble shook the ground beneath their feet. As before, they had trouble keeping their balance and John was slammed against a wall when the ground beneath him became unstable.

And suddenly everything clicked into place for John Blackthorn. The fact that they hadn't seen any sign of the people that set off the mines had been nagging at the back of his mind since he awoke. There was something there, that one little detail he'd been missing that would make sense of it all.

In that moment as the quake began, he understood.

"They're tunneling under!" he shouted as he pulled the sword from his belt and ignited its yellow blade, which glowed in eerie contrast to the blue hue of the Light.

"What?" Crefarn shouted. "Where?"

As if on cue, a nearby rock wall cracked and popped as a large laser drill broke through into the open cave, showering the inhabitants with small rock shard missiles. The driver of the drilling device quickly put the machine in reverse and backed into the newly cut tunnel. Seconds later, the first of the invaders surged through the opening with weapons drawn and ready.

Oglok roared an angry question, demanding to know the identity of the intruders.

Blackthorn shouted a warning. He knew exactly who they were. "War Dogs!"

Blackthorn shouted and charged the enemy, his sword humming with each swipe of its yellow energy blade. Two of the War Dogs were down for the count before the others even knew they were being attacked.

In battle, there were few warriors who could match John Blackthorn's skill with a blade. In his hand, the Sword of Light was a fearsome weapon and Blackthorn's feats already bordered on legend in some areas of Mars. Much like on his home world, rumor spread on Mars faster than wildfire so word of his deeds and exploits had spread far and wide and they seemed to be exaggerated with each retelling. In some stories Blackthorn was a ten foot tall god reborn in a man's body and was able to toss lightning bolts from his fingertips. Other stories painted him as a madman with a weapon and no fear. And then there were some that were so outrageous that, when he heard them, John could only laugh at the ridiculousness of it.

If there was one shred of truth to the stories, however, it was his skill in battle. John Blackthorn was an excellent hand to hand combatant, a fierce and cunning warrior, and a strategist with a unique way of looking at any given situation, probably because he was an offworlder who looked at the Martian landscape with fresh, new eyes. On a normal day, Blackthorn was a force to be reckoned with, but with the Sword of Light in his hand, there were few that could stand against him.

Blackthorn sliced away at the invading horde as the War Dogs poured through the opening, filling the tunnel. The War Dogs wore armor plating, which withstood the blasts from the small energy weapon D'iurk Crefarn had pulled from some concealed compartment inside his clothing. Even a few of Aria's mystic bolts were deflected by the dull, scratched armor.

They did not fare so well against the Sword of Light.

Blackthorn shouted and threw himself into the fray, putting himself directly in front of the opening the War Dogs' laser drill had cut into the thick bedrock of Malador. *The only way you're getting in here is through me*, he thought as he gritted his teeth and sliced through one of the invaders' blaster rifles, which erupted in a shower of sparks as the power pack separated from the stock. A kick to the startled War Dog's chest sent him crashing backward into his compatriots.

Blackthorn was not surprised to find Oglok at his side, using his bare hands to fight off the intruders that managed to get past Blackthorn. Even if they had to swarm the gates of Hell itself, John suspected that his big furry friend would be right beside him the entire time.

In the heat of battle, Blackthorn had lost sight of Aria and Crefarn. Experience told him that Aria could take care of herself and after seeing the little miner going after the War Dogs with his tiny weapon, he assumed the same was true for Crefarn. That didn't stop him from worrying about both of them, but his hands were too full with the invading armored warriors to do much about it.

The Norvallan War Dogs were tall, easily reaching seven feet, so they towered over John and were closer in stature to Oglok. The armor they wore did not completely cover their bodies, but thick black fur covered the exposed areas. He couldn't tell if this was body fur like the Mock-Men or if it was simply an animal skin they wore beneath the armor. Each warrior brandished an energy weapon that resembled a rifle, which fired a pulsed bolt of energy. Each War Dogs also carried a sword in a scabbard on its back. Their faces were covered with masks as well, each one sporting eye holes and nothing more. The masks only covered the Norvallans' faces. Their hair, apparently the same black as the fur beneath the armor, flowed wildly behind them. Beneath the masks, the War Dogs roared with fury as they attacked.

The battle was vicious and although outnumbered, Blackthorn and his companions held their ground until at last the surviving War Dogs fell back in retreat. There was no time for Blackthorn to catch his breath, however, as Oglok started into the tunnel. After bellowing an angry challenge, the Mock-Man was ready to chase the fleeing invaders down like the dogs they claimed to be.

John reached out a hand to stop him. "Hang here, pal," he said, trying to corral the angry Mock-Man. "This tunnel goes under the mines."

Oglok grunted a response that roughly translated as, "*So?*"

"So, they obviously weren't very careful when they drilled under the minefield. You do remember the explosions that brought us here, right?" He pointed down the tunnel where the retreating warriors had fled. "They caused that!"

Even on his best days, getting Oglok to listen to reason was an uphill battle. When he was angry, it was almost impossible to dissuade him from running off half-cocked or doing something reckless. Blackthorn recognized that this was one of those times. Trying to talk the big guy into standing down would just be a waste of breath.

With a roar of defiance, the big Mock-Man tore away from his friend's grip and charged into the tunnel after the War Dogs who were getting away.

Blackthorn cursed.

"Keep an eye on Crefarn!" he told Aria. "We may have to evacuate his people!"

"Where are you going?" the princess demanded, even though she knew the moment she saw Oglok run after their attackers that John would go after his friend.

"Where do you think?" he said. "Be back soon!"

And then he disappeared into the newly-cut tunnel.

It took John Blackthorn's eyes a moment to adjust to his new surroundings.

The tunnel was dark, a stark contrast to the well-lit caves used by Crefarn and his people. The laser drill was still parked inside the tunnel, abandoned in the Norvallans' hasty retreat so he had to squeeze past it. Between the drilling equipment and the bodies of the dead War Dogs that filled the entrance the going was slow. At least until he was inside. He kept expecting one of them to reach out and grab him, like something he'd seen in a horror movie when he was a kid so very long ago, but he passed by without incident. The War Dogs that remained in the tunnel were all dead.

Blackthorn used the Sword of Light to push away the gloom. He kept it on its deadly yellow blade setting instead of switching over to the lantern option. The Norvallan War Dogs were ruthless, a vicious enemy. Better to be ready in case of an attack.

He heard noises ahead and assumed it was Oglok. If his friend had caught up to the War Dogs then he would be outnumbered. Despite his legendary temper and brute strength, Oglok wasn't indestructible.

Blackthorn took off at a run deeper into the makeshift tunnel.

It didn't take him long to catch up.

Oglok was in a rage, slamming two War Dog soldiers against the cracked and jagged tunnel wall. There were two down, two in his grip, and two others just trying to get past him to get away. The others, John assumed, had not stopped to help their comrades. That told him a lot about their enemy. They did not value loyalty. A quick slash of his sword announced his presence and the two War Dogs between him and Oglok turned toward him and roared a challenge. Facing a human must have been far more palatable than dealing with a furious Mock-Man because their swagger returned as they approached with swords drawn for close quarter combat. They must not have considered the human much of a threat, despite what had happened at the tunnel entrance.

Blackthorn was all too happy to show them the error of their ways.

With practiced ease, he extinguished the Sword of Light and plunged the tunnel into complete darkness even though he could still make out the attacking warrior's silhouettes because of the light behind them.

So as not to take out his partner, the War Dog in the rear slowed his pace and let his companion take a shot at the human. That dropped the odds a bit more squarely in John's favor.

He ducked under the first attacker's swing and felt the wind as it passed just inches above his head only to bury itself in the craggy bedrock. The War Dog was caught off guard and as he tugged at his sword to pull it free, Blackthorn leapt back to his full height, igniting the sword in the middle of his swing. The sword's energy blade cleaved the embedded sword in two on the upswing and separated the War Dog's arm from his shoulder on the downswing. The sword handle and the arm hit the tunnel floor simultaneously, one with a *clankity-clank* and the other with a wet *thud*.

The warrior cried out in pain and clutched at the stump where his arm had been only seconds before. Another swipe of the Sword of Light and Blackthorn ended his suffering by separating his head from his neck.

The dead soldier dropped to the cave floor in a heap. His friend let loose a furious roar and charged ahead without a plan, moving only on instinct and emotion. Blackthorn took him down easily.

He was already on the move back toward Oglok when he saw one of the remaining War Dogs toss something that looked suspiciously like a grenade toward the Mock-Man. "Get down!" John shouted as he pulled Oglok away just seconds before the small device exploded in the narrow tunnel.

And for the second time that day John Blackthorn found himself buried underneath the rocks of a cave-in.

★★★

The first thing he saw when he opened his eyes was Aria's face—her tanned, wide-eyed, beautiful face—staring down at him. She smiled when he opened his eyes and he tried to return the gesture, but he couldn't quite manage it.

"I was so worried," she said.

"Yeah. Me too," he said, sitting up far too quickly, much as he had earlier. "Is Oglok okay?"

"He is fine, John," Aria said. "A few bruises and scrapes."

"The big guy's tough."

A bark of agreement came from somewhere behind him, but his head hurt too much to turn. Instead he chuckled slightly. "And the War Dogs?"

"Gone," D'iurk Crefarn said, suddenly standing beside the bed where he sat.

"I'm sorry we couldn't stop them," Blackthorn said.

"Do not worry yourself, J'ahn Blackt'orn," the miner said. "I wanted to thank you on behalf of my people for your help. I shudder to think what might have happened had you not been here."

"Glad to help out a friend, Mr. Crefarn," John said as he got unsteadily to his feet. Aria slipped a hand behind his back to help balance him.

"My people are fortifying the mineshafts now. We've sealed off unused tunnels and have put measures in place to protect the Light."

"How can we help?"

"Your offer is appreciated, J'ahn, but you've done so much for us already. Once we secure the tunnels, we will be sealed below ground for quite some time," Crefarn said. "You and your friends should leave before we do that."

"I understand," John said. "But there's still the matter of that minefield topside. We haven't figured out a way around that yet."

Oglok grunted as he stepped next to his friend and clapped him on the shoulder. It was all John could do not to fall to the floor from the Mock-Man's playful tap. "What do you mean that's not a problem, Big Guy?" John asked.

Oglok barked again and Blackthorn's eyes widened, a smile playing across his lips.

"The laser drill is still sitting right there where the War Dogs left it," Aria said. "All we have to do is tunnel under the field and come out on the other side."

"We would seal the tunnel behind you so the Norvallans cannot return," Crefarn said.

"That's brilliant," Blackthorn said.

"It was Oglok's idea," Aria admitted.

John smiled up at his furry friend. "You're a genius, you know that?" he told Oglok as he slapped him on the arm. The Mock-Man sniffed at the air as if his friend had simply stated the obvious.

This brought laughter from everyone in the room.

"What's to stop them from simply digging a new tunnel?" John asked.

"We have their only laser drill." Crefarn smiled as he delivered the news.

"You're sure?"

"Positive."

"Okay then," Blackthorn said, smiling now that they had a plan. "Let's get it done."

The plan was pretty straightforward.

John, Oglok, and Aria spent the next few hours helping Crefarn and his people *batten down the hatches*, yet another phrase that was totally lost on those not born on Earth. The smaller caverns were abandoned and sealed, herding all of the miners and their families into the larger caverns that made up the bulk of their community. Once they were secured, the miners gathered their tools and headed off to collapse tunnels that led to the surface.

Aria headed back to the chamber where Crefarn had introduced them to the power source for the caverns that their enemies wanted to steal for themselves. The Maladoran miners called this power source *the Light*.

"As I understand it, your people have tapped into the Light to power your tools, heat your homes, and provide illumination for the tunnels and caverns," Aria said as they stepped back into the blue glow of the tunnel leading to the Light.

"That is correct," Crefarn said.

"And it's also a safe bet to assume that the Norvallans are mainly after your power source?"

"Also correct."

Aria smiled. "They don't know, do they?"

Crefarn mirrored her mischievous grin. "No. They do not."

"I didn't think so."

"Would you mind clueing me in?" Blackthorn asked.

"Observe." The princess held out her hand. A soft green glow started inside her lithe fingers and grew in intensity until her hand looked as though it were made purely out of green energy.

"I've seen this parlor trick before, Your Highness," John said plainly, trying to push her to get to the point without the theatrics.

"Watch," she said, and took a couple of steps closer to the glowing blue vein inside the cave wall. As she moved closer her hand glowed brighter. "Remember when I said I could hear it singing to me?" she asked.

"Yes," John said, no longer rushing her as he started. The glow was now moving up her arm and was a sight to behold.

"This vein of ore that they call the Light amplifies whatever energy it is exposed to, such as with my arm," Aria explained. "But as soon as I pull my arm away from it..." She took a few steps back and the glow around her hand faded back to a soft glow, then eventually returned to its normal state.

Blackthorn and Oglok stared at her. Neither said anything.

"Don't you see what this means?" Aria asked.

"Not really," Blackthorn said. "But it does explain why the bad guys want it."

Crefarn huffed and shook his head.

"What am I not seeing here?" Blackthorn insisted.

"The Light," Aria started and patted the pulsating blue vein as she did so. "Whatever this ore is, it is powerful, but it is a localized phenomenon." She looked to her companions to see if they understood.

"Localized?" John asked

"Yes," Aria said and smiled. "The entire place, the caves, the tunnels, even the airshafts all contain the ore. It's all around us. It is also what powers and replicates the explosives buried topside."

Oglok grunted.

"He's right," John said. "I didn't see this blue glow in all of the tunnels either."

"We see the blue glow here because this tunnel cut into one of the veins, and it is right on the surface so it picks up the light from the torches and the overhead lights strung down the line." She pointed to the small bulb lights that ran along the center of the tunnel.

"So that means this section isn't the source of the Light?"

"No, John," Aria said. "This is just one of many veins. The Light is everywhere. The entire community, everything within these caves, is powered by this ore."

"So why not share the ore and be done with it?"

"A good idea, in theory," Aria explained. "If not for the localization field I mentioned."

"So it's localized. As in it only works inside the caves?"

"That's correct," Aria said. "Even if the War Dogs were to come in here and dig out the ore it wouldn't work once they got outside of the Malador cave system."

"We have tried to explain this to the Norvallans on many occasions, J'ahn, but..." Crefarn said.

"But they don't believe you," Blackthorn said, completing the thought.

"No. They do not."

John rubbed his chin. "Something tells me that the Norvallans aren't too interested in living underground, are they?"

"No. They are not," Crefarn said.

"Sounds like a classic 'between a rock and a hard place' situation," John said.

Aria and Oglok exchanged a look, then glanced at the rock walls.

"Never mind," John said before either of them could ask. "We've got work to do."

"You sure you know how to use that thing?"

Oglok snorted derisively at Blackthorn as he shook the laser drill's steering column. Oglok and machinery did not always go well together, especially when the Mock-Man was mad. Blackthorn had to laugh at the thought. The big guy seemed to be angry most of the time. He'd watched with his own eyes as Oglok once pushed the control console of one of the Black Sorcerer's skimmers in on itself with his feet because he couldn't make it work right.

"No. I'm not questioning your skills, pal," John said in response to the big guy's angry retort. "I just wanted to make sure."

Blackthorn turned toward Aria, who was saying her farewells to D'iurk Crefarn. "You ready?" he asked the princess. When she nodded yes he offered her a hand and helped her into the saddle of her horse.

"Good luck, my friends," Crefarn said.

"Thanks," Blackthorn said before reminding him that there remained work yet to do. "Give us five minutes head start then you seal this entrance behind us."

"I will," the old miner said.

"Good luck, my friend," Blackthorn said just before Oglok put the large drill into motion. John nudged his horse and, along with Oglok's monster steed, charged off after the laser drill as it picked up speed through the tunnel. He could have sworn he saw his friend smiling.

The tunnel was long and uneven, but the horses managed to make good time and almost kept pace with the laser drill. John's biggest worry was that once they started drilling they would set off the mines above their heads, much like the War Dogs did when they were making their way to the cavern. One wrong move could bring the roof down on top of them and John Blackthorn had already had that happen enough for one lifetime.

Oglok had the coordinates programmed into the drill and was confident he could handle it so John had faith. At the preprogrammed time, the Mock-Man initiated the laser drill and a high-pitched whine filled the tunnel as they veered off the course made by the War Dogs and started drilling in a new direction.

The plan was simple, but dangerous. If the War Dogs heard them approaching then they would have ample time to set up an ambush as the drill broke free to the surface. On the other hand, John noted if they didn't hear them coming then he and his friends would have surprise on their side.

At the appropriate moment, Oglok increased the angle of the drill and began cutting a shaft upward toward the surface at an angle, but not one too steep so Blackthorn and Aria could follow on their horses. If Crefarn's information about the size of the minefield was accurate then they would come out on the other side of it safe and sound. If his calculations were off, however, then they were on their way to having a bad day.

The tunnel shook as the laser drill broke through the hard-packed Martian clay and came to rest on the surface. Blackthorn and the princess rode out behind the drilling device a second later.

"Oh, crap," John said, looking around at their surroundings. The laser drill had burrowed through the bedrock beneath the mines and deposited them outside of the blast zone.

And right into the center of the War Dog's camp.

"I think we miscalculated," Blackthorn said just before all hell broke loose.

John Blackthorn rolled out of his saddle and hit the ground with the Sword of Light already ignited and in hand. He was already running toward the War Dogs, the sword humming as he swung it back and forth, before they even full realized what was going on. A quick headcount told him that there were at least twenty warriors there and only three of them. *I've had worse odds*, he decided.

Oglok let out a roar that would have put the largest lion on Earth to shame as he, too, attacked the War Dogs. The Mock-Man dove into the largest concentration of warriors with fists flying. The attack caught the War Dogs off guard, as they were not expecting an attack inside their own camp.

Many of the War Dogs were not wearing their armored helmets so John got a good look at their faces. They were feral, almost animalistic, each one scarred from previous battles. Blackthorn had seen it before on this godforsaken world. After the Great Burn, or whatever they called it, fighting was the only thing that many of the Martian survivors understood. Some fought for survival, others fought for power, and some fought because they liked it. It looked like the War Dogs fell into one of the latter two categories.

Blackthorn didn't have long to ponder that insight, however. The War Dogs had been caught off guard by their arrival, but they reacted quickly and were soon ready for combat. He slashed through the stock of a warrior's rifle, sending sparks flying. A quick twist and an elbow to his unprotected face knocked the War Dog backward over a rock with blood spurting from his broken nose.

As Blackthorn moved on to his next opponent, he tried to get a glimpse of his friends. Oglok was easy to pinpoint as he towered over all of them. With his great strength he was hurling War Dogs right and left as if they weighed almost nothing. Aria was also holding her own very well as she fired some sort of mystic bolts from her hands. Each enemy her blasts hit went down and stayed down. John assumed that she was still energized from her exposure to the Light. It was giving her a distinct edge, but they both knew the power boost would eventually fade and her energies would return to their normal levels.

Individually, the War Dogs weren't terribly impressive, but eventually their superior numbers would overwhelm Blackthorn and his friends. The twenty or so in camp were but a small portion. According to Crefarn, there were thousands of the Norvallan War Dogs out there. The odds were too great.

"We've got to get out of here!" he shouted to his comrades.

Oglok snarled a short response as he flipped a warrior over his shoulder and slammed him into the ground, unconscious.

"I was kind of hoping you had an idea," Blackthorn joked. "Cover me and get ready to grab the horses and go!" he shouted before breaking free of the fight to make a run for the laser drill.

"Where are you going?" Aria shouted after him. She blasted a War Dog who had given chase to Blackthorn. The War Dog crumpled into a heap.

Blackthorn leapt onto the laser drill and turned it on. "Just be ready!"

Aria muttered a few choice words as she wove a protection spell. A shimmering blue wall of energy rose from the ground, separating the War Dogs from her and her friends. "You'd better hurry, Blackthorn!" she shouted. "This won't hold them long!"

"Get to the horses!" John pushed the throttle forward and aimed the laser drill at the minefield. The last thing he had promised Crefarn was that he would make sure that the Norvallans never got their hands on the laser drill again. That meant destroying it or taking it with them. The latter was not feasible so destroying the machine was his only course of action.

The laser drill rumbled along at full speed toward the minefield.

Blackthorn leapt from the machine, hit the ground in a roll and came up running as fast as he could toward he companions and his steed. "Go! Go! Go!" he shouted as he vaulted into the saddle and nudged his horse into motion.

The three of them rode away at a full gallop as Aria dropped her protective barrier.

A number of the War Dogs rushed forward, trying to catch the laser drill before it hit the minefield. The rest gave pursuit to the fleeing attackers, but as they were on horseback there was little hope they would catch up to them.

One of the War Dogs, a young and strong warrior and athlete, was able to catch the laser drill. He grabbed hold and pulled himself on board and reached for the controls—

—only to find them melted to slag, a final parting gift from John Blackthorn's Sword of Light.

The War Dog cursed loudly and slammed his fists against the console. He was about to leap away when the drill reached the edge of the minefield and set off a series of explosions that tore through the Martian countryside. He did not survive long enough to feel the second explosion.

The rest of the War Dogs fell back to a safe distance.

It was over.

At least for now.

John Blackthorn was enjoying the peace and quiet.

Once he and his companions had made it safely out of Norvallan territory they made camp, eating a quick meal from some provisions that Crefarn and his people had packed into their saddlebags. It was a modest meal but a good one. John was extremely gratified to eat a meal that he didn't have to kill and skin first.

The next morning they were once again on the move. Another menace to the people of Mars had been defeated but they knew that the First Men—the four sorcerers who dominated this world—were still out there, still searching for them. It wasn't safe to stay in one location very long so they rode off into the Martian dawn, ready for whatever adventure awaited them just over the next rise.

D'iurk Crefarn stood on the small rocky outcropping in the center of the Malador minefield. It had been many days since the strangers had left them, but they had been peaceful days. Finally, he decided to make his way back to the surface, tunneling through the loose debris from the cave-in that had occurred right after he had met Blackthorn and the others.

He knew that this was just a break in the storm. The Norvallans were not the type of people who would give up based on a single defeat. They would regroup, rearm themselves, and try again. The War Dogs would come and they would fight and they would die, but they would never understand just how futile their goals were. They never could possess that which they sought, which was all the more sad. Crefarn would have happily shared the Light with them if he was able, but alas such a thing was not within his power.

Maybe when the benevolent one returns, he thought, dreaming of the day when the great sorcerer who had protected his people would come back and deliver them to their rightful reward.

Until that time, if it ever came at all, he was quite happy to remain underground.

Crefarn sighed at the destruction all around him.

The Malador that had been was no more, but in truth, he liked the new Malador more. His people had found a semblance of peace that so very few on this planet had achieved. That made his people special, Crefarn knew. Perhaps one day, he hoped, all of Mars could find such contentment.

Perhaps if others out there were to meet Princess Aria, Oglok the Mock-Man, and John Blackthorn, then perhaps Mars might just have a positive future after all.

That was also a dream worth having.

CITY OF RELICS

SEAN TAYLOR

He awoke to a brightness so white he thought he'd gone blind. Noises like heavy gears dragging across the floor assailed him from all sides. A hand of only four fingers touched his thigh and he jerked away, banging his head on something hard, then regaining his balance, bracing both elbows against something soft beneath him. A bed? A rapid fire sound of gutturals and hisses sped across the space in front of him and a reply of like kind responded.

"Where am I?" he asked, his voice aching of sand and gravel. He searched his thoughts but came up empty. He could remember days and months and years ago, but nothing from the past few hours. "What happened?"

More gutturals and hisses. Then a sharp response like a knife biting into paper. Then, "Ingliss."

"English?" he muttered, wondering if that was the intended meaning.

"You are in the palace of the Eternal Light of Secunda Provura," a voice said. "You are a guest of the Eternal Light that Shines Over the City."

"The light…" he mumbled. "It's too bright."

"Very well," said the same voice as before. A quick clapping of hands and the gears dragged across the floor again, followed by more of the guttural and hissing sounds.

The room grew darker, and he waited for his eyes to focus. In a few moments the brightness faded into dark spots, then those too finally dissipated into a blurry gaze of an ornate sleeping chamber.

"Why am I here? Where are my friends?"

Eight rough fingers grabbed his shoulders and pushed him flat against a bed that was as soft as the fingers were not. "Rest now, John Blackthorn. Do not aggravate your wounds with movement."

He tried to sit up again, but the hands held him firmly. "Where the hell are my friends?" he yelled.

As he struggled, his captors gradually came into sharp focus. From the waist up, they could almost be considered beautiful, if their nearly seven foot tall stature allowed for it. Skin of pale hues of green, brown and blue, seemingly blending one color into another without clear lines of demarcation. Faces as symmetrically perfect as any he'd ever seen, with lips full and blue, covering a row of sharp teeth that showed gleaming white with every syllable they spoke.

From the waist down, however, anything human about them disappeared. They had no legs, and instead possessed a single appendage much like the tail of a serpent, though without the smooth scales. At the end of the tail the skin split into a small fork like that of an earthly snake's tongue. They wore no clothing, though they seemed neither to notice nor care.

"I want to see my friends!"

Thwack!

One of the heavy tails swatted him across his thighs, stinging like a row of hornets.

"You must quiet yourself, John Blackthorn," the most brown of the serpentine women said in a much softer voice. "You are to meet your benefactress shortly."

"And then I can see my friends?" he asked, realizing that until he regained his strength, he was no match for the creatures holding him. He tried again to remember something of how he had ended up in the castle, of what might have happened to Aria and Oglok, his companions of the past few months since becoming lost on the godforsaken wasteland that was Mars.

The creature made a face that looked like she was laughing, but the only sound to escape was a clicking of her tongue against her sharp teeth.

"My poor human," the creature said, her voice softening again. "Your friends are dead."

The strangers lay as still as the stone around them. Eelia hid behind the shrubbery, watching as Ruuso had commanded him. "Watch the strangers," he had said, "and if they awaken, then and only then come tell me."

So Eelia waited.

He had been collecting twigs for the fire pit when the strangers arrived, and although he had known better, he had left the kindling at the base of the temple and followed the giant creatures who had entered the forsaken land that only his people, the D'Arb-ee, had been cursed with and given as a home.

Eelia munched on berries as he sat obscured by the foliage. The giants did not belong together. He knew that. Even as a young D'Arb-ee, he knew they were of different tribes. The female was dark for her kind and wore her hair short, unlike that of the females of his own people. She was easily the smallest of the strangers, though she was clearly taller than three D'Arb-ee standing on each other's shoulders. Her black clothing covered most of her unmoving body, save for the folds of her cloak that left her legs exposed below her knees.

Eelia wondered if she was as soft to the touch as she looked to be. Surely Ruuso wouldn't mind. Not that Ruuso would ever have to know.

But Eelia stayed behind the green and watched, moving his gaze to examine the largest of the strangers, the beast. The beast had been the last to fall in battle, and it had knocked out four of the even larger temple guards before it too had been overcome and rendered lifeless and left on the dirty stone ground around the courtyard of Eternal Light.

The beast lay curled in a ball, both legs of brown fur matted and bloody as they were bent with its knees pulled tightly to its chest. Its muscled arms lay limp and bruised above its head, covering its face. Eelia had seen the creature's face, and the image had sent him cowering inside the cracked pillars in the courtyard.

But now it no longer moved. And a dead creature couldn't stop him from reaching the female.

The body of the third giant, though—*that* one had still been alive, judging by the rising and falling of his chest when the guardians had dragged him into the temple and slammed closed the rocky door behind them.

That unfortunate creature would no doubt be sacrificed to keep the Eternal Life glowing in Secunda Provura. His dead companions were far luckier to have died in battle, Eelia thought, making two circles over his chest and reciting the Prayer of Light. At least their souls could move to the everlasting mist and not be eaten to fuel the power of the Light Goddess.

But that was no matter to him. He simply had to satisfy his curiosity. He had to cross the beast to reach the woman.

He stepped from behind the foliage and stepped slowly toward the beast, stopping after each one to make sure the creature wasn't moving. He continued, making a wide arc around the beast's legs. The beast didn't move, and Eelia puffed his chest and straightened his back. A rustling behind him, in the foliage from where he'd just come, stopped his proud posture quickly, and he dropped to the ground, covering his curled body with the stone-colored cloak he kept for camouflage.

When the sound stopped, he lifted the cloak just enough to peek out from under it, and saw nothing. Just the wind, he thought. It wasn't yet hunting season for the teeth and claws of the jaggers, and since they had eaten off all the other lower predators, he would be safe. He would. He would have to be.

Hearing the words in his head didn't help.

Instead of puffing and straightening, he crouched low to the ground and all but crawled around the long, thick legs of the beast toward the female.

A soft grunt stopped him. He scanned the world around him and was focusing on the thickest patch of foliage when he heard it again. Behind him.

He turned as quietly as he could.

There was nothing there.

Then the sound came a third time.

And the great beast's chest rose and fell.

The creature was alive.

Blackthorn fought tears as the half-woman creatures prepared him for his appointment with the Eternal Light of Secunda Provura. The pain came not from the claws of the creatures, he knew, for their touch was gentle and their claws never broke his skin, instead giving him a calming massage as they raked across his chest and arms and back as his helpers or jailers—or both—dressed him in a pair of leather trousers and a robe that felt like silk, though he knew of no silkworms on Mars.

No, the tears that threatened to fall came only from the loss of his friends. While they hadn't been together more than a few scant months, many a battle had cemented their companionship in ways that made them brothers and sisters in spite of the days.

It had been the same in the life he now accepted as his previous existence, before his soul—a concept he still struggled with—had been torn from his dying body on Earth and had flown across the silence of time and space to a new home in the body he now possessed. Then he had been a different man—literally he thought—stifling the inappropriate laugh. But, as that man, he had built the same relationships with the men in his Army unit, the 451st. Brave men, every one, he remembered. He'd been proud to serve alongside each of them, and proud to die in their company before being whisked to this world by powers he couldn't begin to understand.

"For a human, you are very handsome," the brownest of the women said. "Had not the Eternal Light chosen you for her own, I would make you my own consort."

Blackthorn shuddered at the thought. The embrace of the creature's passion might prove lethal to most humans, possibly even himself, no matter the shapeliness of their human halves. Then he thought of Aria and how pleasing her shape, both halves, was to him, but the vision was quickly replaced by the scene of her broken body on the ground in the dirt.

The dirt! Dirty ground around a... Around what?

He tried to hold on to the memory that had slipped through the fog. In the corner of the picture in his mind he pushed the edges, just long enough to make out a stone corner of what could have been a temple, judging by the decoration cut into the stone. It wasn't much, but at least it meant his memories might be returning.

He needed to bide his time. Eventually they would all return. He only needed to remain alive and in the good graces of both these snake women and the so-called goddess long enough.

"This Eternal Light, is she like you? Is she the same species, I mean?" he asked.

The brown creature's tongue clicked against her teeth and the lines of her face turned up.

"I'll take that as a no," Blackthorn whispered.

The woman lowered her face to his own.

"It is indeed a 'no,' John Blackthorn. My sisterkind and I are but her servants, and my brotherkind are her warriors, but the Eternal Light is far above our kind, as far as we are above the tiny creatures that hide in the grass around our temple."

"Why does she want to see me? Can you at least tell me that?" He loosened the robe to expose his chest. The material seemed to emanate its own heat, and he had to feel the cool kiss of the ambient air on his skin.

"You prefer to be naked?" the woman asked. "It is the place of the servant to be unrobed."

He thought for a moment before answering. "It is the sometimes the way of my people too, although we are not servants." He straightened his back, listening to the trill of pops that climbed his spine. "We enjoy the air on our skin."

The creature backed away a moment, her face suddenly blank, her mouth closed tightly. Then she slithered toward him, closing the space until her abdomen all but touched his chest. He cut his eyes up to take in her face, but as he did she lowered herself, bringing her face beneath him—he assumed it was a submissive posture and not an aggressive one—almost touching his sternum with her nose. He stood perfectly still, waiting, not sure enough of his assessment to risk an attack from the creature.

Instead of attacking, however, her tongue flicked out and licked his chest, then disappeared again between her blue lips. Immediately after, her form dropped prostrate to the ground before him.

"Forgive me, John Blackthorn," she said. "I have been too forward with the chosen of the Eternal Light."

Blackthorn knelt beside her, and gulped, then lifted her face. "Don't worry about it."

The woman's face upturned into what he hoped was a smile. "You are most merciful, chosen of the Eternal Light."

"What's your name?" he asked.

The woman made a series of clicking noises and gutturals that he could neither understand nor reproduce.

"In English?"

"There is no Ingliss," she said. "I am sorry."

Blackthorn stood and motioned for the woman to stand as well. "How 'bout I call you Sally then?"

"Sal-ee?" she said softly.

"Sure, Sally." He grinned. "If that's okay with you."

"You may call me Sal-ee," she said, lowering her head in what he was sure this time was a bow.

"So, Sally," he said, "when you called me the 'chosen of the Eternal Light,' what exactly did you mean? Chosen as in sacrifice, or chosen as in I need to pick out china from Macy's?"

Sally's face went blank again. "Mae-cees?"

"Nothing. Am I getting killed or getting married?"

Sally turned away and clicked her tongue at the other women-creatures in the room. "Come, John Blackthorn. It is time to meet the Eternal Light of Secunda Provura."

She slithered toward the open doorway of the chamber, and he followed.

"Well?"

Sally lowered her head. "The Eternal Light will answer your questions as she deems necessary."

"I thought we were friends now, Sally." He considered whether to push his luck. His friends were dead, and he was being taken to a woman who was either going to kill him or marry him—or both. What worse trouble could he get into, he wondered.

He reached up and rested his palm on Sally's shoulder. It was almost icy with a single line of heat, like fire in her veins but only in her veins. "Or maybe more than friends…"

Sally slinked a step further ahead out of his reach, and her head dropped even lower.

"So that's how it's gonna be," he said.

"You are the chosen of the Eternal Light that Shines Over the City. I can lay no claim to either your friendship or…" She clicked. A different sort of clicking this time, he noticed. Almost sad, if such a thing were possible.

"Or?" he pushed.

"You are the chosen of the Eternal Light that Shines Over the City." Her arms dropped limply to her side. "And I will take you to her."

"It's okay, Sally. Let's go meet the Eternal Light."

He took a step, then stopped.

"Sally?"

"Yes, John Blackthorn?"

"When I was brought here, I had a weapon."

She sounded three clicks, followed by a final long sound he could only describe as a choked grunt, and immediately a smaller, blue-ish snake woman slid to him and handed him a warm silver cylinder. He took it and nodded.

"Good to see you again, old friend," he said, then he addressed Sally. "Aren't you afraid that I'll try to escape now that I have my weapon?"

She moved into the hallway. "You may attempt what you wish. But it will not matter. The Eternal Light wishes to see you and she has chosen you. It will be as she decrees."

"I beg to differ, but I'll play along for now," he whispered.

127

Sally stopped and turned her head. "Before this is over, you may beg for many things, but it will not matter."

Eelia shuddered in the thick brush as the beast pushed itself up from the ground. Its fur was thick with dirt and blood, clumped together in matted lumps on its chest. As it sat up, it sniffed the air and grunted. The beast looked around as much with its nose as with its eyes.

It stopped when it saw the female.

Then it groaned, loud and long, letting the sound resolve into a roar that burrowed inside Eelia's heart and almost sent him running for the safety of the woods. But some reserve of courage inside him—where it had been hiding, he didn't know—convinced him to stay, and he crossed two circles again over his chest and whispered the Prayer of Eternal Light.

Luckily the beast's noise covered his prayer.

The beast then knelt beside the female and lay its head on her chest. It groaned again, this time cutting it off before the roar. It—*he*, Eelia decided—listened again. Another groan.

He raised his arms and beat the female's chest once.

Listened again.

He beat it again.

Listened.

A third time.

After listening, he groaned even louder than before, and dropped his immense arms to his side.

The female must be dead, Eelia realized. Then again, he had been certain the beast had been dead too. He leaned forward to get a better view of the female, and his back foot, the one with which he had been supporting his crouching weight, slipped and the dry grass beneath it crackled.

The beast froze, his face high in the air.

Then he turned and locked his gaze on the brush where Eelia hid.

The beast sniffed the air, and his mouth scrunched into a snarl.

He growled.

Eelia ran, pushing his tiny legs to cover the distance between the temple grounds and the woods where his people hid. But the beast was too large, too fast. In less than twenty strides, Eelia found himself grappled around his waist, lifted into the air, and shoved face-to-face with the beast.

Eelia bared his own teeth and growled. He was not as large and not nearly as strong, but his people had long biting teeth, and sometimes they could surprise large predators with their ferocity.

The beast didn't respond at first, then he opened his huge mouth and snarled, his breath assaulting Eelia's nose and mouth with its pungent mixture of blood and meat and wild plants.

Eelia shook and went limp in the beast's hand. When ferocity failed, his people could play dead better than many of the land's races.

The beast raised Eelia into the air above his head and shook him.

Eelia held both his breath and his desire to scream. If he died, he would die as one of the brave.

The beast lowered him again till they were face-to-face. Then so close their noses touched. He waited for Eelia to breathe and give himself away.

But Eelia had another idea. He opened his mouth wide and locked onto the beast's nose with his knife-like teeth. The beast let go of him, but he held fast to the beast's nose, shaking from one side to the other as the beast howled and wailed.

"Oglok!"

The beast stopped.

"Put that poor D'Arb-ee down."

The beast turned. As he did, Eelia saw the woman standing, bruised but alive, on the ground on which she'd been lying as a corpse.

Eelia held on with his teeth, afraid of the drop.

The beast grunted and strode to the female.

"Aw-ree-aw," he muttered.

The beast ignored Eelia and almost crushed him in a fierce hug when he reached the female. Eelia smiled as her skin pressed against his back. She was as warm as he had expected, and his own body seemed to steal her heat and claim it as his own.

Just as suddenly though, the heat disappeared and he felt something solid beneath his feet.

"And you, little D'Arb-ee, could you please release Oglok's nose?"

Eelia felt again with his feet to make sure the footing was secure, then opened his maw and let go, then crouched into the female's hands.

The beast leaned down, his bared teeth level with Eelia's eyes, his breath burning rancid against the D'Arb-ee's face.

"Oglok, be nice. I'm sure you frightened the poor thing."

129

"D'Arb-ee, this is Oglok. He is a Mock-Man." The female crouched and lowered her hands so he could step onto the ground. "And I'm Princess Aria." She popped her neck with a long stretch. "Sorry to scare you, Oglok. It's a little trick I learned to slow the heart rate and breathing to something imperceptible to give the appearance of death."

"Greetings in the name of Light," Eelia said weakly, stepping backward to put some distance between them. "My name is Eelia, of the Ris of the D'Arb-ee."

Aria smiled and bowed. "Of the Ris? How very fortunate we are indeed."

Oglok grunted but didn't bow.

"Be polite," Aria said to him. "We are in the presence of Eelia of the Ris."

Oglok grunted again and smirked.

"Fine. One day I will manage to teach you to observe human rites of hierarchy."

Another grunt.

"Eelia," the woman said, still smiling. "We had a companion. Did you see where he went?"

Eelia glanced at the ground and pointed toward the temple.

"Thank you." She gazed at the temple and cocked her head to the side.

Eelia tugged at her long skirt. "Princess, you cannot enter. It is forbidden."

She laughed. "You'll see that very little is forbidden to me and my friends, Eelia of the Ris."

"Please," he said. "It is forbidden."

Oglok growled quietly.

"Does the Mock-Man understand the universal tongue?" Eelia asked.

"He does indeed. His kind was created to serve as slaves, according to the records, and they were taught to understand many languages, as many as there were masters to enslave them." She stood up, and motioned with the fingers of her right hand. A twinkle of lights appeared before her eyes, and each became a small globe that revealed a different section of the temple. She stared at them for a moment, then waved them away.

Eelia fell to the ground, his face buried in the dirt.

"There seems to be no entrance, though it's most likely hidden by sorcery."

"Forgive me, Princess Aria," Eelia muttered, each word allowing more dust into his mouth. "I did not know you were one with the Eternal Light."

"It's okay, Eelia of the Ris. Stand up."

"I cannot. The D'Arb-ee are forbidden to enter the presence of the Eternal Light."

"I assure you, I'm not one with anything, much less the Eternal Light, whatever that is."

"But you possess the power…"

"Tricks and spells, little D'Arb-ee, nothing else."

Oglok grunted.

"I cannot. You are testing me, and I will be obedient to the old law."

"Oglok," Aria said.

He made a sound like that of a grunt starting up but getting caught in his throat and stopping before it could commit to the noise. Then Eelia felt a giant hand gripping the back of his shirt and lifting him from the ground.

"And suppose I *am* one with the Eternal Light. I'm sure you don't want to disobey me, do you?"

"No, Princess."

"Then look at me. I promise not to smite you or punish you in any way."

Eelia raised his head and lifted his eyes until he was gazing— shaking all the while—into the Princess' warm eyes. He had been chosen—he the smallest of the house of Ris—*he* had been selected as prophet, the first in more than six generations.

"Thank you, Princess," he said.

"Now tell me about this temple and why you believe it is forbidden."

Oglok set him down, and when he again felt the safety of solid ground beneath his feet, he sat down and crossed his legs. "As you wish, Princess of Eternal Light."

"I —" Aria started, but stopped and nodded at him. "Please, carry on."

"The temple houses the Eternal Light of Secunda Provura, one of your sisters in the Light. She too has the power you possess."

"Another sorceress…"

Oglok glanced sharply at Aria.

"It's okay," she said. "I'm sure John is fine. It's not like he hasn't gone off by himself and left us to catch him up before."

Oglok moaned softly.

"I know. I miss him too." Aria turned to Eelia. "I'm sorry. Please continue."

Eelia fought the chattering of his teeth and cleared his throat. "For six and twenty generations of the D'Arb-ee, she had lived inside the temple, served by the temple guard and her maidenservants."

Oglok growled.

Aria nodded and scrunched her face in thought. "The creatures we fought."

"Yes, Princess."

"Please, you can call me Aria."

"As you wish, Princess Aria."

Aria sighed. "Whatever you're comfortable with, Eelia of the Ris. Carry on."

"Once in every generation, the horn will sound from within the temple, and seven of my people will enter the temple. The ritual is the only time we're allowed to enter. The few of the D'Arb-ee adventurous and stupid enough to disobey were found dead the morning after, and then the clan from which they came was stricken with disease for several days until enough of the clan lay dead. So we learned that the Eternal Light is not to be disobeyed."

"And my companion?"

Eelia pointed at the temple again.

"He found a way inside?"

Eelia shook his head.

"He fell into a trap?"

He shook he head again. The Mock-Man crouched beside him and pushed his eyes together and bared his teeth.

"He…"

"What happened? It would be just like him to chase those creatures into a locked temple."

"He did not chase them, Princess Aria," Eelia said. "He was overcome. And the guards dragged him inside."

Aria jerked up and turned toward the temple. "Then we must rescue him."

Oglok raised up beside her.

"Show us," Aria said.

Eelia pulled at her skirt, shaking his head. "Please. I cannot. It is forbidden."

"Am I not a sister of the Light?"

"It is forbidden."

"I can make you."

"My clan will die. I cannot." Eelia shuddered and shook and he felt the little warmth he had taken from the Princess turn cold inside him. "Please."

"I'm sorry, Eelia, but I have to. My friend is inside, and Oglok and I have to save him."

He tugged again at her skirt.

"What now, my friend?" she asked.

"He is not your friend anymore," he said. "If she hasn't devoured him, she will have emptied and refilled him to make him her own, as the legends state."

"What?!" she said, waving her hands in a wide arc, and lifted the terrified D'Arb-ee on a cylinder of light.

Eelia fell to his knees and bowed prostrate before the princess' hardened face.

"I'm sorry, Princess, but if your friend is not dead, he will soon wish he had died in battle."

Whatever preconceptions Blackthorn had possessed about his hostess vanished the instant he entered her throne room.

"Enter, most favored among mortals," her voice echoed through the gargantuan white chamber.

Sally led the way, and he followed. Two of Sally's sisterkind brought up the rear. Before them, the room was flanked by a row of plain, undecorated columns on each side, partly reflecting their images as they passed and partly absorbing the image and stealing it away from view. The walls themselves were polished glass, and it appeared as though they were a single piece at least sixty yards long rather than segments pasted together. There was not a seam to be seen, just the outer edges. Instead of reflecting their image, however, the walls apparently emitted their own light, flooding the chamber with a glow not unlike the one he had awakened to hours ago, only ten times more brilliant.

The floors were paved with the same polished glass, and were cut into frescos and figures that dotted the floor between the columns rather than the simple geometric shapes that decorated the most of the structures he had seen on Mars. He recognized many strange beasts from the landscape of Mars, but also some creatures from Earth, mostly the large cats of Asia, and even a few mythological beasts from the mythologies of the Greco-Romans, the Norse, and Hindu pantheons.

At the end of the frescos and figures were a set of steps leading into a pit. The steps were cut from simple, base stone and were weathered and already showing signs of erosion. The floor of the pit lay littered with sand and dirt and small bones that covered most of the stonework. The pit was at least six feet deep and ten feet wide, and across it stood a second set of steps that led up to a raised pedestal. The base of the pedestal was crafted from the same common stone as the pit, but from the point it reached above the pit, the rounded sides were covered with the same polished glass as the walls and floor.

On top of the pedestal sat a throne of the blackest stone he had ever seen, darker even than the darkest onyx he'd seen at home on Earth, and yet it seemed to be on fire, like a black flame rather than something burnt and consumed and leftover from a fire. He wondered if it would burn him if he touched it.

"Please come, John Blackthorn. Your appearance here has been foretold, and it would do your young legend no favors to prove your exploits no more than mere stories by showing fear now in my chamber."

The voice spoke softly, but with such command that the serpentine attendants who flanked him backed away, leaving him alone at the first step into the pit.

On the throne sat a being who appeared to cast a light like that of the walls. He waited for his eyes to adjust so he could make out her features, but his eyes refused to cooperate. She remained a featureless silhouette of light instead of shadow.

"Surely the great Blackthorn, whose very name already thunders across this world, is not afraid."

He cleared his throat and straightened his shoulders. "There is a difference between fear and caution."

The attendants let out a loud gasp. No doubt, he thought, they had never heard their goddess spoken to in such a manner. Good. It would only bolster his legend and perhaps give him the edge he'd need to survive.

"Then step into the pit, warrior. You have nothing to fear from me. Have I not chosen you?"

"That's what Sally told me," he said, placing his foot on the first step.

The being shifted in the throne, leaning forward.

"Sorry," he added. "Sally is what I named her. Apparently I can't make the sounds to say her actual name."

The being laughed loudly.

"So much like a mortal. You must name everything you fail to understand. It is your way of controlling the world you see and touch."

He shielded his eyes with one hand as he took two more steps into the pit.

"It is never enough to let what exists remain unknown and unknowable." The voice laughed again. "It is but a pretense, but it amuses me to honor it." The being of light raised what he assumed was her face to the brown attendant who had accompanied him. "From this time, until I command otherwise, you are to be known as Sally."

"Sal-ee," the half-woman said, bowing low. "It is as you decree, Eternal Light."

"And if it pleases my chosen, you will remain his helper until such a time as he no longer requires one."

Blackthorn stared up at the light, then shielded his eyes again. He wasn't sure if no longer needing a helper would be a good or bad change. And he couldn't wait around to find out. But first he had to fill in the missing gaps in his memories.

He took the remaining steps until both feet stood fully in the pit.

"You now stand where no unbound creature save myself has ever stood," said the voice from the light. "You in your ignorance have been honored higher than any of my worshipers have ever been."

"So, do I get to see your face?"

"No mortal sees my face and lives."

"I've read that before," he said.

"Silence. Your honor doesn't grant you complete clemency, John Blackthorn. You would do well to remember that."

Another gasp filled the back of the great chamber.

"Sally!" the voice snapped.

Sally responded by rising from her prone position and spoke in her native clicks and gutturals to the being of light.

"Take your sisterkind and prepare a cleansing for my chosen."

Blackthorn watched as the three serpentine women turned away. Sally paused for a moment to let her gaze linger on him before she too slithered away through the doorway. After they passed the arc, a large stone slab descended and filled the opening so fully that it appeared to be nothing more than solid wall.

No sooner had the 'door' closed than the light began to fade in the chamber. But not completely. It stopped at what felt akin to an overcast day in the Fall on Earth.

"She likes you, you know," said a voice much like the one from before, but less rigid, more soft, less deliberate.

"Now that the charade is over," Blackthorn said turning to face the being, "I'd like to know just what the hell is going on, if you don't mind."

But the woman was no longer on the throne. In fact, he realized, she was no longer anywhere in the room.

"You should feel very special," the voice said, coming as much from inside his head as into his ears. "The Gausheen are a race that only thrice before has mixed with any other. For Sally to risk not only my wrath but the banishment of her own sisterkind says a lot about you."

"Where are you?"

"I am the Eternal Light of Secunda Provura. I am anywhere I want to be."

"And I'm the backside of a desert worm. Your snake people might buy that garbage, but don't expect me to."

"Your bravery is commendable, John Blackthorn, and it makes you an ideal candidate for my needs. But do not be deceived—I will not tolerate mockery from you any more than from the lowest beast that crawls in the dirt outside my temple."

A blast of light hit him in the chest, and he fell back, but quickly regained his footing. "Now we're talking," he said. "Battle is a language I speak far better than deception and false religions."

"False?!" the voice shrieked.

Another blast raced toward him, and he reached at his side for his Sword of Light. In an instant, the sword leapt to life and he blocked the burst with a sweeping motion that sent it into the glass wall. But instead of reflecting it, the blast merely disappeared into the glass, leaving a dark spot that faded quickly.

"My god..." he muttered. "What kind of tricks are you playing at?"

"No tricks," said the voice in and around him. "Are you still so blind, man of Earth?"

"What do you know of Earth?"

No response.

He surveyed the room. Still no sign of the woman. The sword stood in front of his chest and face, guarding against attack.

Something struck him from behind and he toppled forward, falling to one knee.

"Show yourself!"

"Very well, my chosen," the voice said. "I am here."

This time there was warm breath in his ear along with the words, and he raised the sword and spun around to strike.

Then he stopped cold.

Standing before him was a woman barely five feet tall. Her long red hair hung like liquid fire over her shoulders down to her waist. She wore a robe similar to his and a flowing skirt made from the same 'silk' as the robe. The robe gapped open just below her neck and the expanse of her milky skin almost matched the white of the robe, save for the smattering of freckles that lay scattered across it.

Her lips parted and he saw her speak for the first time. "Is that better, John?"

He stepped back and held the sword between them.

"Put that away," she said.

"What the hell is going on? Who are you?"

She raised her hands, held them palm out to him, then moved them toward each other so the palms touched. She smiled then moved them apart again.

The Sword of Light faded, leaving Blackthorn holding little more than a dead flashlight.

"H-h-how…" he stammered.

"I am the Eternal Light of Secunda Provura, and I am not to be taken lightly, even by my chosen."

His sword arm hung limply at his side as she stepped forward and stood up on her toes, leaning forward and resting her palms against his chest. The surprise of her lips meeting his held him fast as they pressed and parted his own slightly.

"Welcome to your destiny, man of Earth," she said, and he felt his eyes grow heavy.

Aria watched as the tiny D'Arb-ee edged into the woods. Eelia glanced back to them once, then gazed wide-eyed, begging without words, before turning away and completely disappearing into the heavy ground cover.

"Very brave," she said.

Oglok grunted.

"For a D'Arb-ee, he was practically a warrior."

Another grunt. Oglok scanned the distance and sniffed the air.

"Anything out there, my friend?" Aria asked.

The giant Mock-Man shook his head.

"Good. The last thing we need is a surprise." She interlocked her fingers and stretched them out with a loud series of pops. "And it's a good thing we left the horses at the tavern in Ostravarne, or we would have lost them for good after that battle earlier."

If Oglok had heard her, she couldn't tell. He instead walked a few yards ahead of her toward the temple, his nose up, and his head sweeping back and forth slowly. He stopped every few steps, waited for a moment, then continued toward the temple.

"One of these days I'm going to have to teach you to speak the universal tongue. I love the sound of my own voice as much as anyone, but even I get tired of hearing it sometimes. Between you and Blackthorn, a girl can wear a blister on her throat trying to keep a conversation going."

Oglok stopped, turned his head toward her, nodded, then continued onward.

"Especially since I can only guess as what you're trying to say. I still don't understand how Blackthorn does it."

Oglok let out a short groan that ended in a sort of whinny.

"What's out there?" she asked, locking her hands in a gesture to quickly bring up a shield should one be needed.

Oglok made no sound.

Only the breeze whispered its song.

Then the Mock-Man burst into a run not toward the temple but away from it, toward the opposite side of the clearing, at a full sprint toward the woods.

Just as quickly he disappeared into them.

Aria ran after him, but knew he'd leave her far behind before he realized he'd left her alone. His instinct to protect—a trait uncommon for the normally docile and kind-natured Mock-Men—had taken over, and all other considerations were temporarily forgotten. She'd seen it before.

Oglok's devotion to his new friends, she thought, was both fierce and deep-set. Somehow, thanks to his loyalty to herself and to Blackthorn, the creature who was supposed to be genetically incapable of being warlike had become perhaps the most accomplished fighter among the trio.

Just as she reached the edge of the woods, she heard a long shriek followed by a loud roar. Oglok's cry, she recognized—but what of the shriek? That was unlike anything she'd heard before.

Brush trampled beneath heavy feet, and the sound grew closer. Thump. Crackle. Thump. Crackle.

Finally the sound stopped no more than a few yards from within the copse of weeds as thick as trees and twice as dense.

"Let go of me!" came a voice she recognized.

"Oh, Oglok, you've caught a wandering warrior of the Ris."

The Mock-Man emerged from the thicket carrying Eelia by the scruff of his collar.

"I thought you were going home, little one," Aria said with a smile.

"Put me down, beast-man," the D'Arb-ee whined.

"Put him down, please," Aria said.

Oglok set him on the ground.

"So, what made you change your mind, Eelia of the Ris?"

The little manling stood as tall as he could and puffed out his chest. "It's true that we D'Arb-ee are forbidden to enter the presence of the Eternal Light. But if you are also of that Light, then merely by being around you, I have already brought ill upon my people. Perhaps the only way to prevent it from coming to pass is to follow and obey the Princess Aria of the Eternal Light until I can earn your favor enough to substitute my service to avoid the punishment."

Aria leaned over and rubbed the little creature's head. "You are indeed the bravest of your people, Eelia. It may be that you will have your own legend sung in the years to come."

"Do you think that —" he began then stopped. "If the Light wills it, it will be," he said instead. Then he strode toward the temple with faltering steps.

Aria grinned at Oglok. "He may be as brave as you, my friend."

Oglok snorted.

"Almost as brave then."

"There is little time," Eelia said, taking three steps to walk the distance his companions covered in one. "It may not actually exist, but I have heard legends that speak of a hidden passage into the temple."

The darkness cleared in blurry patches, and Blackthorn cursed whatever fate had consigned him to passing out and waking in strange places on this day.

As consciousness came into focus, he noticed a soft touch against his back, cool and smooth and moving in a slow back-and-forth motion that caused goosebumps to rise along his skin.

"You have awakened, my chosen."

Damn. Memory hit his mind and he winced. The so-called goddess of the snake women had poisoned him with a kiss and now he was in her bed. It was a good thing Aria wasn't around to...

But she couldn't be around. Nor would she ever be around again.

He sat up and pulled away from the woman's massaging touch. But before he could speak, she moved back to his side, her hand resting on his thigh.

"What bothers you, John Blackthorn?"

He turned, brushed her hand away from his leg, then wrapped his own hand around her throat. "Why did you kill my friends, you witch?"

Rather than answer, the woman glared at him. Then a heat burned along his hand. He held his grip on her throat until he saw smoke rise between her neck and his hand.

"I told you I was not to be taken lightly, John." She coughed and brushed her fire-kissed tresses from her face, then pulled it together in a ponytail behind her and tied it off with a band of light that appeared between her thumb and index finger. "I do not appreciate being taken lightly."

John clenched the bedclothes in his fists. "And I do not appreciate having my friends murdered."

"John. My precious, silly man." The woman's face softened, and she sat on the bed beside him. "I did not order your friends to be killed. It was simply the way of the Gausheen—what you called the snake-people. They guard the temple and were only performing their duties as decreed of old. They would have killed you too had I not commanded them to bring you to me." She turned away. "I would have stopped them sooner, had I known…"

"Had you known what?" Blackthorn spat.

"Had I know that you too oppose the great wizards of Mars."

Blackthorn lost his grip and almost fell off the bed.

"What?!"

"Had I known you were allies in the overthrow of the four charlatans who rule this world, I would have tried to spare you all, but alas, you are the only ally I have left, John."

He rose from the bed and stood over her, reminding himself that no combination of loveliness and curves could bring back his friends.

"So you let them die?!"

"They—you—were invaders on the temple grounds."

"And what of the bones in the trench in your throne room? More unfortunates you were too late to save?"

She laughed. "Simple animals, the prey of the Gausheen. An intriguing type of hominid, much like a primate, but from a more blurred genetic line. It keeps the Gausheen placated and helps to hone their hunting instinct."

"Like they hunted my friends?"

"You were the invaders. They did what any trained guard dog would do."

"I should kill you where you sit, witch." He raised his fist to strike, but she made no motion to either block the blow or evade it. He stopped, letting his arm hang in the air, fist clenched but not hammering down onto the woman.

She gazed up at him, her eyes moistening. "Paula," she said.

He glared at her, but unclenched his fist.

"Paula Winterbourne," she said.

"What?" His arm fell to his side.

"My birth name was Paula Winterbourne. I too am from Earth, John."

She stood up and walked across the room, waved her hand over a pale orb on the wall, and cupped her hands. No sooner had her hands formed a seal than a thin stream of water sprayed from above the orb. When she pulled her hands away to drink the water, the spray ceased.

"You were right, John," she said. "I am a fake, a charlatan, the leader of a false religion."

"I – I…" He stepped toward her, but stopped after a single stride. "Earth?"

She nodded.

"So I'm not the only one?"

"I thought *I* was until I discovered you."

"Why tell me this now?" he asked.

She turned to face him, then closed the distance between them. She rested both hands against his bare chest and he fought the urge to flinch away. "Do you feel this heat in my hands?"

"I don't get how that answers my question."

"Do you feel it?"

A sort of electrical current coursed from her palm to her fingers tips and back again.

"I feel it."

"It is the power of this world, John." One hand rose from his chest to his shoulder, still pulsing. "Mars is a conduit. At least that's the best way I can think of to explain it. The wizards of this place aren't really magical at all, no more than I am. But to the people on this planet, they certainly seem to be. It's difficult to describe, but know that there are ways of channeling that energy and using it."

The other hand climbed to his shoulder as well.

"If I let my guard down around the Gausheen, I would be killed instantly. They are a simple race, and will either worship me or

141

destroy me." She looked up into his face, her eyes heavy and bordering on tears, or at least so it seemed to Blackthorn. "This moment, here, now, with you. This is the first time I've been able to be Paula Winterbourne again since I ended up on this godforsaken planet."

Her hands roamed around his neck and her fingers intertwined and clasped together.

"I need you, John."

Her chest heaved a noticeable sigh.

"I need you as a very lonely woman and I need you as an ally against the sorcerers who will destroy this planet with their petty rivalries."

Coming to himself again, Blackthorn tried to push her away, but her grip held fast and he dragged her with him as he backed away. She lost her footing and fell against him, her lips brushing his chest.

"Stop. Please," he said.

"Are you not lonely too, John?"

She kissed his chest gently.

Not like this, he thought. Not like this.

"My friends are dead and you're trying to seduce me?!"

He wedged her arms loose from him and pushed her back. She fell to the floor in a disheveled heap. After gaining her balance, she locked her eyes on his and made her hands into fists. Instantly they were surrounded by white flame.

He held his place and didn't look away. If his adventure ended here, at the hands of a psychotic sorceress, then it would only serve to rush him to his friends' side that much sooner.

But her gaze softened, and the flamed faded from her fists.

"I'm sorry. I've been a goddess so long that I've forgotten how to be a woman." She reached up, obviously waiting for his assistance to stand. "Please forgive me."

He stepped forward and helped her up.

"I'm also sorry for you loss. You have to believe me that I would have saved your friends if I had known. It is a small consolation, I know, but it's all I can give you."

Taking his hand, she led him to the bed, and they sat down. "You probably want to know how I came to be here," she said.

She waved her hand across the air between them. Instantly a holographic image of a city appeared, but a city unlike the ones Blackthorn had seen on Earth.

"My Earth was not your Earth, John." She paused to let the words sink in. "The city you see is New Pittsburg, built on the remains of what you knew as just Pittsburgh. It's the city where I was born, John." Her other hand gripped his then released it. "Where I was born in the year 2234."

"I…" he started

"Please, allow me to finish before you ask anything. I've been waiting to tell my story to someone for so long." She smiled.

Warm, he thought. Sincere.

"I was a physicist at the University of New Pittsburgh. I returned after leaving it as a child when they offered me a position in research. Sadly, that's what killed me."

Blackthorn didn't respond.

"There was an explosion, and I was in the midst of it. I lost most of my body, I remember that, but I didn't die immediately. No, some sick joke of fate thought it would be fun to let me lie as a burnt torso for several hours, slowly dying while the lab lay in rubble all around me. I don't remember the actual moment I died, but I do remember waking up here, in this body in the traveling fortress of the Sorcerer of Fatal Laughter."

"He doesn't usually work with flesh, just robots."

"Yes, that's right."

"But…"

She turned away. "How do you think I have been a goddess so many years, John? I have lived six human lifetimes in this artificial body, never aging, never changing." Her voice grew low, almost a whisper. "No matter how soft and natural it may feel thanks to that monster's craftsmanship, it can never be real flesh."

"The dog of a devil! He'll pay for this."

She turned to face him again. "Thank you. And now you know my secret, the only living creature on this planet besides the one who created me who knows the truth."

"But my friends?" Blackthorn said.

"I *am* very sorry, John, and if I could change the past, I would save them," she said, her voice fading almost to a whisper. "I have been a goddess so long, and a robotic slave before that for many years. I'm afraid it may take a long time to teach me how to be genuinely human again." She grabbed his hand with both of her own. "But I am willing to try if you are willing to teach me." She lifted his hand to her chest and pressed it against her pounding heart. "And if you can be patient with me, I can be a suitable companion for you in time. After all, this body will not grow old and lose its beauty, nor will it succumb to disease or become ill. We can have a lifetime of happiness when…" Her voice trailed off.

"I…" he stammered. "We…" He let the words go.

"Perhaps I should continue." She let go of his hand and let it fall to the bed again. "I wandered a long time after I escaped, and I eventually found this temple and a mostly dead race of the Gausheen living in the woods as predators. I hid from them for years, learning the history and secrets of this temple—it was built by the Black Sorcerer, John, as a conduit to gather power to rule over the other three First Men."

"Him I know very well."

"Yes," she said. "Your escape from him is already part of your legend on this world."

"Then you also know I have no love for him or his kind."

"On that we agree." She continued. "But he couldn't channel the power in this temple, so he eventually gave up and moved on. But that's where he failed, John, and I succeeded. He didn't know how energy worked on Earth, so he couldn't know fully how it worked here either."

John cocked his head to the side. "I don't understand."

"Oh," she said. "I forgot. In your time, they hadn't seen through the magic to understand the science of it either." She stood up, clapped her hands in front of her, and energy shot from the floor to her hands then finally around the room in a wide spiral. Just as suddenly it dissipated. "Ley lines, my brave and backwards man. Mars is built, just like Earth, on a series of interwoven lines of energy, and this temple is built on the nexus they all flow into. And since the Sorcerer of Fatal Laughter filled my artificial body with the same filaments that allow him to channel the 'magic' of this world, I can do the same, thanks to my understanding of physical laws of energy. My knowledge of Newton, Einstein, Kaku and Mugur-Schächter will succeed where his knowledge of so-called arcane arts has failed."

Blackthorn nodded. He was a warrior, a man of battle, not of science, and he had seen enough in the past few months to know he was way out of his league intellectually, but this woman, Paula, she believed it and seemed to know what she was talking about. And he would have to trust in that.

"So I became a goddess and revealed myself, and formed what few Gausheen remained into a powerful race again, and in return they chose to serve and worship me. And even if we have to annihilate this world to do it, we will finally destroy the four charlatans who think they rule Mars."

She grabbed his hand and he let her take it.

"Come, John Blackthorn. Let's go to my throne room. I need to show you the fullness of my power."

He followed, his penchant for military strategy taking hold of his emotions. There was little else to do, and he would need allies, strong allies. And no matter her power, her heart was wounded, and he could either rebuild it or manipulate it to help him tame the planet he now called home.

It was the most expedient plan. The lump in his throat begged him to reconsider, but he ignored it.

"There is so much to show you," she said, pulling him along the hallway of lit glass walls.

"Ssshhh," Aria said, motioning from her companions to stop. "Something's moving, but for the life of me, I can't say what exactly."

"Guardians," said the D'Arb-ee.

"The snake people?" she whispered.

Eelia nodded. "The males."

They waited, not moving or speaking until the sounds disappeared in the distance.

"The ones that defeated the three of us earlier," Aria said. "And that was taking Blackthorn's strength into account."

Oglok moaned.

"It's okay," she said. "They caught us by surprise then. We're expecting them this time."

Aria lifted her palm to her face and stared at it. It looked like it held a constellation connected by lines of white-hot light. She shook it. The lights remained.

"There's power here," she said. "And it's more than I've ever sensed before." She turned to her companions and smiled. "If I'm right, then I don't think we're going to have to worry about the guardians this time."

Then she braced both hands above her head and locked her feet and legs wide, making a living 'X' in the tunnel. "Brace your eyes," she said.

She waited to see that Oglok and Eelia had indeed closed their eyes and covered their faces. Then she spoke in a tongue she hadn't uttered since leaving the Black Sorcerer's fortress.

The tunnel erupted in light, and the brightness raced through the path of stone for nearly a mile. Bathed in the light herself, she felt the fading energy of every creature it encompassed on its journey, felt them fall to the floor unconscious, felt the tunnel fill and empty again until nothing stood between them and the entrance to the temple.

She spoke again in the old tongue and stood silent for several breaths as the light flowed back to her body and the tunnel grew dark again. When at last all the energy was back inside her, her legs gave way.

Oglok caught her before even one knee touched the stone floor.

"Thank you, my friend," she said, glancing over him to see how the D'Arb-ee was doing.

Eelia lay prone, his own tiny body an 'X' on the floor, mumbling in his people's prayer-language. Aria couldn't make out all the words, but she did catch something about a "wish for death" and "the great mother."

"Stand, Eelia of the Ris of the D'Arb-ee," she said with as much royal decree as she could muster to comfort the little warrior. "You have faced the Eternal Light and have been found deserving. You are now Eelia-Kan of the Ris of the D'Arb-ee."

"Eelia-Kan?" he asked feebly, not moving.

Oglok raised his bushy eyebrows at Aria, and she whispered, "I know what I'm doing."

Oglok held on until her footing was secure.

"Rise, Eelia-Kan. Rise and serve."

Eelia practically leapt to his feet. "There has never been a Kan among the D'Arb-ee." He didn't wait for a response, but instead he disappeared into the darkness and led the way down the tunnel. "Come, come," he shouted. "Come."

Oglok gave her a quizzical glance. "Kaaahn?" he grumbled.

"They probably didn't teach you the old tongues, did they? Not needed for slave labor, I'm sure they thought." She patted his shoulder. "Kan is an ancient title bestowed by the first men. It means warrior-prince, and it makes the recipient an heir to the power of the sorcerer he serves. In this case, me, or the goddess-princess he seems to think I am."

Oglok grunted.

"Come on," she said. "Let's go get Blackthorn."

"This throne," Paula said as she climbed the steps from the trench, "is here because beneath this spot is the single point where all the ley lines of Mars intersect. You wouldn't believe the amount of power that flows through this place." She turned to Blackthorn and smiled. "And this throne has been so infused by the energy that it changed the stone to a new element entirely. It's the same type of new stone that covers the walls of this room."

Blackthorn followed and placed his foot onto the first step out of the trench. "I suppose it works like a prism."

"Just the opposite, John. Instead of splitting the energy it focuses it even tighter, and sends a single, laser-light beam into the filaments that line my body. Had I a body of flesh, I'm sure it would melt away to nothing with this much power coursing through it."

He took another step. "Sounds painful."

"Stop!" she yelled. Then said in a softer voice, "I do not know what the energy would do to you, John. And besides, the Gausheen would not understand to see another standing beside me as an equal."

"Figures," he said.

"Only where they are concerned." Her face disappeared in the brightness that took over her form. "You and I know the truth. It is..." she paused, let the emptiness hang between them for longer than he felt was comfortable. "...*expedient* for now."

The lump returned to his throat.

"Are you sure you didn't serve in the 451st too?" he mumbled to himself.

She answered anyway. "Your unit. You honor them in this, John. You will help me bring peace to an entire planet. How can you not honor *all* of your fallen friends in this?"

Blackthorn felt something twist in his heart. "The enemy of my enemy..." he whispered.

She either ignored her or didn't hear him. "Watch, John Blackthorn. Watch as we announce our power to those who mistakenly believe they rule this world."

Paula raised her arms and the doors of the chamber opened. Hordes of the Gausheen slithered in, and he couldn't help but smile when he saw Sally. She paused at his gesture, but did not return it and kept her head low. Within minutes, the room was filled with the clicking gutturals and sliding scratches of the half-women.

Paula spoke in the clicking language and the creatures grew silent. Then she said softly to Blackthorn. "We are safe. The brotherkind patrol the hallways and tunnels. Should even the First Men oppose us, we should see victory."

He nodded as it seemed she waited for some acknowledgement from him.

She stood, then stepped onto the seat of the throne, standing like an 'X' as her body appeared to burn alive with a flame so hot it was almost crystalline in its whiteness.

"Sisterkind!" she yelled. "Bring in the sacrifices." Then she turned her featureless face to Blackthorn. "Remove yourself from the pit, John Blackthorn, for the time of power."

"Theatrics," he mumbled to himself as returned to the main temple floor, surrounded by the snake-women.

But he changed his mind when the mass of Glausheen parted and a group of six tiny human-looking creatures were led to the front and into the pit by two large, dark blue Gausheen females. As they walked, the tiny creatures chattered and trembled, cowering before the giants behind them.

The Gausheen stopped at the edge of the pit, but with a swish of their tails, they shoved the sacrificial creatures inside.

"What's the meaning of this?" Blackthorn yelled.

"They are the sacrifice." Paula rose almost a foot above the throne, a comet's tail of light following from her feet. "They trigger the release that will bring peace to this world."

He stepped back into the pit. "No!"

The creatures looked up at him. One shook its head. "No?" it said.

"Are these the 'simple animals' you spoke of? Are you so far gone that you no longer recognize sentience?"

"It is necessary, John Blackthorn. Do not interfere."

"No." He reached the floor of the pit. The creatures pressed in upon his legs, their trembling almost shaking him. "You will not kill these little men and women."

"Do not interfere, chosen of the Eternal Light," she said. Then after a paused, added, "...please."

The Gausheen gasped and backed away from the edge of the pit. No doubt, he thought, they'd never heard their goddess plead for anything.

"Tell me why not?"

"The power has been made known, and even now, the First Men could be amassing themselves to approach."

"Then kill me as well."

"No." Paula descended to the throne, and her feet lit upon the glowing seat. "You will remove yourself from the pit, human."

Blackthorn stepped onto the first step leading to the throne pedestal. "I'd like to see you try it, lady."

Paula stood calmly, and let her face lose some of its glow, enough that he could make out the pain her eyes. "Please," she whispered. "I know you don't understand, but I only do what I have to do to save this world."

"Not this way," he said, taking the next step as he grabbed the Sword of Light from his side.

It lit up with a crackle and the Gausheen slithered another foot or so back.

"What will it be, Paula?" he whispered. "I may hold no love for the bastards who rule this planet, but I will not let myself become like them—not even to defeat them."

"Please."

"No."

There was only the quiet shifting of the Gausheen's tails against the stone floor, and the chattering of the sacrificial creatures as Blackthorn took the last step to reach the pedestal and stand before the so-called "Eternal Light."

He saw a tear fall across Paula's cheek as her face faded again into a sheer wall of light. "So be it," she said flatly.

The first beam hit the sword and deflected into the front row of the Gausheen, sending four down to the stone. Dead or alive, he couldn't tell. The second he deflected as well, but sent it away from the snake-women. No need to kill unless necessary.

The third however, hit the sword and the blade disappeared.

A fourth just missed him as he dove for the pit.

A fifth hit him mid-leap and carried him above the pit and above even the Gausheen and into one of the shiny walls at the back of the temple.

The wall didn't crack, but he wasn't so sure his spine was as fortunate, and he tumbled from the wall into a heap on the ground.

"Stay where you fall, John Blackthorn, and my servants will care for you after the ceremony."

Through his blurring vision, he made out a wide circle of the snake-women around him. In the front, already approaching him, was Sally. She motioned with her very human-looking hands for him to stay down.

Several others of the women slid toward him, but she clicked at them loudly and they stopped.

"I can't do that," Blackthorn said, already trying to rise to his feet.

"So be it," said the voice from the light. "But we warned. No man can survive two such blasts and walk away."

"Thanks for the warning," he said as he pushed weakly to a squat, then forced his aching body to stand. "I'll keep that in mind."

He looked at Sally. She motioned more fervently than ever for him to stay put.

He smiled.

Then he walked toward the pit again with slow steps.

As he did, Paula rose into the air again, and what he could only describe as a puddle of light drained from her, though it never diminished the light inside her, and spilled from the floor of the pedestal into the pit.

Blackthorn broke into an uneven run and wove between the snake-women until he reached the pit again.

He powered up the sword and lunged for the pit.

"Blackthorn!" Aria yelled as the great stone door lifted high above her.

They stood before a huge, glowing cavern, surrounded by hundreds of the same kind of creatures her magic had left unconscious in the hallways behind them. But as those had been all males, these were all females. They turned as she yelled and bared their sharp teeth.

Oglok braced his stance beside her.

Little Eelia, braver by far after she had titled him as Kan, stepped in front of them both.

There was a flash of light, and John Blackthorn disappeared from her view as the sea of snake-women engulfed him.

Sal-ee, for that is who she was now, until the Eternal Light no longer demanded it from her, spun immediately when she heard the name of the human male . It was no longer the Eternal Light who spoke the name, nor one of her sisterkind, but one of his own kind, one of those he had called his friends, one she had told him lay dead outside the temple.

Then the blast of light from the throne, and she turned away from the intruders.

John Blackthorn sailed through the air toward the rear wall again, his form awash in the Water of the Eternal Light.

She had to act fast even if it meant risking the anger of the one she served.

150

151

Sal-ee darted across the floor, clearing a path among her sisterkind, until she stood between the wall and the approaching human.

She closed her eyes and waited for impact.

Blackthorn smashed the wall a second time, but something absorbed the brunt of the impact. He opened his eyes to find Sally lying beside him on the ground.

"Sally?" he asked.

"I could not let you die, John Blackthorn."

"Can you move?"

She clenched and unclenched her fingers, but made no motion from her waist down. "I fear not."

"You saved me," he said. "Why did you do that?"

"I could not let you die, John Blackthorn, chosen of the Eternal Light."

She smiled weakly.

"Will you live?" he asked.

"Perhaps."

"Stay here."

He stood up and, for the first time, saw the battle raging around him. The rest of the Gausheen had become like demonic doppelgangers of the gentle species that had cared for him in his chamber. They had surrounded something in the center of the temple, though he could not make out exactly what.

Raising the sword to life, he ran headlong into the battle, caring less this time how many of the snakelike creatures fell dead around him. Their goddess was insane, he knew now, and as long as they served her, they could suffer the same fate he reserved for her.

He heaved the blade left and right, making what seemed to be little headway, when he heard a familiar voice cry out his name.

Aria!

Bless all the gods of every religion he could name. She was alive!

"Aria!"

"Close your eyes tight, Blackthorn," she yelled, and he barely had done so when the temple chamber disappeared into a light not unlike that of Paula on her throne.

He waited as the light faded behind even his screwed-tight eyelids. Along with the light, there was a degree of heat, though not painful, that faded as well.

"You can open them now," Aria said.

He opened his eyes and all but fell into a powerful hug around the companion he had thought dead. "It's wonderful to see you," he said. "I was told you were dead."

Oglok grunted behind him.

"And you too, my friend. I've missed you as well."

He gazed over the floor of the temple around them, as the surprise of seeing his companions faded. It lay littered with the bodies of hundreds of Gausheen. Some lay as though asleep, while others lay hacked in pieces by the Sword of Light.

Among the bodies lay one miniscule by comparison.

"Eelia?" Aria said, kneeling beside the tiny body.

The body raised its head and tried to smile, but just barely.

"I…" it said in the common tongue. "I… I was brave."

"You were very brave, Eelia-Kan," Aria said.

"Will I serve you even after I die, Princess?"

Blackthorn watched as Aria stifled a tear. "You're not going to die, little hero."

"Touching," said a voice behind them. "But you're too late. The power has been awakened, my chosen."

Blackthorn strode to the front of the temple and gazed into the pit. The puddle of light had dissipated, and six new tiny skeletons lay on the eroded stone floor.

"You're as vile a creature as any of the First Men," he spat.

"You will come to know me as a friend, John Blackthorn, and perhaps more."

He looked at the being of light, then to Aria and Oglok. Oglok held the tiny creature called Eelia-Kan in his arms. "I don't think so, Paula."

His sword flashed to life before him.

"You still believe that toy can harm me?"

"Aria?" he asked without turning.

"I'll do what I can."

"This toy by itself, no," he said. "But I don't have to defeat you by myself, false goddess."

Paula threw a blast of light at the sword, but it held fast. Another. It held again. And another. The sword didn't even flicker.

Blackthorn laughed. "It seems that my sorceress can channel this power as easily as you."

"No," Paula cried. "It isn't possible. Not unless…"

But Blackthorn was no longer listening. He leapt from the edge of the pit across the chasm until he stood just below Paula's fully lit form.

"Taste my power, Eternal Light!" he yelled, and swung the sword until it bit through the full shape of her left leg.

The false goddess screamed, and as her features returned to her face, she glared. "You've ruined everything, John! Everything!"

Then she fell from the throne, into his arms, her all-too-human face grimacing in pain as she fainted.

Blackthorn carried her across the pit and to his friends. "Can you save her?" he asked.

Aria smiled and rested her hand on his shoulder. "That's what I don't understand about you, Blackthorn. You fight like all hell itself to destroy an enemy, then have the audacity to be concerned about your foe once all is done."

"She wasn't always evil," he said. "What she went through could make anyone go crazy." He laid the unconscious woman on the ground in front of Aria. "In her own misguided way, she was trying to save this planet from the First Men."

"I'll take your word for it," Aria said, looking over the woman. "Her wound is already cauterized. And her body is strong. Her power is saving her all by itself. She doesn't need me."

"Then there is another I want you to save, if you can."

He led Aria to the back of the chamber. Sal-ee lay barely breathing in the same place he had left her. Her chest heaved and fell only once or twice every minute.

"You… you are… alive, John Blackthorn," she muttered faintly.

"So are you, Sally." Then to Aria. "Can you save her?"

Aria felt the air above the dying snake-woman, then let several flickers of blue light dance along the woman's form. Then she gazed at the ground. "I can keep her from dying, but she will never move on her own again."

"Let me die," Sal-ee said. "Please." The snake-woman smiled. "Let… let me die with… Goddess."

"She is no goddess," Blackthorn said. "She never was."

"Let me die with kiss," she asked, her breath losing strength.

He leaned into her. "I would be honored, Sally," he said. He pressed his lips to hers, and she pulled away weakly, then her tongue darted out and flicked against his heaving and sweaty chest.

"You…" she started.

"I…" he said.

"You… taste…"

He leaned in. Her voice grew quieter. His ear all but rested on her lips.

"Taste like salt," she said, and her chest stopped forever.

He closed her eyes.

"Can you destroy this place?" he asked Aria. "There is power here, where the ley lines converge. We can't let anyone access this kind of power ever again."

"I still don't understand why you had to take her," Aria said.

"Only as far as the outer cities." Blackthorn glanced behind him at the still-sleeping form of the Eternal Light who lay over Oglok's shoulder. "Doesn't look so eternal, now, does she?"

"That doesn't explain anything," Aria said.

Oglok spoke a long series of grunts, punctuated by a sharp hiccup.

"We must never become like our enemies, my friend," he said. "When you rerouted the ley lines, you destroyed the temple's source of power." He cleared his throat. "Her own abilities will be no stronger than yours now. She will still be formidable, but the Gausheen would have killed her for deceiving them, and left to herself, she would be found and returned to the Sorcerer of Fatal Laughter to be either killed or enslaved again." He looked off into the distance. "I couldn't allow that."

"I sometimes wonder if I want to understand you or not, Blackthorn."

Oglok made another series of grunts.

Blackthorn nodded and turned his head toward the forest miles behind them. "Yes, I bet that Eelia would enjoy the monument."

"He deserved more," Aria said. "Perhaps a stronger sorceress—"

Blackthorn cut her off. "No. He died in the glory of battle. He died with a smile." He took her hand gently. "Don't dishonor him with regrets."

She forced a smile. She couldn't hide the truth from him. Battle had erased those masks.

"We should all hope to have so noble a death when our time comes."

Oglok brayed and raised his fists into the sky.

Aria sniffled and nodded.

Blackthorn pushed on into the fading sunset.

INDISTINGUISHABLE FROM MAGIC

JAMES PALMER

John Blackthorn rode easy in his saddle, his horse moving at a lazy trot. His two companions rode beside him through the strange ruins. Steel girders jutted from the ground, twisted by time and chaos, like the bones of some prehistoric beast. The remains of strange vehicles—sleek, wheel-less teardrop shapes with cracked bubble tops—were scattered about like toys. The horses' hooves clacked atop a crumbling stretch of road shot through with green tendrils of weird vegetation. There was an eerie pall about the place, and Blackthorn realized that this ancient town or city had been abandoned for a very long time.

Tiring of the dreary surroundings, Blackthorn turned his attentions skyward. It wasn't much better. An ugly, potato-shaped moon hung limply in the sky; the sun looked smaller and too far away.

Blackthorn glanced at his companions. To his left, Princess Aria rode calmly beside him, her small mouth curved in a perpetual smirk, her close cropped dark hair waving in the breeze that wafted in from the east, billowing her green cloak behind her. Her jeweled necklace glinted brightly in the sun. On her left sat perhaps the strangest sight of all, Oglok the Mock-Man, atop an equally strange horse he'd recently acquired: a lithe, chitinous animal with a golden, fan-like mane. The Mock-Man was shirtless and his golden pelt seemed to glow in the sunlight that washed this plain in light.

The quiet afternoon was soon punctuated by the sound of galloping horses and a woman's cry. Blackthorn and his companions glanced at one another before spurring their horses into a gallop. They led the animals around a pile of stone and steel and came to another ancient road, this one reduced to little more than a dirt lane between the skeletons of buildings. There they saw the source of the noise.

Four large, armored men on strong black horses were running down a woman and a small boy, both dressed in little more than rags.

The four men had herded the woman and child into the middle of the lane, where they circled them menacingly. The woman gripped the child protectively while the horsemen prodded at them with long rods affixed with some sort of cylinder at the end.

Blackthorn slowed his horse to a stop and Princess Aria and Oglok did the same. They still hadn't been detected by the horsemen.

"The Master demands tribute!" said one of the horsemen. "Everyone gives their part!"

"The crops have suffered!" the woman cried back. "We have nothing to give!"

"Then tithe with your life!" replied the horseman, lowering his stick and unsheathing a crude yet lethal-looking sword.

"I've seen enough," said Blackthorn, unhooking his Sword of Light from his belt. Touching the yellow square, he caused a pillar of light to erupt from the end of the metal cylinder with a crackling hiss. Spurring his horse, Blackthorn surged toward the group of horsemen, his friends galloping right behind him. Princess Aria's color-changing dress turned a violent shade of crimson as they closed on the men. Oglok growled a guttural battle cry and sent his own horse into the fray.

The horsemen turned at the sound. Blackthorn could now see that their masked helmets were made to look like gleaming skulls. "Who dares interrupt the Skeleton Corps in the execution of their duties?" cried the lead horseman. "These rabble are criminal tax evaders and must be sorely punished!"

Blackthorn could see the leader's eyes darting furtively back and forth, sizing up the black-clad stranger with his Sword of Light blazing, the dark-skinned woman and Mock-Man who now threatened him.

"They must be dangerous criminals indeed to require four strong warriors to apprehend them," said Blackthorn as he brought his Sword of Light down in a blazing arc that severed the leader's long prod in half.

"Kill these strangers!" the leader ordered, and his three companions forgot all about their prey and turned instead to face this new threat. Their leader lunged at Blackthorn with his crude iron sword, but Blackthorn simply held out his light sword and let the horseman's blade melt in half as it struck the concentrated energy beam.

"What sorcery is this?" rumbled the horseman.

"More than you can handle, I assure you," quipped Blackthorn. He lashed out with his weapon, cutting across the horseman's breastplate, causing the bottom half of it to fall off and hit the ground with a clang.

The other horsemen had fanned out now to attack Blackthorn and his companions, while the woman and child they had hunted ran inside one of the derelict buildings and watched from the shadows.

Oglok the Mock-Man eagerly joined the fray. He leaped from his mount and tackled the nearest armored bully, knocking him from his own black steed. Oglok sat atop him and dealt a heavy blow to the horseman's faceplate that cracked it in two. The rider lay motionless. One of his companions charged at Oglok, holding the strange staff like a lance. The Mock-Man grabbed it and effortlessly lifted the rider from his horse and tossed him into a nearby pile of debris, then gripped the prod in both hands and bent it double before tossing it aside and starting to scavenge the first toppled horseman's clothing and armor. The man he had pulled from his horse stood shakily and, unsheathing a crude sword with a serrated blade, marched toward the unsuspecting Oglok, who had busied himself with acquiring a new costume.

Princess Aria pulled the dagger from the sheath behind her neck and threw it, hitting Oglok's would-be attacker squarely in his sword hand. He screamed and dropped the blade, which alerted Oglok. The Mock-Man stood and growled an epithet at the rider before hurling a nearby hunk of metal at the horseman. He narrowly avoided the heavy piece of debris before screaming and disappearing into the ruins.

The last rider charged at Aria, his strange pole raised like a lance. Aria held out her right hand with her thumb, index and little fingers extended while touching her necklace with her left hand. A purple orb of light formed around her hand, while a similar energy field appeared around the horseman who approached her. Suddenly he was flung violently from his mount and hurled fifty feet into a metal girder that jutted from the broken ground. He did not attempt to get up.

Only the lead horseman remained, held at bay by Blackthorn's light sword and unable or unwilling to attempt further assault. "The Master shall hear of this!" he said at last, his deep voice quavering.

Blackthorn smiled. "I hope so," he said. He slashed his sword easily and expertly through the air directly in front of the lead horseman. The remains of his black armor fell apart and thudded to the ground, leaving only his helmet and a few protective undergarments in place.

Without another word the disrobed horseman turned his horse and sent it running deeper into the ruins.

"We should stop him," said the princess.

Blackthorn touched the yellow square again and the deadly energy beam vanished. "No, let him go and tell his master. I would like to meet the villain who would send cowards like these to victimize women and children." He turned around and said, "You can come out now. We won't harm you."

Slowly, almost reluctantly, the woman and child appeared in the darkened doorway of the ruined building. They stepped out, the woman shielding the child behind her. "Who are you?" she asked.

"My name is John Blackthorn. These are my friends, Princess Aria and Oglok."

The woman stared at Oglok. "A Mock-Man. I haven't seen one of your kind in years." Oglok growled something and nodded as he climbed atop his horse.

"I thank you for helping me and my child. I am Marna, and this is Zak." She patted the boy's head and he peered up at them from his mother's shadow but said nothing.

"Who were those men?" asked Blackthorn.

"The Skeleton Corps. They are in the service of Lord Valaron, our ruler."

"That must be the master they referred to," Princess Aria said to Blackthorn.

"This Valaron of yours rules with an iron hand," mused Blackthorn.

"He provides us with much," said Marna. "He uses his magic to light and heat our homes. But sometimes the tribute he demands in return is more than we can bear." She glanced down at Zak and stroked his brown hair.

"Your children?" asked Blackthorn, startled.

Marna nodded. "Sometimes. They are put to work as slaves deep in his lair, or are trained to become Skeleton Corps like those blackguards who hounded me and my son." Her voice was tinged with hurt and anger.

She looked up at Blackthorn, smiling brightly. "Return with us to our village. I can repay your kindness with what food we have, and rest and nourishment for your horses."

Blackthorn and his companions graciously accepted the invite and, once Marna and Zak were riding behind Aria on her steed, the woman directed them to her village.

Marna's village was the most advanced Blackthorn had seen since awakening in this strange new world. Crude yet usable houses had been constructed from wood harvested from the nearby forest that grew to the south, and Blackthorn heard the buzz of what could only be a saw mill. "You mill lumber?" he said, amazed.

"Yes," replied Marna. "Water from the river powers the blade. It is very ancient magic. Lord Valaron showed us how to harness it."

"This Valaron of yours is very clever," replied Princess Aria.

"That is nothing. His true power is beyond all understanding." She pointed a shaky finger at a large dark shape in the distance. Atop a hill on the other side of the river was a monstrous metal hulk rising from the crumpled metal of some ancient ruin. It was in the shape of a skull. "That's the Keep of Lord Valaron."

Marna ran into the village, Zak following closely on her heels. The other villagers who were working or milling about stopped what they were doing to eye these bizarrely-clad strangers and listen intently as Marna told them what had happened. Blackthorn kept his sharp eyes on the Keep, watching for signs of movement, wondering about the petty tyrant who dwelled there.

The village eagerly shared what food they had, which to Blackthorn's reckoning was quite plentiful after subsisting on meager travel rations for hundreds of miles. Small game, fruits and berries gathered from the forest, and water collected from the river were given to them freely, while someone tended to their horses. Blackthorn was surprised to learn that the people of the village even farmed and turned strange-looking wheat into a sweet-tasting bread. The younger villagers marveled at Oglok, who stood stoically in his newly acquired makeshift armor while they stared at him or touched his golden fur. The young girls of the village stared at Blackthorn, giggling and running off when he returned their gaze. The men and women of the village asked Blackthorn and Aria about their magic and where they came from.

Blackthorn, Princess Aria and Oglok the Mock-Man were escorted into a large, open high-roofed building. Low benches hunched in neat rows along the hard-packed dirt floor. They were invited to sit and were given more refreshments. Blackthorn was handed a plate containing a leg of meat he recognized, a small animal that resembled a rabbit that looked like a failed experiment concocted by some long dead—and quite mad—geneticist. Blackthorn had encountered many such animals on his journey, but this one appeared to have been raised in a cage and fattened. He bit into it ravenously.

"You must leave now!" came a shout from the building's entrance.

Blackthorn and his companions turned toward the sound. A frail older man stood in the doorway, lean, sun-bronzed arms outstretched, gesticulating wildly. "They can't stay here," he said to the villagers who served them food and drink. "Lord Valaron will punish us severely for harboring these, these..." here he stammered. "Strangers."

"These strangers saved my life and that of my son," said Marna proudly. "Valaron and his Skeleton Corps torment us, but these brave people stood up to them. They deserve our thanks."

The room erupted in cheers.

Princess Aria stood. Her cape, now a peaceful green along with her dress, billowed out behind her. "We mean you good people no harm," she said. "But this Lord Valaron of yours is a tyrant. We have seen his kind before, in the First Men. And all over Mars people are crying out for freedom."

Blackthorn rose and placed his right hand on Aria's shoulder, silencing her. "We won't be starting the revolution, today, Your Highness."

She turned to look at him, her face grim, but Blackthorn was smiling.

"We want to help you," said Blackthorn. "This Valaron appears to be quite powerful, his army many, his gifts great. But I have seen nothing he has wrought here that you could not learn to do on your own."

An excited murmur rose from the small group assembled around them.

"You would ask cattle of Lord Valaron to become gods?" asked the old man. He had stepped into the building now, and was pointing a long bony finger at Blackthorn.

"I would ask Valaron's cattle to become men," countered the general. "And I swear by the moons of Mars that your master shall pay with his life for what he has done to you."

More cheers from the assemblage now. The old man simply lowered his head and shook it slowly. "And what do you ask of us in return?"

Blackthorn shrugged. "Nothing. Except to run your own village and your own lives, and stand up for yourselves. One day a revolution will come to Mars, and you must all be ready."

"Who is that man?" asked Princess Aria, her voice low.

"That is Dar," whispered Marna. "The oldest person in our community. He knows the horrors of Lord Valaron's reign better than anyone. The Master killed his three sons and took his wife to serve him in his Keep. She died there."

The old man stood before them, his bony frame quivering slightly, but he said nothing more. A moment later the cheering died as they heard the galloping of horses approaching.

"It's them!" cried Marna. "The Skeleton Corps!"

"Stay here," said Blackthorn. "We'll see to this." The tall soldier motioned for his two companions to follow him outside.

Six heavily armored men were approaching on horseback, their strange rods brandished high.

Blackthorn pulled his Sword of Light from his belt and ignited it, a column of pure energy extending from its tip. Oglok beat his chest and growled a warning to their attackers. Princess Aria touched the diadems on her necklace and stretched out her hand.

The lead horseman held up his hand and the men stopped. "Are you the strangers that disrupted Lord Valaron's men while they conducted their duties?"

"We are," said Blackthorn.

"Then it has been decreed that you and everyone here must die," replied their leader. "Burn the village!"

At his command the men fell out of their tight formation and sent their horses galloping through the streets of the village. To his horror, Blackthorn saw that some of the horsemen carried a weapon he not only recognized, but had thought long vanished. These Skeleton Corps held out long black pipes that spat flames onto the wooden buildings, setting them ablaze.

"Flamethrowers!" he shouted. His memories of his past were gradually fading, but this weapon he remembered all too well.

"We really should have some kind of plan," said the Princess.

"I'm open to suggestions, Your Highness," said Blackthorn. "For now, let's take out their leader and see what fearsome fighters they are without him."

Smiling, Princess Aria touched a sequence of jewels in her necklace. A second later, a bolt of energy erupted from her outstretched hand with concussive force. The purple beam struck the leader of the Skeleton Corps square in the chest and sent him flying backward off his mount with stunning speed. He landed twenty feet away with a heavy thud. He did not get up.

Blackthorn arched an eyebrow at the Princess, who simply grinned and shrugged.

This sent the remaining attackers into a frenzy. They had no doubt heard of the trouble caused by these powerful strangers, and they would leave nothing concerning them to chance.

They rushed Blackthorn and his companions with their horses, forcing them to scatter or risk getting trampled. The general touched one of the men with his sword as he passed dangerously close, and the man screamed and fell from his mount, unmoving.

"Oglok!" Blackthorn shouted. "Help me dismount these thugs. Aria! Can you put out those flames?"

The Princess nodded and touched another sequence of jewels across her neck and pointed at the flaming buildings. Purple spheres enveloped the burning structures and the flames sputtered and died.

Oglok was already hard at work relieving two of the Skeleton Corps of the burden of their horses, grabbing their prods and lifting them into the air as he had done earlier. Another horseman circled around behind the Mock-Man and thrust his staff between Oglok's shoulder blades. Oglok convulsed in pain, dropping his opponents to the ground.

"Those are cattle prods!" said Blackthorn, amazed. Considering the strange and powerful machines and weaponry he had seen since awakening on this post-apocalyptic Mars, he had expected something a bit more exotic. Spinning on his heels, the general caught the horseman who bounded down upon him on his right side, knocking him from his mount, his armor smoldering.

Blackthorn touched the yellow square and his light blade vanished. He aimed the metal cylinder at Oglok's assailant and activated the energy beam setting, sending a bolt of yellow flame into the attacker's chest. Oglok growled his thanks and went back to pummeling the other two Skeleton Corps fighters senseless.

The Skeleton Corps' numbers were great, but they were not prepared for Blackthorn and his companions. At least, that's what

164

Blackthorn thought when the armored horsemen had first appeared to ransack the village.

Two more horsemen rode up behind Oglok, hefting a thick net between them. Before Blackthorn could shout, they tossed the heavy webbing over the Mock-Man and began poking him with their electrified prods. Oglok yelped in pain while futilely trying to free himself.

Blackthorn prepared to send out another energy pulse with his light sword, but an unseen force snatched it from his outstretched hand.

"I have seen enough!" said a booming voice. The sound came from a glowing golden orb that was slowly dissipating into nothingness. A man stood where the orb had been, tall with dark features. He wore a blue suit similar in style to Blackthorn's, and a great red cloak swirled about him. On his left hand he wore a leather and metal gauntlet with hundreds of tiny metal studs arrayed upon it. In his right hand he held Blackthorn's Sword of Light.

The dark man touched one of the studs and a powerful blast of energy erupted from his gauntleted fist, striking the princess and knocking her to the ground. The Skeleton Corps were upon her then, snatching her up and giving her a few shocks with their terrible prods. "Bring me her necklace," the dark figure commanded.

Before Blackthorn could protest, many powerful arms grabbed him. Something heavy struck the back of his head and he saw stars dance before his eyes. The next thing he knew, he was on his knees and struggling with his captors. He looked up at the cloaked man, his eyes narrowed to slits. "Lord Valaron, I presume."

The man walked toward the general, regarding the sword of light coolly.

"An interesting toy," he remarked casually. "How did it end up in the hands of a pathetic barbarian such as yourself?"

"You call me pathetic while attacking defenseless women and children?"

Lord Valaron ignored Blackthorn's retort. "I asked you a question, stranger. Where did you get this?"

Princess Aria was thrown to the ground beside Blackthorn, her jeweled necklace ripped from her throat by one of Valaron's cursed Skeleton Corps. From him it floated through the air into Valaron's other hand.

"Another powerful trinket," said the evil sorcerer. "Fascinating. And is the hairy brute similarly armed?"

"No, your Lordship," said one of the horsemen.

"What a shame. I suppose these items must suffice for my collection. Tell me: How do they work?"

"Give them back and we'll show you," said the princess.

Lord Valaron reared his head back and laughed.

"Such gumption! And from a woman, no less! Are you the leader of this merry band?"

"Leave her alone, you petty tyrant!" Blackthorn looked up at his captor, gritting his teeth.

Valaron gave the general a thin smile. "Your presence here will no longer be tolerated. Bring them to my Keep! We'll see if some time in my prison levels will still your insolent tongues."

Valaron turned and addressed the villagers. "Let this be a lesson to you. Harboring strangers who attack me or my men will not be tolerated. Next time I will not be so lenient."

Blackthorn and the princess were snatched off the ground, their hands and feet bound tightly. Oglok was still a prisoner of the thick, heavy netting that had been thrown over him like a shroud. The three of them were unceremoniously thrown onto the backs of horses as Valaron touched another stud on his gauntlet and vanished in a bright yellow orb of light.

John Blackthorn did not remember losing consciousness, but he awoke in a dimly lit, grey chamber. The walls and floor were metal, and there were strange machines all around him though, unlike the lair of the Black Sorcerer, where he had first come to awareness in this strange time and place, these machines looked almost brand new. He could feel the steady vibration of machinery around and below him, and the smell of ozone wafted through the slight breeze that blew through the place.

His hands were lashed above his head by hard, metal restraints that came down from the high ceiling above. His feet were similarly fettered. The bands around his ankles were raised off the metal floor a few inches by sturdy looking metal rods.

"Interesting place," said a voice to Blackthorn's right. "Though I can't say much for our host's hospitality."

Blackthorn turned his head. "Princess! You're all right."

Princess Aria was shackled the same way as Blackthorn, her necklace gone. "It would appear so," she said. "At least for now."

"Where's Oglok?"

Aria looked about the room in which they were imprisoned. "I heard one of Valaron's Skeleton Corpsmen say our furry friend was to be used for fighting practice."

"We must get to him soon," said Blackthorn. "That is, if we can get ourselves free of these bonds."

Blackthorn tugged uselessly at his shackles while his keen eyes scanned the large room, looking for something—anything—that might help them escape. At the far end of the vast room he spotted his sword, along with Aria's necklace. They were each sitting on two disc-shaped platforms mounted atop short, hinged arms that jutted out of a control panel. Blackthorn could barely make out tiny electric sparks flashing around the jewels on Aria's necklace.

The princess followed Blackthorn's gaze. "It appears our Lord Valaron is trying to plumb our weaponry's secrets."

"Either that or drain them of their power."

"That may be possible with your Sword of Light, but not with my necklace," countered the princess confidently. "But if he decodes the spells stored inside the gems, he'll be even more of a nuisance than he is already."

"Let's not give him that chance, then," said Blackthorn. "There must be a way out of these blasted bonds!" He put one last bit of effort into freeing himself, and succeeded only in swaying back and forth between the shackles that bound his hands and feet.

"Perhaps we should wait until our host returns," offered the princess. "He obviously has plans for us. We should formulate one of our own, for when he releases us from these shackles."

"And what if his plans involve using us for target practice where we stand?" said Blackthorn. "If we wait until he comes back we'll have lost any element of surprise. The time is now or never, Princess."

"If that's the case, then I'm out of ideas," she replied tersely.

"Just give me a minute. Princess, can you use your magic without your necklace?"

"No. My magic is stored in the diadems in the necklace. I still have my knife safe in its neck sheath, but I can't reach it with my arms fettered."

Blackthorn heaved a heavy sigh. Their situation seemed dire, and yet he couldn't accept the fact that there was no way out. Ever since awakening on this strange, time-blighted Mars he had faced countless foes and encountered bizarre situations. But he had always found a way out. With his friends and his Sword of Light by his side, General John Blackthorn felt that he could conquer any foe.

He strained against his bonds again, throwing everything his new body had into one final effort. Then, without warning, their shackles mysteriously opened, sending Blackthorn and Princess Aria sprawling to the floor.

"Ouch!" cried the princess. "You could have warned me first."

Blackthorn blinked. "I don't think that was me. Look."

He pointed across the room. Standing near a darkened doorway was an old woman clothed in rags similar to those worn by the villagers. Her long white hair spilled past her shoulders, and she had a time-hardened look about her. Slowly she ambled toward them as quickly as her creaking joints would allow.

"You must hurry," she said. "If the Master finds out what I've done he'll surely torture me."

"Who are you?" asked Blackthorn.

"I am called Lorna."

"Why did you set us free?"

"Because I heard the men talking about your attack on them earlier today, and saw the look in the Master's eyes when he learned of your presence in the village. They are afraid of you." Her toothless mouth stretched into a weak smile.

"If your master asks," said Princess Aria, returning the old woman's smile, "We'll tell him it was our magic that set us free."

"Speaking of which," said Blackthorn as he stood and strode to the raised platforms holding his sword and Aria's necklace.

"Careful, Blackthorn," said the princess. "They could be booby trapped."

"Let me," said the old woman. She stepped to a control panel and flipped a switch and the Sword of Light and the necklace dropped into Blackthorn's waiting hands. He tapped the yellow square and the energy blade flared to blazing life. Princess Aria took her necklace and put it once more around her slender neck. She touched a sequence of gems and extended her right hand, her index and little fingers extended. After a moment the shackles that had restrained them exploded in a shower of sparks.

"Seems to be in working order," she said. "Let's find Oglok and teach Valaron a lesson he'll not soon forget."

"The Mock-Man is being held outside," said the crone. "In Lord Valaron's proving grounds. The Master's skeleton men are having much fun with him I fear."

"Show us the way," said Blackthorn.

Lorna began walking back the way she had come, followed closely by Blackthorn and the princess. "I will lead you to the proving grounds, and to your friend. I can do no more than that."

"We understand," said Blackthorn.

"Thank you for helping us," said the princess. "How can we repay your kindness?"

"Just free my people from the Master's yoke," she replied.

"With pleasure," said Blackthorn. "Let's go, Princess."

Blackthorn and Princess Aria followed the old crone through the darkened doorway. They emerged in a dim corridor with a low ceiling, lit only by some sort of bioluminescent or phosphorescent blocks set into the walls at irregular intervals. Expecting danger around every twist and turn, Blackthorn kept his sword ignited and ready. They passed through a large area with piles of enormously thick wire coiled about in heaps. "Those are the great worms that built this place," said the old woman. They have many teeth instead of eyes. But they have slumbered since the Keep was finished."

They wandered through dimly lit corridors for an interminable length of time, and for large portions of the journey Blackthorn felt the floor curve slightly downward, as if they were actually going underground, instead of up and out as the general would have imagined.

"How close are we?" he asked Lorna, his voice echoing loudly in the tunnel. "Not long now," she said over her shoulder.

The glowing blocks, combined with the light from Blackthorn's Sword of Light, gave them just enough illumination to navigate the metal maze, but the crone moved quickly through the dim recesses with practiced ease. After a time Blackthorn decided to shut off his energy blade so he would still have plenty of charge left when he actually needed it, which he hoped would be soon. Princess Aria said nothing as she followed Blackthorn and the old woman through the long, eternally winding tunnels.

"How much farther, Lorna?" said the princess, growing annoyed.

"This is definitely the end of the line for you," said a voice up ahead.

The three stopped in their tracks. A flash of light was ebbing in the tunnel before them. Standing in its place was Lord Valaron.

"Fools! Do you think I don't know everything that goes on within my Keep? I've been watching to see how far you'd get, and I've decided this is far enough."

Blackthorn unsheathed his light sword and ignited it. "You'll play no more games with us today," he promised.

"Right you are, barbarian." Valaron touched one of the studs on his gauntlet, and immediately a great rumbling could be heard from the direction they had come.

"Enjoy these tunnels. For they shall be your tomb!" With that, Valaron disappeared in a flash of light.

"That is really getting annoying," Blackthorn grumbled.

The rumbling was getting closer, the sound of something impossibly heavy dragging itself snakelike along the metal floor. There was another sound just beneath the rumbling, a sort of high-pitched whine.

In the light cast by Blackthorn's light sword, they saw what was making the horrible sounds.

"The great worms!" cried the old woman. "The Master has awakened them from their centuries-long slumber! We are doomed!"

Blackthorn could see them now, two snakelike shapes that slithered up the shaft toward them, wide, diamond-shaped heads encrusted with spinning blades.

"Moons of Mars!" the general swore. "I see what you meant by eyes instead of teeth."

"This Valaron is a crafty devil," said Princess Aria. "I'll give him that."

"I don't think Valaron created those things." To Lorna he said, "Get behind me!"

The old woman ducked behind him and cowered. Blackthorn held his light sword out in front of him, hoping it would block a strike from one of the mechanical devils.

Princess Aria touched the diadems on her necklace and raised her left hand in the air, her fingers splayed. A spinning disc of purple energy formed above them.

One of the worms lunged for it, the spinning, diamond-hard blades pulverizing when they made contact with the whirling energy field. The tunnel filled with the tang of burned metal as the worm flinched backward, its sightless, mangled head just sitting there above them as if weighing its options.

Suddenly the second worm dived into the tunnel floor, the rapidly spinning drill that was its head making short work of the metal surface beneath their feet. The whole tunnel shook violently.

"It's going to come up beneath us!" shouted Blackthorn. "Run!"

The metal floor buckled and bent, and the spinning head of the snakelike machine emerged directly behind them with a shower of sparks and the smell of burning metal. The first serpent thing came

171

after them again too, its bent blades and teeth useless, but its large diamond-shaped head still serving as a deadly flail. It thrashed at Princess Aria, who was barely able to get out of the thing's way in time. It left a huge dent in a metal floor that was already rent beyond repair.

"These things will dog us until we are dead," said Blackthorn. "If you have some bit of sorcery that would be helpful, best deploy it now."

"I have to do everything," she replied sarcastically. Touching her necklace again, she raised her right hand and sent out coils of purple energy that writhed like tiny snakes. They insinuated themselves around the first mechanical worm, entering it through small holes and flaws to strike at its inner workings. Suddenly, the worm spasmed as a shower of sparks flew from it, then fell heavily to the floor.

The second worm dove for Blackthorn, but he was ready, leaping backward, pushing Lorna along with him. The thing's head buried itself in the floor where he had stood seconds earlier. Blackthorn gave a shout and leaped into the air, igniting his light sword and severing the drill bit head cleanly from the thick cable that was its body. The headless coil lurched, spat sparks, and fell and lay still.

"*That* was fun," said Blackthorn, deactivating his sword.

"Let's find Oglok and get out of here," said the princess. "Before Valaron sends more of his mad machines after us."

"I will stay with you," said the crone. "The Master knows I aided you now, and he will surely kill me."

"Not while the princess and I draw breath," Blackthorn assured her. "Now, which way to Valaron's proving grounds and our friend?"

"This way," the old woman pointed.

They walked twenty feet or so. Finally the old woman stopped and pointed to a hatch above her head. "That opens out in the middle of the proving grounds," she said. Beside her on the wall a series of metal rungs led up to the hatch.

Blackthorn understood now why they were taking the long way around. The old woman Lorna had led them directly below their enemies' feet.

"We thank you," said Princess Aria. To Blackthorn she said, "How do you want to play this?"

He considered that. "Well, the element of surprise is certainly on our side." He unsheathed his light sword and set it ablaze. "Let's go in, guns blazing."

A sly grin played across the princess's mouth. "It's simple, but I like it."

A quick energy blast from Aria's outstretched hand sent the hatch sailing high into the air, with Blackthorn, the princess and the crone right behind, levitated up and through the narrow portal by Aria's sorcery.

The Skeleton Corps were too busy torturing Oglok to notice the round hatch door soaring twenty feet into the air and Blackthorn and the Princess floating down toward them, their bodies surrounded by purple auras of energy. The old woman was set down near the hole and she slunk away to a door set in the wall of Valaron's compound. She passed through it and fled to return home to her beloved village.

The Mock-Man was lashed to a post while the men taunted and jeered at him, occasionally giving him doses of electricity from their cursed cattle prods. Oglok snarled and hissed back at them, but could do no more.

Princess Aria had no sooner set herself and Blackthorn safely on the ground that she went straight to work on Oglok's jailors, causing the cattle prods and swords to fly from their hands. The dozen or so men turned in confusion toward the princess and the general.

Blackthorn raised his light sword, its energy blade glowing and throbbing with power. "We'd like a rematch."

Princess Aria raised her hand once more and the chains binding Oglok to the wooden post became enveloped in purple light. They appeared to melt away and vanish, leaving Oglok free. The Mock-Man stretched his powerful arms and growled.

"Yes, my friend," said Blackthorn in reply. "You may have at them." The general grinned, then added, "With extreme prejudice."

Usually a peaceful sort, the torturous guards had riled the ordinarily good natured Mock-man, spurring him to violence, and he lashed out at them with relish, tossing them about like rag dolls.

Blackthorn went to work, slicing their electric prods in half and relieving the rest of their swords, staffs, spears, maces, and any other weapon they dared raise toward him.

Princess Aria used her magic to bind Valaron's soldiers, twisting chains, weapons and anything else nearby into sturdy shackles and binding as many of the fleeing men as her sorcery could grab. When every member of the Skeleton Corps either had been captured or had fled, a flash of light appeared in their midst.

"What is the meaning of this outrage?" Valaron demanded. He scowled. "You three have proven to be formidable opponents. I was going to let my men practice their skills on you. Now I shall have to destroy you outright." He glanced at Aria menacingly. "Except for you, my princess. My machines have completed their analysis of your physiology, and I see that you will be of great value to me."

"What are you talking about?" Aria snapped.

"You'll not lay a hand on her, tyrant," said Blackthorn, his Sword of Light held at the ready.

Valaron laughed. "I'll do what I like, barbarian." He touched a stud on his gauntlet, and the shimmering blade projecting from Blackthorn's Sword of Light suddenly winked out.

"Moons of Mars!" blared the general. "What have you done?"

"Merely shut off that troublesome little toy of yours before it hurts someone."

"I'll handle this." Princess Aria touched the diadems on her necklace and an energy field coalesced around her, then crackled and faded. She tried again. Nothing.

"By the First Men!" she shouted. "How dare you interfere with the powers of a Princess of Mars?"

"I dare because I can, my dear. Your necklace was difficult to crack, but plumb its secrets I did."

"Those discs," said Blackthorn. "They must have scanned our weapons and given Valaron a means to control them."

"You are very clever," said Valaron, "for a barbarian. The technologies beneath my Keep allow me to do any number of things."

Oglok had finished with the last of Valaron's Skeleton Corps and now focused his attentions on their leader. He lunged toward the wizard, but another touch of his gauntlet and the sorcerer had the Mock-Man and his companions contained within a cage made of pure energy.

"Your puny efforts to dispatch me have grown tiresome," said the sorcerer. "Now you will watch while I strip the princess's abilities and transfer them to myself—and then destroy each of you with my own hands!"

With a flash of light the energy cage containing Blackthorn and his companions was transported back down to the vast room filled with machinery that they had recently escaped. Valaron was nowhere to be seen.

"This is depressing," said the princess. Oglok growled in agreement.

"This is maddening," said Blackthorn, stabbing buttons on his lifeless light sword. "Why won't our weapons work?"

"Valaron is more powerful than we gave him credit for," said the princess. "Or at least his gauntlet is."

"That's it!" said Blackthorn. "Valaron's gauntlet is the source of his power. If we can destroy it, we'll have him by the throat."

"That is easier said than done without our weapons," said the Princess.

"Indeed," Blackthorn replied. "Let us think on it a while. I am sure an opportunity will present itself."

"We may not have much time. I'm afraid I know what Valaron intends to do to me, though I don't know how it's possible."

Blackthorn said nothing to this, merely nodded. The princess had been very secretive about her origins up to now, and any questioning would probably just cause her to raise her guard even more. And if it was like most everything else he'd seen since awakening on this ancient Mars, he probably wouldn't understand it anyway. The energy cage throbbed around them, which seemed to have awakened the machinery within the chamber, for it pulsed and vibrated in rhythm with the hum of the cage.

"I wonder how long Valaron can keep up certain levels of power?" mused the princess after a time.

"What do you mean?" asked Blackthorn. The Mock-Man, too, regarded the princess quizzically.

"We know that every time he uses his gauntlet, the machines down here come to life," she said. "At least, that's my theory. But for how long? Even your Sword of Light can't be used indefinitely, and must be periodically recharged."

"So the same must be true of Valaron's gauntlet," Blackthorn mused.

Princess Aria smiled. "Perhaps. If we can get him to use it more than he should and overload his equipment, he'll be powerless."

Oglok growled excitedly.

"That too," said Blackthorn. To the Princess he said, "Oglok thinks once Valaron's machinery is out of commission we'll have the use of our weapons."

Princess Aria shrugged. "It's worth a shot. What do you say, General?"

"Anything beats standing in this cage waiting to die."

Suddenly the incomprehensible machinery within the chamber flared to life, gears whirring and lights flashing. In the midst of this chaos Valaron appeared.

"Well, my pets, how do you like your cage?"

"Let us out and we'll show you," said Blackthorn.

Valaron laughed. "Such spirit. Even powerless you choose to defy me."

"It is you who are powerless compared to the might of the First Men," said Princess Aria. She cast Blackthorn a sidelong glance.

The general gave a slight nod. "You are nothing to them."

"We'll see about that!" snapped Valaron. "Within this chamber lie the secrets of the ages. It was technology like this that spawned the First Men! It can unmake them as well."

Princess Aria laughed.

"You don't believe me? Then allow me to demonstrate."

The sorcerer touched a stud on his gauntlet and the section of cage in front of the princess vanished. An invisible force snatched her and pulled her from the prison. Oglok, who was closest, tried to leap through the breach but the missing section reformed as soon as the princess was free.

Princess Aria was hurled through the air and then spun around so she was facing Blackthorn and Oglok. She was pushed against a raised slab of metal and shackles shot out from it, gripping her wrists and ankles.

"What is the meaning of this?" she screamed.

"You'll know soon enough, Your Highness," said Valaron mockingly. "We shall now see who is greater than whom when I strip you of your abilities."

"Impossible!" exclaimed the princess.

"Not to me!" Valaron touched a button on his cursed gauntlet and walked calmly to the side of the room where Aria was being held prisoner, while a structure similar to the one that held her seemed to grow out of the floor of the chamber. He ascended a set of metal stairs to stand level with the princess and only a few feet away from her.

"I analyzed more than your weaponry," said the wizard. "You, my princess, are a remarkable creature. You have the sorcery of the First Men running through your veins."

"If you mean I'm wired, you are correct. But what was given to me cannot be tampered with by the likes of you."

"That is where you're wrong, Princess. I have learned a great deal during my time in this Keep. Things that have made me master of this valley. Things what will soon make me Master of Mars as well."

"This tyrant is worse than the First Men and Morningstar combined," said Blackthorn. Oglok growled in agreement. The general turned to the Mock-Man. "We must do something quickly, my friend. Aria is in great danger."

Valaron placed his hands on two metal orbs that had risen from the platform on transparent rods and closed his eyes. The machinery within the chamber went wild, pulsing lights beating in time to a deep rhythmic hum coming from somewhere deep within the ground.

Aria screamed then, her face a rictus of pain. Dark lines began to show under her skin, bulging out in places. A spider web tracery appeared on her face, like cracks in porcelain. She continued to scream.

Valaron too appeared to be in some discomfort. He winced as if punctured, and the same lines began appearing under his skin, crawling up his arms from the metal orbs, tracking through his veins like poison.

"Stop, villain!" yelled Blackthorn, powerless to halt this horror.

Oglok howled and beat his chest, then rammed his shoulder into the energy cage.

Blackthorn started to grab his friend, get him to stop such a foolish, futile gesture. Then he realized what Oglok was doing. The glowing of the machinery around them increased in intensity when Oglok attacked the cage. He reversed tack immediately. "Keep it up, old friend," he said as he punched one of the bars with his fist. It didn't burn. Instead it was more like touching a rapidly flowing stream of water. Slowly he slid the metal hilt of his light sword into one of the beams, breaking a portion of the cage, which quickly reformed. The machinery about them grew brighter momentarily, then faded somewhat.

"I don't know what we did, exactly," said Blackthorn, "but keep it up!"

Oglok acquiesced and continued his onslaught, while Blackthorn assaulted the bars of their energy cage with fists, boots, and his deactivated light sword. As they worked, the bars of the cage seemed to fade, growing less intense with each of their prods. Finally it was enough that Blackthorn believed they could break through. "On my mark, Oglok. One...two...three...jump!"

Blackthorn and Oglok leapt through the shimmering bars of the cage, which faded into nonexistence behind them. Some of the machinery overheated and shorted out, assaulting their nostrils with the scent of ozone and burnt wiring.

Blackthorn tried his light sword hesitantly, and the familiar pillar of heat and light erupted from the weapon's tip once more.

"Now you will pay, villain!" said the general as he and the Mock-Man strode across the room toward Valaron and Princess Aria, violently dismantling machines as they went.

"Stop, you fools!" Valaron shouted, but he was powerless to stop them, lashed as he was to his machine that was even now inserting the weird metal threads that ran through the princess' veins into his own.

"Whether this is science or sorcery, I have no idea," said Blackthorn. "But I know only brute force can stop it. Come, Oglok. Let us end this madness once and for all."

Blackthorn stormed Valaron's platform while the Mock-Man ascended Aria's. With a swipe of his light sword Blackthorn melted the struts holding the metal orbs aloft.

Valaron screamed as electricity danced around him, and thin tails of silvery thread trailing from his outstretched hands whipped through the air.

Blackthorn's onslaught had freed Princess Aria from her shackles, and Oglok had flung her unconscious body over his left shoulder and was descending the platform while lightning danced around them.

"You think you have stopped me, barbarian?" Valaron shouted. He laughed maniacally as more machinery in the vast space exploded.

Dodging stinging thread, Blackthorn leaped from the platform and joined Oglok. "Let's go," he said, and they made their way through the maze of crumbling machinery to the opening the crone had shown them earlier.

The whole place thundered and shook, and it seemed as if the entire Keep would come crashing down around them. Princess Aria stirred and demanded to be put down at once.

"Are you all right?" asked Blackthorn.

"I-I think so," she replied shakily. "I've never had my wiring mapped before. That hurts."

Blackthorn didn't have a clue what the princess was talking about, but he didn't push for an explanation. "I believe it was painful for Valaron as well."

"Serves him right, meddling in powers he can scarcely understand."

"We need to get out of here," said Blackthorn as the entire building shook suddenly.

The princess looked around the now-familiar tunnel as they ran along its length. "I think we should look for a more direct way out," she said. "One that takes advantage of speed over stealth."

"Good idea," said Blackthorn.

Suddenly Oglok veered down a side tunnel as he barked excitedly.

"He said he smells something," Blackthorn told the princess.

The two of them followed the Mock-Man to a sort of galley. A well-stocked kitchen filled with food preparation equipment greeted them. It looked as if it had been thoroughly ransacked. Cabinets stood open and bits of bread and fruit lay on the floor.

"Looks like Valaron's beloved Skeleton Corps decided to get out while they still could."

Blackthorn nodded, marveling at the level of technology present here. It reminded him of a modern mess hall back on...*where?* He struggled with the name. *Earth, of course.* He had the feeling of having been in a room very similar to this one, but he couldn't call up the image. It was just...gone.

"They must have felt the vibrations and feared the worst," said the general. "Unless they know something we don't. We'd better find a way out, quickly."

Oglok, banging around in a far corner, gave a high-pitched growl.

"He found stairs!" Blackthorn translated.

The three companions bounded up the stairs as fast as they could while the Keep continued to shake and shudder around them. Once they found the way blocked by a piece of metal debris but Oglok, with some magical assistance from Aria, easily moved it aside. At the top was a door designated *01* by a faded red stencil. Blackthorn rent it in two with his Sword of Light and they were free of the Keep. The late afternoon sun was beginning its dip into evening when they emerged from the side of the skeletal Keep's massive jawbone.

An armed melee greeted them as they emerged. The remains of Valaron's Skeleton Corps did battle with Marna's people, who had managed to completely surround them. The villagers attacked from the cover of the trees that ringed the front of the Keep, hurling rocks, sticks, rough-hewn spears, and more than a few arrows at their one-time masters.

Caught completely off guard, and having prepared only to flee, the Skeleton Corps were in no shape to fend off their attackers.

"These Skeleton warriors are being shown for the cowards they are," said Blackthorn proudly.

"And Marna's people have finally decided to defend themselves," Aria added. "Let's give them a hand, shall we?"

The three companions dove into battle, surprising the already perplexed Skeleton Corps' rear. The already retreating soldiers were no match for them, and shortly every member of Valaron's army was either down for the count or had fled on foot or horseback.

Marna's people cheered their victory, as well as the safety of Blackthorn, Princess Aria and Oglok.

"We are glad you are safe," said a thin but wiry young man with blond hair. Blackthorn remembered meeting him back at the village, and recalled that his name was Tarn.

"What are you doing here?" asked the general.

"We thought about what you said," Tarn answered. "When Valaron's forces carried you away, we feared the worst. Some of the younger ones, along with myself, suggested we take up arms to rescue you, but Dar and the others forbade it. Then Lorna returned to us and told us about what you did for her. She is Dar's wife. The Skeleton Corps lied to us all these years, told us she was dead. The sight of her brightened Dar's countenance, and he finally agreed that we should fight. We have decided to stop being cattle, John Blackthorn."

Blackthorn smiled. "I am glad to hear it. You've done well for your first battle. But we haven't won the war yet."

Just then they heard a rumble of thunder from within the keep, and lightning seemed to dance in the huge skull's cavernous eyes. After a minute of this, a silvery figure appeared, standing in the right eye socket, its arms outstretched and wispy silver threads whipping around it.

"You think you could best me so easily, barbarian?" the figure blared. "Your pathetic sabotage of my equipment has only served to make me even more powerful."

"By the Pale Lord's cloak, who is that?" asked Tarn.

"Valaron," said Blackthorn.

"Yes!" said the thing that had been Lord Valaron as it rose into the air on arcs of blue flame. "Your Master as returned, rabble!"

"Moons of Mars!" Blackthorn swore as he got a closer look. "What have you done to yourself?"

Lord Valaron was no more. In his place was a thin, silvery mummy wrapped in burnt flesh and wire. Cold, mad eyes glared out at them from a face puckered and made hairless by an intense heat. The wires whipping around him seemed to grow out of his very skin like sentient worms.

180

"I have become more than myself. More than human. Now not even the First Men will be able to challenge me."

"Another would-be dictator," grumbled Blackthorn. "I'm getting really tired of this."

Valaron grinned at the general. "Then you can be the first to die!"

The tyrant thrust his right arm toward Blackthorn and a series of wires shot from his fingers, ensnaring the general. Blackthorn raised his right arm and brought his Sword of Light down on the stinging threads, severing them.

Valaron lashed out again, and this time hundreds of the tiny wires wrapped themselves around Blackthorn, pulling at him like a marionette. He severed three, and four more took their place.

"The mapping process was ended prematurely," said Princess Aria. "That's why I'm still alive and he's...become *that* thing."

"I'm listening," said Blackthorn as he continued to hack and slash at the threads, even switching hands when a series of strands wrapped around his right arm.

"He's wired, but only partially," she said, "but he seems to be able to control the wiring mentally, or by pumping power through it."

Oglok growled and lifted one of the heavy rocks the villagers had used against the Skeleton Corps, hurling it up at Valaron, who dodged it easily.

Princess Aria's eyes narrowed to slits and she touched her hand to her necklace. Behind her, Tarn and his warriors watched in fear and awe. She knew she would only get one shot at this.

The Princess closed her eyes. Concentrating, she could feel the energies transmitting to Valaron from the Keep's machines— energies that were keeping Valaron alive, feeding him whatever power he needed. But there was a limit to that power. She formed a mental image of those machines in her mind, and let her necklace do the rest.

A low rumble issued from deep within the Keep, a muffled explosion, and Valaron's body spasmed. Blackthorn broke free from the last of the silver threads and jumped back, joining the princess, Oglok and the villagers.

Blue orbs of energy erupted from the Keep, enveloping Valaron. He gave one final scream and then he disappeared in a huge flash of light. The great skull lurched to one side, groaned, and collapsed in upon itself, silent at last.

For a long moment no one spoke. The villagers looked on in awe.

Finally Blackthorn turned to the princess. "You want to explain to me what just happened?"

"I simply attacked what was left of Valaron's machinery," she replied. "It was feeding him power, but the connection was unstable. I knew it wouldn't take much for me to overload his equipment, thus overloading *him*."

"That's what we tried to do back in Valaron's chamber," said Blackthorn.

Oglok growled something and the general snorted at it. "Exactly," he said. "Great minds, and all that."

"Is the sorcerer gone, then?" asked Tarn.

"Yes," replied Princess Aria. "But he was no sorcerer. Just a man meddling with science beyond his understanding."

"What is science?" asked Tarn, a confused look on his face.

Blackthorn smiled. "Let's return to your village and talk about it."

The villagers celebrated their victory long into the night. Blackthorn left the party and wandered up a small hill overlooking the cluster of homes, their windows filled with the glow of electric light, a small miracle amid this ancient landscape ravaged by time. He sat down and admired the view, deep in thought.

A short time later Princess Aria appeared beside him. He had not noticed her arrival.

"Penny for your thoughts?"

"What?" Blackthorn stared up at her.

She smiled. "I believe that is an expression from your time."

Blackthorn thought about it a moment, then slowly shook his head. How could she possibly know that? But he knew better than to ask. After all this time together, the princess was still full of surprises.

"I was thinking these people party to excess."

Princess Aria sat down beside him. "Let them have their fun," she said. "They've earned it."

"I was actually thinking of Valaron," said Blackthorn after a long moment. "A clever man who used the ancient technology around him to become a despot. Just like the Black Sorcerer and the other First Men. Just like David Morningstar. How will this world ever get back on its feet with people like that running around?"

"They won't be running around much longer," said the princess. "We'll stop them. And people like this will show mankind the way." She gestured toward the village below. "You taught them well, told them the difference between science and sorcery, and encouraged them to not give into their fears about either."

Blackthorn nodded. "Science is a useful tool in the proper hands." He sat quietly for a few minutes, then said, "If everyone else we meet is only half as resilient as these people, the Black Sorcerer won't know what hit him."

Princess Aria smiled. "So what's on the agenda for tomorrow?"

Blackthorn looked straight ahead, his keen eyes on the line of trees that grew beyond the village. "Tomorrow we ride. There are other settlements we must rally, and possibly more upstarts to take down a notch or three. Care to join me?"

Princess Aria nodded. "I wouldn't dream of doing anything else."

QUEST FOR THE EYE

JOE CROWE

Two raggedly-dressed men scrambled, desperately gasping for breath, through the ruins of a broken-down building. Masses of tangled overgrowth and twisted metal blocked their path.

The one in front, the larger of the two, cradled a wrapped package to his chest.

"Here!" He pointed with one filthy hand. "Our safehouse is here!"

A dusty concrete wall stood at the end of the hallway in front of them. With his free arm, the larger man touched the wall gingerly.

For a moment, nothing happened. Then a door slid open directly ahead of them, grinding on gears long unused.

"Quiet, Bothar!" yelled the second man, as he yanked his reed-thin arm from a briar outgrowth. "They will hear us!"

Bothar sighed. "I cannot make this door quieter, Tumblos! Now hurry!"

As the door continued to grind open, Bothar crawled in and exhaled. The room inside was brightly lit, clean, and free of debris. Bothar sat on the spotless floor and laid down the wrapped package.

Tumblos scurried through the now-half-open door. He turned and stared back at it, wide-eyed, as it continued to grind loudly on its track. His hands were shaking and sweat trickled down his face.

"Come here, Tumblos," said Bothar, seemingly oblivious to the sound. "Come and see our prize! Behold The Eye of Tecafu!"

"But the door! The door is still opening! We must close it!"

Bothar sighed. "Now who is loud? Now who is to blame for alerting our pursuers?"

"This door!" Tumblos whispered. "I will blame the makers of this safehouse for their terrible screeching door!"

Bothar shoved past Tumblos and gently touched the door again. It stopped. Then it began to slowly close—at the same loud, grinding pace.

"No! No!" Tumblos wailed. "Our fate is cast into the pit!"

Bothar sighed.

"Lord Ruin will retrieve us in moments. These safe rooms are invulnerable and all are tracked and numbered. His escape agent will take us back to his lair—" and his bloodshot eyes glinted greedily, "—where our payment awaits."

Tumblos didn't seem to hear, or to be swayed by the reassurances. He frowned and nervously paced the room.

Shaking his head impatiently at his friend, Bothar returned his attention to the package on the floor. Carefully he unfolded the cloth wrapping around it. "Calm yourself, tiny one," he whispered. "Gaze upon the Eye of Tecafu. See how its chrome gleams!"

"Tumblos is not tiny! Tumblos is the God of Gravity itself!" Tumblos stopped in mid-pace and inhaled, raising himself to his full height, a shade over five feet. "I will summon the powers of gravity and shut this door! Then we shall determine which of us is tiny!"

Tumblos spun around and faced the door, just as it clicked closed.

Bothar sighed.

"Your mastery amazes even me, Bothar Bearsbane, mightiest of the Bearsbanes."

Tumblos ranted incoherently at Bothar's back as Bothar gazed down in awe at the Eye of Tecafu.

"You bulbous buffoon! It was only thanks to I, Tumblos, that we escaped from Blackthorn and his gaggle of hooligans!"

"Indeed," Bothar replied without looking up. "I knew it was time to make our escape when you ran past me, stumbling and screaming."

Tumblos was about to launch another scathing rejoinder when the very air flickered before them. Moments later, a human shape came into focus.

"Our escape agent arrives!" exclaimed Tumblos with great relief. "Present the Eye of Tecafu as required!"

"Yes—*yes!*"

Kneeling on all fours, head bowed to the floor, Bothar held the package out before him as the shape became solid.

"Thank you," came an unfamiliar voice, "on behalf of the gaggle of hooligans."

Bothar looked up slowly. He saw a woman standing before him, dressed all in black. Her hair was short and dark; a cloak flared about her and a jeweled necklace sparkled at her throat.

Tumblos lurched backwards, yelping.

"It's the witch! It's the witch!"

Tumblos clawed the wall behind him. "The door," he cried. "The door! Open the door!"

The wall to his left caved in, revealing a big, fur covered beast. It stood tall like a man, and was clad only in boots and black trunks.

Oglok the Mock-Man slapped Tumblos with an enormous left hand. Tumblos flew into the far wall and fell to the formerly dustless floor.

The princess touched a jewel on her necklace. Glittering ribbons of light coalesced around Bothar, binding his arms.

She tossed the Eye of Tecafu toward Oglok. The beast-man snatched it from mid-air and looked it over. He grunted.

"You're right," the princess replied with a wry smile. "It was nice of those villagers to let us borrow their water faucet for an hour or two. We'll let John return it."

Oglok slung Tumblos' unconscious body onto his left shoulder.

"We should get these guys back to their so-called *secret lair*," the princess said. She grinned. "I want to make sure they get their payment." Then she narrowed her eyes in a way that Bothar found remarkably menacing for such a nice-looking lady. "And I have a little something to give Lord Ruin, as well, once their agent is good enough to show us the way there."

Bothar sighed.

GHOSTS OF ACHERON

I. A. WATSON

The lizard-men hunted in packs, racing along the broken ground almost as quickly as horses for short distances, their claws churning up the red grass of the Lycos Plains as they closed on their prey. Blackthorn looked east and saw another column of them ranging round to cut them off from the side.

"Looks like we really annoyed the Black Sorcerer this time!" the displaced Earthman grinned. "Are there any minions left on that floating city of his that he hasn't thrown at us?"

Oglok the Mock-Man growled as he scented the closeness of the hunters. He waved his long hairy arms in protest as he steered his mount after John Blackthorn's own grey steed.

Princess Aria brought up the rear, keeping her sleek thoroughbred under perfect control despite its exhaustion. "I can only understand about one word in four of what the Mock-Man grunts," she said, "but I comprehend enough to know he agrees with me that attacking the Harmony Needle was a bad idea."

Blackthorn leaned lower over his racing horse and pushed it to a last dash. "The idea was to prick the Sorcerer into focussing his attention on us and away from the gathering resistance elsewhere. Blowing the hell out of one of those ancient tech-towers sure managed it."

"It was vandalism," snapped the Princess. "Those constructs date back before the First Men, to the time when this world was tamed. The secrets of constructing them are lost even to the Sorcerers."

189

Another pack of lizard-men broke from cover less than a hundred yards to the left. The horses smelled the rank odour of the predators and raced on with the last of their strength.

Blackthorn didn't like the odds but he didn't want to show it. He'd pushed Oglok and Aria hard over the last three days, knowing he'd made them all targets, knowing it was important they had the Black Sorcerer's full attention. It was too late to doubt his strategies now.

Oglok called out mournfully, his muzzle-like mouth ill-suited for language, his words a mixture of snarls and groans. As always, General Blackthorn found he could comprehend the words of the Mock-Man.

"We can't get to that pass we were headed for," Blackthorn responded. "We're being forced too far off track. We'll to have to find another way down the cliffs—and fast. We can't be far off the ridge now."

"We'd better be," warned Princess Aria. "The horses won't hold out much longer!"

The lizard-men packs were closing. Blackthorn slid his Sword of Light from his side and thumbed the red square on it to project an explosion behind them. The nearest hunter packs squealed and separated as the red-grass plain burst into sudden flame.

Another two packs appeared in the distance.

"Any idea where we are?" Blackthorn shouted across at Aria.

"Now you want my advice?" the Princess asked angrily.

"Not dying would be nice, yes. I need intel."

Aria shook her head. Her black hair streamed behind her as they rode. The angry setting sun cast the fugitives' shadows wide across the grassland. "I don't know this area. If we'd kept on course we'd have got down the cliffs into the Amazonis canal basins."

"If we'd kept on course we'd have been blown to pieces by those spider-legged war machines."

"We're too far north now. I can't even see the Erebus Mountains."

The wind almost carried Oglok's mournful snarling away, but Blackthorn thought the Mock-Man noted that they were all unlikely to see anything for much longer.

Suddenly the seemingly endless grass fields came to an abrupt termination. Blackthorn had to rein his steed in hard as they crested a shallow rise and discovered the sudden cliff at the edge of the Lycos Plains.

"Watch out!" he called to the others.

Aria and Oglok managed to turn their horses too, but now the hunters had the advantage. The three horses were forced to run along the edge of the high cliffs perpendicular to the closing lizard-man packs, towards the red sunset.

The chase was almost over.

Aria looked down at the mist-swathed gloom at the bottom of the trench and shuddered as she realised where she was. "John!" she shouted. "That's Acheron! Down there... it's Acheron!" She said it as if Blackthorn should know how terrible that was.

Then the cliff edge beneath Aria's horse crumbled, dropping princess and steed alike sliding down the steep embankment into the thick mists below.

Alerted by Oglok's roar, Blackthorn forced his terrified stallion to turn back. Then the lizard-men were upon them.

The first attack gutted Oglok's huge mount from neck to belly. The Mock-Man rolled free and rose fighting, first with his massive hairy arms, breaking the neck of the nearest lizard-man, then with the antique bastard sword he'd scavenged back at the Harmony Needle.

Blackthorn managed to roll off his own horse before it pelted away in panic and was lost across the plain. He pulled his Sword of Light just in time to fend off the lead lizard-men that came at him full pelt from the high grasses.

It occurred to the soldier that another General named Custer has faced a very similar situation on the plains at Greasy Grass. He was surprised that he could remember military history when he no longer knew his parents' names.

"We're not going to win here!" he called across to Oglok. "Follow me!"

He paused until he was sure that the Mock-Man had heard him then slid himself down the steep shale bank where Aria had disappeared. Even if the descent killed him it was a kinder end than what the lizard-men would do.

Blackthorn tried to control his slide down into the mist-filled gorge but the incline was too steep. His decent became a helpless tumble, rolling him over and over down the jagged steppes. He bounced down the sandstone embankment, crashing through dead bushes. A heavy fall winded him. A sharp outcrop grazed the side of his head.

He tumbled like a broken puppet and didn't feel it when he hit the bottom.

★ ★ ★

The lizard-men camped out along the ridge. As night fell they gathered up dried grass and started small campfires—not to cook food, because the predators preferred to eat their meals raw and preferably alive, but so that sacred herbs could be sprinkled onto the flames to ward off evil.

It didn't work. The sinister clank of old chain-drives and the rough hiss of pistons alerted the outrunners to the arrival of the war crawlers long before the stilt-legged tripods loomed out of the gathering gloom. A lizard-man runner raced to warn the pack-chiefs that the master had come.

The trio of crawlers made their way to the cluster of camp fires, then hissed down to a rest position so the occupants could disembark. The lizard-men gathered, silent, knowing they had failed in their hunt. Their long tongues flickered agitatedly over their serpentine faces as they watched the hot-bloods alight from the crawlers.

First came the robot master, his pale flesh laced with the technological implants that interfaced him with the crude battle robots trailing the crawler convoy. Then a delicate ebony-skinned woman shrouded in a shimmering web of sensor-threads alighted, her milk-white eyes flickering with each input from a thousand data feeds. But the only one that mattered was the gaunt black-robed wizard with the serpent staff; the Black Sorcerer had arrived.

Nash'Tak the Many-Warred moved forward and grovelled his obedience. The lizard-man commander feared for his life and people.

"Report," commanded the Black Sorcerer. The runners' intelligence had been lacking in both senses. The electromagnetic fog generated by the great machines that maintained Mars' gravity and atmosphere prevented long-range radio communications. So the wizard-king of the West had come himself to take command of the hunt.

Nash'Tak's speech implant allowed him to use the human tongue. "They ran fast on their four-legss," he hissed. "All acrosss the great grasss. We chassed. We cornered."

"And then they jumped off the cliff?" scorned the wizard. "Into Acheron?"

"Not jumped," the lizard-man winced. "Fell. Accident."

The Black Sorcerer peered down in to the darkened chasm. "All of them? The Princess Aria?"

"Sshe fell first. Others followed."

The wizard turned to the ebony creature in the sensor-webbing. "Malethea?"

She turned to the gorge and focussed arcane senses into the stygian darkness. "Nothing, master. The emanations from the psychotropic mists prevent all scanning, even mine."

The Black Sorcerer scowled down into the blackness. He held out his snake-staff and tried to sense the princess' implanted arcane-net himself but could find nothing. That might mean that Aria was shielding, or it could mean she was out of range; or she could be dead.

"You did not pursue," the wizard said to Nash'Tak. It was not a question.

"They are dead," the lizard-man commander replied as if it was self-evident. "Iss *Acheron!*"

"Your orders were clear," the Black Sorcerer replied. "You were to capture Aria and Blackthorn and kill any with them. You failed."

Nash'Tak trembled and pointed down the gorge. "Acheron!" he objected.

"You fear Acheron more than you fear me? That must be rectified." The Black Sorcerer randomly pointed to half a dozen of the lizard-men. "Kill yourselves," he ordered them. "But slowly. Open a vein so you bleed to death."

The other lizard-men watched as their pack-mates obeyed their master.

"If Aria is dead many more of your number will die," the Black Sorcerer warned Nash'Tak. "Prepare for a descent. We will continue the hunt in Acheron."

Nash-Tak the Many-Warred knew not to argue. Six of his comrades bled out their life on the red grass around him. Many more would die if they entered the forbidden lands. But the Black Sorcerer had spoken.

They broke camp and began to climb down into the fog.

A sticky wetness woke John Blackthorn. He opened his eyes and looked right into the hairy face of Oglok the Mock-Man.

The General raised a hand to his wet cheek. "Did you just lick me?" he asked.

Oglok growled that the saliva of his people had antiseptic properties.

"Well thanks – I guess."

Blackthorn dragged himself to his feet and checked his new body for breaks and sprains. He had bruises and abrasions but the black leather-like material of his outfit had protected him from the worst of the fall. He found his Sword of Light where it had bounced a little way from the edge of the cliff.

The choking mist filled the gulley. At night the fog was faintly luminescent, painting everything with an unsettling purple glow. The fumes obscured the sky and made the top of the cliff invisible.

"Why didn't the lizard-men follow us?" wondered the General.

Oglok uttered a worried growl that spoke of superstitious fears of magic. Blackthorn remembered the catch in the princess's voice when she'd spoken of this place. Ravening lizard-men packs had been closing in on her but her fear had all been focussed on discovering that they had stumbled upon Acheron.

"We'd better find Aria," Blackthorn said.

The white square on his Sword of Light turned the tool into a simple light. Its pure bright illumination was strangely comforting in the silent purple mists.

Blackthorn and Oglok followed the base of the escarpment until they found the place where Aria had fallen. They found her horse, its neck broken, but not the princess.

"She must have been able to walk," Blackthorn reasoned. "Otherwise she'd be here."

Oglok growled, noting that something could have dragged her body away. The Mock-Man's fur was raised along his back ridge.

There was none of the lush red plains-grass here in the ravine. Rather the ground was choked with sharp grey thorns. The vegetation looked dead. Only one clear path led away from the cliff. It was the only feasible route that the princess could have taken and it coiled off even deeper into the valley of Acheron.

"The lizard-men might fear this place," Blackthorn told Oglok, "but it won't stop us."

They moved deeper into the mist swiftly but cautiously. The only sound was their feet crushing the dead barbs. The air was rank with dust and decay, a dead stench. The glowing fog parted as they moved and closed in behind them thicker than before.

Oglok shivered. The Mock-Men feared magic, feared the dark things and dark places of past-haunted Mars; and perhaps they had good reason.

"Aria!" shouted Blackthorn. "Aria, where are you?" His voice echoed back, distorted, hollow.

A light glimmered in the distance.

At first Blackthorn thought it was an illusion, or some concatenation of the luminescent fog. The light was of the same purple sheen as the mists, or else it was filtered through the tainted vapours. Then he saw another point beside it, and a third.

"Over this way!" he called to Oglok. "There's something there."

They pushed their way through the banks of thornweed. Blackthorn used the Sword of Light to cut through the sharp tangles and carved a direct path towards the glowing points.

The nearer the explorers got the more lights were visible. As Blackthorn approached he realised they formed an ellipse, a circle. And then the lights moved.

Oglok growled as the illuminations shifted, as they rotating as if on a wheel.

Not *as if* on a wheel, the General realised; they *were* on a wheel. As he approached the lights he could see them reflecting off struts. He could see two parallel circles joined by interconnecting lattices. He could see…

Blackthorn blinked. He could see a Ferris wheel! The fairground ride shimmered like a purple ghost in the choking fog, turning noiselessly. Empty cars rose and fell as the wheel spun.

And beyond it, picked out by points of light like strings of bulbs, was the rest of the carny sidewalk. More rides, and booths, a ghost train, a house of mirrors; but all insubstantial, all painted out of the purple mist.

Oglok whimpered in confusion and terror.

"It's a carnival," Blackthorn told him. "An… an amusement park. A holiday place. It's… it's from my world. I recognise it."

He recognised what it was, at least, and how impossible for it to be here, on Mars, however many centuries since such a thing might have existed on long-lost Earth. He wondered if he might have known exactly what carnival he was seeing the ghost of if he'd had his memory. Had he been here, once? Had it been important to him?

The lights shimmered through the omnipresent mist, re-enacting the scene from another world. A deserted phantom carnival replayed over and over, mocking John Blackthorn.

Oglok howled and fled. John called the Mock-Man's name and chased after him.

The huge humanoid ploughed through the thorn thickets heedless of his hide. Oglok was the bravest of fighters. He would have stood against the lizard-men until they tore him down. Only the stench of magic robbed him of his courage.

Blackthorn struggled to keep up with the fleeing Mock-Man, then almost slammed into him when Oglok suddenly dropped to his knees.

Ahead of them the fog had coalesced into another array of lights. This time the pinpricks of luminescence approximated the candle-saucers of a Mock-Man village, picking out the wattle and daub domes of the servitor race. Between the beehive huts were the trellises where the Mock-Men cultivated their food, the heavy jars where they fermented their thick liqueurs, the shallow water-basins where they grew their spices.

Oglok moaned and trembled then began to crawl towards the illusion.

"Hold it!" Blackthorn called, trying to hold the huge Mock-Man back. "Oglok, it's not real!"

Oglok kept moving forward, crawling, but slowly as if reluctant to obey. Now Blackthorn saw that unlike the ghost carnival this phantasmal village was peopled. Translucent silhouettes of Mock-Men walked the spectral streets, silently accomplishing the domestic work of the day.

Perhaps if I'd remembered anybody then there would have been folks at the carnival, the General speculated.

Oglok was almost at the edge of the lightshow now. Something warned Blackthorn that if his friend passed that perimeter he would be utterly lost.

The Sword of Light was in his hand. He thumbed the red button that set it for a projected explosion. He regretted the energy cost, for here in this stygian gloom the weapon could not recharge, but he saw no other way of disrupting the illusion. It fired. The purple fog evaporated as the radiant flash seared the ghost town out of existence.

Oglok turned on Blackthorn and hurled him to the ground before the general could even react. The huge Mock-Man caught the human's neck in an unbreakable grip and squeezed.

Then he stopped. The madness left Oglok's eyes. He pulled his hand from Blackthorn's throat and scrambled away as if he'd been burned.

The purple mists gathered again.

"It's alright," Blackthorn assured the Mock-Man, albeit breathlessly with a rasping voice. "It's this place. Acheron. We have to find Aria and get out of here."

Oglok growled his agreement.

★★★

The Black Sorcerer descended into the valley with three score of Nash'Tak's finest warriors, hand-picked by the Many-Warred himself. He brought Malethea the Sensorine and Robot Caller Charn with him, flanked by half a dozen of the clanking combat drones.

The lizard men clustered together nervously, unhappy to be in such a cursed and ill-omened place.

"Keep them in order, Nash'Tak," the wizard warned. "I am warding them from the worst of this place, but there is a limited range at which I can do it."

The lizard-man leader barked sharp sibilant orders and the packs formed up. The Black Sorcerer raised his staff and concentrated. The vaporous wisps of purple fog were brushed aside as if by invisible hands.

It was harder than the Black Sorcerer remembered. The Acherim were growing stronger.

"Which direction?" he demanded of Malethea. Her white eyes flickered like static and her pale finger pointed. "I am blindest when I look there," the Sensorine reported.

"Take point, Charn."

The Robot Caller gestured, the orange lights implanted in his forearms flickering as he sent commands to the machines he controlled. The largest of the robots pressed forward, trampling through the thick barbed undergrowth, forcing a path.

The Black Sorcerer followed, flanked by Nash'Tak and the largest of his guards, trailed by another pair of battle robots. Just beyond the edges of the fog-free space the mists churned and twisted into strange shapes, but the wizard's barrier prevented any of the lizard-men's fears being etched on the shifting vapours.

The Sorcerer sensed rather than saw the half-buried monolith of black steel and silver circuitry somewhere to his left. Malathea directed her gaze at the overgrown pile of crusted metal and confirmed his find. He had the lizard-men hack their way through to where a great abandoned slab rotted and rusted where it had been dropped a thousand years ago.

"A plague drone. One of Ruin's," the wizard decided with a sniff. "Overengineered, overpowered, inelegant, unimaginative. No wonder he abandoned it." He turned his back on his fellow First Man's discard with professional contempt.

They pressed on through the forest of dead thorns. Whenever the lizard-men began to mutter Nash'Tak hissed them to silence. Silence seemed to be the natural state of this grey wasteland.

Ahead a faint set of glowing lights attracted the Black Sorcerer's attention. He diverted towards it and paused to take in the last glimmering afterimages of a giant rotating wheel.

"An old-Earth image," he recognised, "like the ones I recorded from Blackthorn's mind. So he at least survived his fall. And he passed this spot."

The lizard-men dropped to all fours and sniffed the ground. Finally one of them lifted its snout and hissed excitedly. It had found a scent trail.

"Move on," the Black Sorcerer commanded. "I will not be denied."

It was the lights that led them to Princess Aria.

Blackthorn and Oglok had lost track of how long they had foundered through the coiling mists. Sometimes solitary will o' the wisps drifted past them, tempting them away through the gloom. Other times whole landscapes formed up in luminous purple to draw them in. The carnival appeared again, this time with shadowy silhouettes of men and women on the boardwalks. Oglok's village came to them, and some sacred place by a waterfall, and a tall arena with a gathering ghost crowd. Blackthorn recognised a railway station and a military base. But always the travellers turned away and carried on.

When the lights formed something neither of them was familiar with they dared to edge closer.

The purple glows picked out a high towered structure like a glass cathedral. Free-floating platforms circled around it. Soaring crystal tines jutted from the earth at the cardinal points. The walls were composed of filigree latticework.

"This has got to come from someone else's memories," Blackthorn told Oglok. "It's a good bet it's from Aria's."

The Mock-Man reluctantly skulked behind the General as they approached the lightshow.

"Maybe this is Aria's lost distant kingdom?" Blackthorn speculated. "The technology and architecture are a bit similar to the Black Sorcerer's."

Sword of Light in hand, Blackthorn crossed the first threshold of the glowing illusion. He suppressed a shudder; it was considerably colder inside the lightshow. Oglok followed, his hair almost straight up, a low constant growl in his throat.

Close up the translucent purple memory was amazingly detailed. Every cornice and moulding was reflected in the eerie purple glow. Delicate traceries of wire and glass – perhaps decorative or maybe advanced circuitry – roped and ribboned over the graceful walls. The floor was a patterned polished mirror that reflected the lights from above.

Blackthorn ventured through the arched entranceway to the structure's interior. The purple mists twisted round his legs, disturbed by his passing.

Aria sat in the very centre of the cathedral, her legs folded under her. She stared into the distance, rapt, unaware.

"Aria!" called Blackthorn. Then he fell silent.

There was something there. Something else. His senses screamed it, some atavistic instinct warning him of danger. Not the cloying fog. Not the mesmeric twinkles that painted lightshows to beguile. Something else. Something worse.

At the doorway Oglok paused. His lips were drawn back, his bestial teeth bared.

"We're seeing things that aren't there," Blackthorn reasoned out loud. "What are we not seeing that *is* there?"

He thumbed the white button on his Sword of Light and flooded the citadel with its illumination.

And he saw them.

There were three of them ranged around Aria, almost close enough to touch her. They were man-sized and robed, and they floated a few inches above the ground. Their dark mottled cloaks had a serpent sheen. And where their heads should have been…

Oglok howled and raced forward, intent on attacking.

Where their heads should have been floated transparent jellyfish, detached from the bodies below, their dangling tentacles twitching and twisting.

The Mock-Man's attack caught their attention. The jellyfish heads glowed with the same lurid purple as the mists, then launched searing bright balls at the charging Oglok.

The Mock-Man shivered as if he'd been tasered and was hurled back to the ground, twitching and helpless. Aria did not react.

Blackthorn raced in, shifting his Sword of Light to a searing sabre. When the purple orbs shot out at him he sliced through them and kept on coming.

The jellyfish-heads were disconcerted and fell back, panicking. Blackthorn cut through the first one easily, slicing detached head and body both. It fell heavily, unravelling like a loose thread, leaving little but rotted rags and a foul odour. It died silently. The second creature tried to avoid the Sword of Light but was taken in the chest.

The third launched a simultaneous pair of purple orbs, each twisting in a different arc to take Blackthorn from both sides. The General dropped and rolled, barely avoiding their assault, then cursed as they each twisted round for another approach.

The glowing balls closed in, but now Blackthorn was ready for them. He rolled into a crouch to slice the first and ducked the second. The jellyfish-head didn't expect the warrior to suddenly reverse his thrust and slice into the transparent goo of its floating cranium. The body crumbled and the last orb flickered out as it died.

Blackthorn had no time to catch his breath. The second jellyfish appeared able to move without its destroyed body. Now it was dragging itself across the floor towards the entranced Princess Aria. The General hurled his Sword of Light and transfixed the horror inches away from her.

The luminescent cathedral shivered and melted away.

In the resultant darkness it took Blackthorn a few moments to locate his Sword of Light and shine it to seek the fallen Oglok; but the Mock-Man had gone.

"John?"

Blackthorn turned. The princess was awakening from her trance, confused and frightened.

"Aria. Are you alright?"

The woman blinked and came to full consciousness. She looked at the thin mists and the banks of thorns. "We're in Acheron!"

"I guess."

"Then I'm not alright." She struggled to her feet then staggered. "We have to get out of here."

"Oglok's missing. He was right there, but some jellyfish things zapped him with these glowing balls..."

Aria's eyes widened as she remembered what had happened. "They were here! The Acherim! They'd got me!" She glanced around as if expecting to see them swarming through the fog. "And they've taken the Mock-Man!"

"Taken? How?" Blackthorn wasn't certain how anyone could have crept up while the fight had raged.

Aria rubbed her pale face like someone waking from a nightmare – or into one. "This is Acheron. The haunted land. Even the First Ones don't venture here without good cause."

"We have good cause. We need to find Oglok."

The princess waved her hands to dispel the clinging mists. "These vapours are a medium for the corpse lights. You've seen their arrays?"

"The ghost places? Oh yeah. They tried to suck us in."

"They did suck me in," Aria confessed, "and I actually knew what they could do. When enough of the... the energies have suffused a person, the Acherim can transport that body to their realm. The lights beguile and bedazzle so they can accumulate enough energy to allow a transfer."

"Those jellyfish things – the Acherim? – they generated concentrated light-zaps," realised Blackthorn. "That's why they were able to take Oglok."

The princess bit her lip. "And now the Mock-Man is lost."

Blackthorn shook his head. "We'll find him."

Aria shuddered. "Even the Black Sorcerer would not seek to retrieve one taken by the Acherim."

"Well in case you hadn't noticed I'm not the Black Sorcerer, princess. Oglok was terrified but he followed me to help you. We're not leaving him to be jellyfished to death or whatever those things do."

Aria's lips curved into a tiny smile. "No, you are not the Black Sorcerer," she agreed.

Blackthorn looked around. Apart from the omnipresent vapours there seemed no immediate threat. "So tell me who these guys are and what they do. Then we'll figure how to stop them."

Aria sighed. "I told you that attacking the Harmony Needle was a bad idea but you ignored me and did it anyway. I'm telling you now that facing the Acherim is a bad idea."

"But when I ignored your advice you came with me to the Needle anyway. And we achieved our objective and distracted the Sorcerer while word of our resistance was spread across Arcadia and Ceraunius."

"I suppose if I'd wanted a quiet life I could have stayed at home," admitted the princess. "Very well. Where you came from, ancient Earth, they had places where they put dangerous waste? Places where toxins could be sealed away for a hundred thousand years while they decayed."

"Sure. They were controversial."

"Just so. Well, back at the rise of the First Men such places were needed here on Mars. Wastelands. Such is Acheron."

Blackthorn stared at the dead needle-bushes. "This place is radioactive?"

"Not any more. The nuclear poisons, the discarded bioweapons, the psychic sludge, the quantum detritus, all of it has evolved in this place." The princess hugged herself as she looked about. "This is why the First Men do not come here. Who wishes to squirm down his own cess hole and crawl about to see what his defecations have become?"

"The Acherim?"

"Born of this, or else attracted here from elsewhere. No one knows. They take the bodies of some they lure in and use them – you've seen it – as we might use horses. Except we don't remove our horses' heads the better to control them. What else they do, or how, or where, nobody has ever fathomed who has returned sane to tell it."

"Cheery."

Princess Aria braced herself and stood up tall. She turned to face the General and met his gaze. "This is why I feared Acheron, John Blackthorn. I will follow you into its nightmare depths, but we will never ever return."

It was a high school gym, but the banners and bunting had transformed it to something special. The purple fairy lights glinted down on the homecoming dance and the translucent revellers who swirled across the hall in silence had no faces. The purple mists danced with the students.

Blackthorn wondered if this had been his prom. Had he brought some date here to this important rite of passage? Had he taken her home to her folks afterwards, or parked somewhere secret and become a man? Had he met his wife here? Had this been a treasured memory of the man he'd been, a recollection of disaster of delight? He would never know.

The girl in his arms now was the Princess Aria, and her turquoise dress was as graceful as any prom gown. They swirled across the dance floor with the others as the fog closed around them and the purple light bored into them.

And before the dance was done the mists folded over them and they were gone.

★★★

Malathea halted. Her pale perfect skin was sheened with sweat as she strained to the limit of the sensorware threaded through her flesh. "I'm getting something," reported the Sensorine. "A trace of the Princess."

The Black Sorcerer looked around the dim light remnants of a fading high school gym. *So Aria is alive,* he thought, *and she is still with Blackthorn.* His scowl deepened.

The lizard-men clustered together and hissed in agitated undertones. Nash'Tak growled them to silence.

Charn fussed over the remaining four battle robots. Two had already burned out in the electromagnetic churn that the damned purple fog caused. The whole valley was inimical to any technology save that of the Acherim.

The Black Sorcerer prowled over to the place where the grey soil was most churned and pressed the tip of his serpent-staff into the ground. "They were taken," he decided.

Nash'Tak waited for the wizard to announce that nothing more could be done, to give the order to return to the safety and sanity of the grasslands.

Instead he turned to Charn. "Set the robots to dig here. There are cavern chambers beneath. Burrow down. Malathea will direct you."

Even the Robot Caller hesitated a moment. "We are to break into the Halls of the Acherim?"

"Have I not commanded it? Am I not the Black Sorcerer?"

While the purple mists churned angrily outside the wizard's barrier the grinding robots began to cut down through the crumbling sandstone to invade the caves beneath.

The searing white light snapped John Blackthorn out of a turbulent dream of torment. He sat up suddenly, startled. His hand found the Sword of Light at his side.

And then he remembered: Acheron, the mists, the loss of Oglok, the dance…

The princess! "Aria?" he called.

She was there beside him, on the next slab, blinking awake as she went through the same trails of thought as he had. "John? It worked?"

It had worked. The only way to follow Oglok had been to let the lights take them to the Acherim. Aria had used her sorcery to roll the dice in a desperate gamble.

"Oh, I'm good!" the princess told herself. "I locked up the brilliance of your Sword of Light until my spell degraded and then the concentrated flash purged our systems of that purple glow. It worked!"

"And now here we are in Arkadim-ville," Blackthorn noted.

The two of them looked around. They were underground, in natural caves that had been polished off where flat floors and smooth walls were required. Lurid violet illumination came from veins of luminous fibres threaded through the stone. The roof was obscured by a choked tangle of roots, presumably from the dead briars that clogged the canyon above.

It was chillingly cold. Aria did something to her multihued gown and was suddenly cloaked.

"No sign of Oglok," worried Blackthorn. "We'd better recon."

Aria nodded and kept close beside the warrior.

There was no mist here, but a thick purple-grey dust coated the floors and rose in clouds as it was trodden on. The tunnels twisted along channels made by water back before Mars' molten core had cooled and its dying magnetosphere had allowed the solar wind to strip it of atmosphere and life. These passageways had been hundreds of millennia old before ever humans had come to the red planet to remodel it to their tastes.

For the first time John Blackthorn wondered if there had been sentient life on Mars before men. And if so, what ghosts of them remained in forgotten chambers here in buried Acheron?

Aria pointed ahead, to where a wall was inscribed with dim-glowing purple glyphs. "We're moving out of the storage bays into more important areas," she guessed.

"Good. We need to find one of those jellyfish and ask it a few questions," responded Blackthorn.

The princess shook her head. "They're all connected. For all we know they're all one intelligence. Attack one and you alert all of them."

Blackthorn remembered that when Oglok had been suffused with purple energies he'd been transported somewhere below; when Princess Aria has been beguiled the Acherim had come to her. "How do you know so much about them?" he wondered.

"Everyone knows about the Acherim. Everyone knows to stay out of Acheron."

"Why were they specially interested in you, enough to make a personal collection?"

"Sometimes the Acherim go hunting, even beyond the mists." She paused nervously. "They specially favour taking those who have an aptitude for magic."

The explorers passed through a carved archway into a larger chamber. The light from Blackthorn's sword sent long shadows over the walls and root roof. "What do they do with these captives?" the General wondered.

Aria shook her head. "I don't know. I... I don't want to know."

There was a hesitance in her answer that made Blackthorn turn back. "Aria?"

She looked at him and blinked back tears. "Can't you feel it, John? This hall? Can't you tell the answers to your questions?"

The warrior looked about, ready for danger. The cavern was large and dark but he could see nothing.

"Very well," the princess said. "Come here." When Blackthorn stood by her she reached up, pulled his head lower, and softly kissed his eyelids. "Look now."

Blackthorn forced himself to forget the touch of her lips and opened his eyes. He was surrounded by horrors.

"What?" he demanded, taking a defensive stance and raising his Sword of Light. "What's this?"

None of the horrors moved. He could see them now, see them as Aria has perceived them all along, a series of tableaux picked out in three dimensions with lurid lines of pulsing purple. Each one was different, and each depicted some grotesque scenario of utter misery, degradation and torture.

Blackthorn approached one of the images. Each different perspective on it shifted the whole, offering some new atrocity.

"I said, what is this?" Blackthorn demanded.

"It's what the Acherim want people for," said the princess in a small voice. "My father..." she blurted, then reconsidered.

"Yes?" Blackthorn asked. Aria didn't mention her family often.

"My father once said that the Acherim kept the heads because they want the brains. Or the minds. That they sculpted them, like artists use clay or stone, twisting them to make their statues." She pointed round the gallery of grotesqueries. "These statues."

"There are people's minds in these, suffering?" Blackthorn asked, horrified. "People's souls?"

"You know the technology exists to extract such things, John," Aria pointed out. "These sentiences weren't housed in new bodies.

They were... sculpted. That's what they were going to do to me. They were probing my mind to find out what horror would hurt me most, would make me the most delicious to their perceptions."

"This is what they'll do to Ogruk if we can't save him?"

"That's... that's what they'll do when they catch us, John." She shivered again despite her cloak. "Please kill me first."

The sculptures were now growing dim to Blackthorn's sight. Aria's gift had been temporary. Even for a touch of her lips Blackthorn did not want another.

They hurried through the gallery and past more of the wall-writing. Beyond that was a network of corridors, a whole maze.

"We shouldn't go too far," Aria reasoned. "When we were transported here we woke up in a holding space. It makes sense that those spaces aren't a long way from wherever captives are taken."

There was an intermittent cold breeze in this corridor. It took Blackthorn a moment to realise that it stirred first in one direction then in the opposite one, as if a giant was sucking icy breaths.

They were wondering which route to take when the corridors started screaming.

The robots had tunnelled perhaps thirty feet down into the grey sandstone when the counterattack began. The first of the machines flared then toppled over as livid purple energies lanced into it from below. Before Charn had a chance to shout a dozen thick tentacles rose through the broken rock and wrapped around him. The largest of the war engines went berserk, turning its cutting tools on the lizard-men beside it.

"They're here!" screamed Malathea redundantly, her unpupiled eyes wide and suddenly bloody as she sensed the approach of the Acherim. The Sensorine's capacity to process the data she was receiving overloaded and she fell back in an epileptic spasm.

More of the tentacles burst from the ground around the lizard-men, growing and coiling. The tips of the writhing protuberances grew through the reptile warriors' flesh as easily as around it.

Some of the packs broke and scattered, running beyond the perimeter of the Black Wizard's protection, racing into the waiting fogs. Nash'Tak screeched at the others to hold, cursed their breeding nests and tried to marshal some coherent defence.

The Black Wizard's lips curled back in an angry snarl. He held his staff vertically with both hands and closed his eyes in concentration.

Charn cried out for his master as the tentacles wormed their way into the Robot Caller's belly. Already the purple fire that danced around the exposed nerve clusters of the questing tendrils was sparking memories of agony through his neural interface. The robots ran mad.

Nash'Tak seized up an energy lance and burned out one of the machines' core processors. A second robot caught the commander from the side, tearing a deep gash that bled green ichor.

The lizard-men in the mists realised their mistake too late. The thick vapours closed in around them, flaring into ghost-images that seared their sanity, reducing them back to the atavistic killers they had been before they had emerged from the Black Sorcerer's evolution vats. They turned on each other with fang and claw, no longer pack-brothers but merely dying animals desperate for one last taste of blood.

Tendrils grew around Malathea as she spasmed, wrapping her tightly and drawing her down through the ground.

Charn screamed one last time as the tentacles growing through his body popped waving cilia out through his eye sockets.

And the Black Sorcerer slammed his staff through the nearest tentacle and into the ground. "*Enough!*"

Black energies crackled from his stave and tore across the member it had transfixed. Each of the tentacles blackened and blistered as the surge of power radiated outwards. They calcified then shattered into dust. A sonic boom slammed out, flattening the dead thorn forest for five miles in every direction. The purple mists dissipated.

When the maelstrom was over Nash'Tak tried to rise. The great gash in his side still pumped ichor but the lizard-man commander needed to know which of his packs had survived, which had held their discipline. His body betrayed him and he stumbled again.

The Black Sorcerer surveyed the devastation. Shattered robots and torn minions littered the broken field. The remaining lizard-men ran insane over the midnight wasteland. He walked over to General Nash'Tak.

The lizard-man chieftain tried to rise but failed once more. "Master," he recognised.

"Your people ran," the Black Sorcerer declared. "I will cull a thousand of their kin for their failure."

Nash'Tak closed his eyes in shame and defeat.

The wizard loomed over him. "You stood. I will allow their children to live."

"Thank you, master."

"You may die now," said the Black Sorcerer.

Nash'Tak drew his knife and cut his throat.

The Black Sorcerer stood alone amidst the devastation of his army. Beside him the broken ground formed a maw down to the Halls of the Acherim. He folded his mantle around him and descended.

"I am coming," he announced.

Princess Aria and John Blackthorn backtracked through the gallery and found another cavern with slabs identical to the one they'd awoken in. There were piles of discarded clothing and equipment on the floor – Blackthorn took a cloak – but no signs of the Mock-Man.

"We've moved some way from where you were beguiled and Oglok disappeared," reasoned Blackthorn. "Perhaps we should try and find the chamber nearest to where he vanished?"

"Good idea," agreed Aria. "How?"

The General had no answer. He realised that they were trekking around blindly on an impossible mission. He had to redefine his objectives. "This isn't working. We need an edge."

"An edge is good," agreed the princess. "You have the Sword of Light."

Blackthorn considered the universal tool in his hand. "The Acherim don't seem to get on well with its rays," he admitted.

"It was no mistake that of all the treasures in the Black Sorcerer's lair I directed you to that one. But you must husband its power for it cannot recharge here in this eternal night."

It occurred to the Earthman that Aria must have spent quite some time as the Black Sorcerer's prisoner to know so well the secrets of her captor's lair. He wondered again why the wizard-king had demanded her as tribute – unless it was the obvious reason any evil warlord might want a beautiful princess. He wondered what Aria had suffered at the Black Sorcerer's hands.

He pushed his morbid speculations aside for a better time. He had a rescue to accomplish. Oglok the Mock-Man's life, perhaps his very soul, was in peril right now. Blackthorn did not want his loyal friend to join that gallery of grotesqueries, tormented for all time in some clever cruel frozen moment like so many other victims...

"So many other victims," the General said out loud.

Aria turned from inspecting the runes on the wall. "John?"

Blackthorn shook his head. "It's not right, Aria. It's not enough."

"What isn't enough?" The princess looked at the warrior suspiciously. "What are you thinking, John?"

"It's not enough to rescue Oglok and escape."

"Fortunately the chances of doing that are miniscule anyway. In truth, John, I was thinking the best we could do was to find and kill him cleanly and then take our own lives before the Acherim catch us." Aria indicated the direction her best guess suggested might lead to more holding chambers. She wondered again why she followed the mad Earthman on suicide mission after suicide mission. It seemed to reflect badly on her psychological condition.

Blackthorn followed her down another twisting tunnel lit by thin stripes of glowing purple. "I mean it's not enough to save our friend just because he is our friend. What about all the others they've destroyed who we didn't happen to know and care about? These Acherim jellyfish things are evil. The things they do, the things they've done for centuries... It's not enough to just escape them. We have to destroy them."

Aria's face reflected her despair then her irritation. "John, the Black Sorcerer avoids Acheron. Lord Ruin, the Sorcerer of Night, even the Lord of Fatal Laughter all leave this place alone. Nobody goes after the Acherim. They just leave them well alone."

"That's how bullies get powerful," Blackthorn argued. "Look, you wanted me to do things, to make Mars a better world, right? You wanted me to fight the tyranny of the Black Sorcerer and the others. So why should I keep these cruel terrible Acherim off the list? Why not take them down with all the rest?"

"Because it's impossible!" the princess cried. "Honestly, John. The Black Sorcerer wanted you to marshal his armies in his wars with the other First Men because he thought you understood strategy and tactics. But you seem unable to distinguish between viable resistance methods and no-hope charges! You just..."

She fell silent as Blackthorn clapped his hand over her mouth and hauled her into an alcove. She struggled momentarily as he wrapped her in his arms and pulled her close, then relaxed as she realised he'd heard something moving along the corridor.

They stood motionless, pressed together in a cramped niche as one of the Acherim floated past, feet hovering above the floor, serpentine robes flapping unsettlingly, jellyfish cranium floating separate above a circuitry-topped head stump. Behind it shuffled three battered lizard-men, beguiled and obedient, their eyes glowing with that unholy purple aura.

Aria expected Blackthorn would follow them. It seemed like the most stupid and dangerous thing to do. She was mildly impressed when he instead elected to look into the cavern from which the slave train had emerged.

This cavern was more refined than most. Machine-shaped flat walls were laced with a web of organic circuitry that pulsed as if to a heartbeat. The roots that choked the roof of the cruder corridors were replaced by more of the tentacle-like cilia which dangled down into bulbous machines. There was a stench of bodily fluids and an underlying odour of decay.

Aria gasped as she recognised the woman dangling from the dissection crib. "Malathea!" She rushed forward to examine the captured Sensorine.

"You know her?" Blackthorn asked. He checked the gutted husks in the other tentacle cradles but they were all lizard-men and all dead.

"She's one of the Black Sorcerer's creations," the princess replied. "How could she be here? Unless…"

The General reached the same conclusion. "I guess we annoyed the old bastard even more than we realised. He's so mad he's chased us right into Acheron."

Aria swallowed hard. "Why would he do that? Why would he send his people in here? He wouldn't come himself. He wouldn't."

"He must have really cared about that Harmony Spire."

"Yes. Yes he must." Aria's eyes evaded Blackthorn's gaze. "We need to get Malathea free. We can't leave her here."

Blackthorn was conflicted. On the battlefield he'd have been pleased to deny the Black Sorcerer one of his prime assets. Yet he was reluctant to leave even an enemy to the torments of the Acherim. In the end he let Aria decide for him and used the Sword of Light to sear through the network of tendrils binding the Sensorine in place.

Malathea toppled down into Aria's arms, barely conscious, bleeding from a dozen places where the tentacles had burrowed through the sensor-net across her skin. The Sensorine looked up dazedly and saw her rescuer. "Princess?"

"It's me," agreed Aria. "Did you come to Acheron with others? With the Black Sorcerer?"

Malathea managed a nod. "There was an attack. They put thoughts into my mind… overloaded my inputs." She stifled a sob.

"You have to keep going," Aria told her. "Look at me. Focus. We need your skills."

"Skills?" asked Blackthorn. "What skills?" He looked more carefully at the ebony woman with the silver circuit-board tattoos. "What is she?"

Malathea realised who he was. "You are John Blackthorn, the apostate," she said. "The one who stole Princess Aria."

"He is our only chance of escaping, Malathea," the stolen princess argued. "John, Malathea's a Sensorine, a living diagnostic device. Her entire nervous system is a living sensor grid. If anyone can detect Oglok for us it's her." She turned to the woman. "Malathea, we need you to scan for a Mock-Man. Find him."

"A Mock-Man? Why?"

"Because he's our friend," snarled Blackthorn. "So if you don't want me to push you back inside one of those tentacle nests, just find him."

In the central cavern of the Hall of the Acherim the glowing organic veins that laced the complex twisted together like the roots of a great tree. Shimmering with eye-watering purple light they pulsed rhythmically around the great central brain of the pain sculptors. A huge central mass of linked jellyfish, knotted and grown together like a Medusoid rat-king, emitted the psychic vapours that choked the haunted valleys above.

The Black Sorcerer stalked to face it. This close to the Acherim hivemind his personal shields could push the writhing mists no further than three feet from his body.

Why do you disturb us? asked the Acherim. *Why do you challenge us?*

"You've taken something that belongs to the Black Sorcerer. I want her back."

The Acherim did not even pretend to believe the wizard sought the Sensorine. *Your princess transgressed into our territory. She will be ours.*

"If I must destroy you I will."

You do not know if you could.

"I am ready to find out. Are you?"

You are strong. We are the Acherim, and this is our place.

The Black Sorcerer considered this. A battle here, now, could go either way. It might destroy both combatants alike. There was a better way. "We might resolve this by other means," the wizard suggested slyly. "A test. A wager."

How so?

"I want Aria safe from here. You dream of adding her to your gallery of atrocities, of admiring her screaming soul for eternity. How then if we leave her fate to other circumstance?" The Sorcerer smiled thinly. "There is a man in your Halls, Acherim. He calls himself John Blackthorn. If you can destroy him in, say, the next hour, if you can bring his shattered mindless body to me, then I relinquish my claim on my princess. She will be yours to degrade and torment forever. But if you fail to end him in that time then Aria may leave, free and unimpeded."

The Acherim considered this. The ancient hivemind pulsed as it extended its consciousness through the rootweb and mind-mists until it located the intruders in its Halls. It laid its plans and made its choices. *Your terms are acceptable. We will bring the broken human to you within the hour.*

The Black Sorcerer nodded his satisfaction and leaned on his staff to wait.

Malathea led them to the Mock-Man. Oglok was trussed out on an operating slab, held down by more of those intruding tendrils. Nerve secretions rendered the huge beastling unable to use his massive strength the wrench free.

A pair of Acherim leaned over Oglok, enjoying his growls of terror while they prepared for surgery.

Blackthorn knew that the time for stealth was over. He sliced through the first jellyfish before it had even sensed his presence, then splattered the other while the purple battle-orb still formed in its translucent cranium.

"Now they'll all know that we're here," Aria warned.

Blackthorn cut Oglok free. "We're here for you, buddy," he calmed the terrified Mock-Man. "Can you fight?"

The Mock-Man staggered to his feet and roared that he was not dead; of course he could fight.

Malathea shuddered. "They are coming," she sensed. "Many of them."

Blackthorn turned to Aria. "Right," he said. "Are you ready? Can you do it?"

"An edge," promised the princess. "Just like you wanted." She pulled the Sensorine over to the nearest cluster of wall-threads then touched her fingers to Malathea's forehead. "Concentrate on the readings you're getting from John and me," she commanded.

Oglok growled, warning that foes were near.

Aria touched her other hand to the slimy rope of luminous tendrils that snaked around the operating cave. She pressed the readings from Malathea into the Acherim sensor net. "They thought they were dredging my mind when they caught me," the princess spat. "As if I wasn't doing the same to them! Who do they think I am?"

Throughout the Halls of the Acherim sensor dendrons misfired. Suddenly a hundred Blackthorns with a hundred princesses seemed to leap out and race away from the confused jellyfish.

"They're reaching out!" shrieked Malathea, clutching at her bleeding nose and ears. "They're reaching out again with their minds!"

Blackthorn clubbed her unconscious and heaved her over his shoulder. It was better that the sensitive Sensorine was not awake when the Acherim unshipped the full fury of their hive-brain.

He gestured for Oglok to flank him and began his charge down the corridor. The Mock-Man ripped a heavy metal pipe from the floor to use as a club and raced after the General.

There were Acherim in the next cave, still reacting to the false images Aria had transmitted through the rootweb. That gave Blackthorn the advantage. His Sword of Light sheared through the jellyfish heads, popping them like pus-filled balloons. Oglok roared approval and squashed more in his huge leathery hands.

"Keep moving!" Aria shouted. "I don't know how long that illusion will hold."

Blackthorn nodded and made quick work of the flailing tentacles blocking the next doorway. They ran on, following the route suggested to them by the Sensorine before she'd been knocked out.

Three headless Mock-Men, massive and menacing, loomed out of the darkness, driven by the Medusazoa hovering over their necks. Oglok howled his fury and set upon them with a terrible wrath.

Tentacles burst out of a wall and wrapped themselves around Princess Aria. Blackthorn swung his blade and sliced through the squirming appendages. Aria wriggled free.

"They're refocused now," the princess warned. "In fact they've channelled all their awareness into pinpointing us through the psychic chaff I sent out. I think we have their full attention."

"So it's time for part two?" Blackthorn checked.

His wicked grin was infectious. Aria returned it. "It's time for part two. You lunatic."

They pelted down the icy breathing hall, Blackthorn at point still hefting Malathea, with Aria close by him and Oglok running interference at the rear. Ahead of them the whole cave tunnel shifted and flexed like a swallowing sphincter, gushing out thick purple mists to billow over the fugitives.

Blackthorn thumbed his Sword of Light to its maximum setting, located the central locus of the tentacles, and stabbed his weapon deep. Searing light flared into the highly-sensitive psychic network; it was like a burning needle stabbed into the Acherim's eye.

The Halls of the Acherim twisted and screamed.

"Half an hour," said the Black Sorcerer to the jellyfish hivemind. "How would you say it was going?"

The Acherim were blinded, reeling from the light that had seared through their collective perception. The purple mists floated in ragged streamers, unable to coalesce. Blackthorn and Oglok pressed into the great mass of the creatures, tearing their way through with a savage abandon.

The General had not quite surrendered to the same berserker fury that possessed the Mock-Man. While Oglok expressed the terror that had possessed him as a captive of the Acherim by savaging his way through hordes of the monstrosities, the General suborned his loathing and anger at the creatures and kept pressing towards the goal that Malathea had detected.

It took a long time to fight his way to the great central Hall where the Acherim hivemind pulsed and squirmed. Too long, maybe. The Acherim were recovering, their attacks becoming more coordinated again. A few managed to summon and project the beguiling purple energy balls that could end the fight with one single hit. Aria focussed her attacks on them.

Blackthorn powered through the rallying Acherim drones and headed straight towards the brain. He checked the dwindling charge on his Sword of Light and hoped it would be enough the sear the gestalt monster from existence.

"Impressive, isn't he?" the Black Sorcerer whispered to the Acherim. "I knew he would be when I chose him. Once he has been fitted with an obedience disc he will be my finest general. And Princess Aria almost defeated you in her own right."

The hivemind bubbled angrily, stirred and wounded as it had not been in a millennium. It focussed its remaining psionic energies and reached out to the upstarts that charged towards it.

Blackthorn and Oglok stumbled and ground to a halt, held in their tracks by the will of the over-brain. Aria managed two paces more before her own psychic defences were overcome.

Then all three stood immobile, helpless at the last before the mind of the Acherim.

"Have you learned a lesson, Acherim?" the Black Sorcerer wondered as the ancient intelligence turned its malevolence on the prisoners that had nearly destroyed it. "About how even in your place of power there are things that can threaten you?"

We are the Acherim. We triumph.

"So you're still missing the point," sighed the Black Sorcerer. Then he jabbed his snake-staff into the essence of the hive-mind. Seething black energies discharged into the writhing Acherim collective. "I told you: even in your place of power there are things that can threaten you. *I* am the worst!"

Blackthorn broke from the mental thrall that bound him. The Acherim's attention was elsewhere. He sprinted forward and dived for the massive collective brain that twisted and shook in front of him. His Sword of Light sliced into it, discharging the last of its stored power in one massive pulse.

The psychic backlash sent everyone spiralling away into unconsciousness.

Blackthorn's headache woke him. A clumsy giant in hob-nailed boots had moved into his skull.

"Drink this," instructed the Princess Aria. She lifted a water-skin to the General's lips.

Blackthorn rallied enough to sit up and look around. It was day again and they were in red canyons beyond the valley of Acheron. "Did I miss a chapter?"

"You were nearest to the psychic detonation. You were out the longest. Oglok dragged you from the tunnels before they collapsed?"

"They collapsed?"

The Mock-Man made a complicated noise indicating how satisfying it had been to see the Halls of the Acherim reduced to rubble even while fleeing for his life with the human across his shoulders.

"I think we destroyed the Acherim hivemind," admitted Aria. "That should have been impossible, but..." She shrugged. "Impossible seems to be what you do, John Blackthorn."

Aria looked better than any woman had any right to after being dragged through tentacle-filled tunnels fighting sadistic psychic jellyfish. He'd gone to hell for her and then she'd followed him deeper in. The General smiled despite his splitting head. "Impossible is what we do, Princess Aria. And we're only just beginning."

Malathea the Sensorine struggled awake with a sob. She looked around and found herself back in the Black Sorcerer's laboratory.

The wizard-king himself turned from his studies to regard her. "Go to the data-sump," he commanded. "There is much valuable information you have absorbed in Acheron that I can use."

Malathea ignored her hurts and rose obediently.

The Sorcerer stopped her. "Wait," he called. "Before that, tell me... You saw the princess. How was Aria?"

The Sensorine considered her answer, unsure what to say. "She seemed..." Malathea perfectly recalled every nuance of Aria's behaviour, her speech, her body language, "...more."

"More?"

Malathea nodded helplessly. "More confident. More powerful. More Aria."

The Black Sorcerer pondered her words. "I see. Did she seem... content?"

"It is hard to say, master. We were in deadly danger in the Halls of the Acherim. But she... her biometrics changed when she... when the warrior was near her."

"Blackthorn."

"Yes, master. And his readings..."

"I do not care to hear about General Blackthorn for the moment. It is clear now that his foray to the Harmony Needle was a mere diversion. Word of his dissent is spreading across Mars. His futile ideas of liberty and peace sprout like weeds, unwanted and unneeded. He no longer amuses me."

Malathea bowed low.

"Has she told him?" the wizard asked. "Does he know who she is yet?"

"I do not know, master. I have no data on the subject." The Sensorine bowed again.

The Black Sorcerer turned to the balcony where he could look out over the red landscape of his wide domain, from the heights of Nix Olympus to the vast canal plains of Arcadia, the Ceraunius jungles to the Amazonis Ocean expanse. They seemed tranquil enough but now rebellion was brewing, and war on the borders beyond. Events were taking a life of their own, and the balance of power that had held for a thousand years was shifting and changing.

"Go to the data-sump," he dismissed Malathea. "Leave me to forget about John Blackthorn for a while. And to consider the problem of my daughter."

EPILOGUE: RED PLANET BLUES

VAN ALLEN PLEXICO

John Blackthorn dropped his tired frame into the rusted old metal chair at the head of the long table and looked up, regarding the others arrayed on either side of him. They made for a most interesting congregation: chieftains and priests, pirate lords and rebel leaders, some human and some...*not*. Then, his mouth forming a tight smile, he nodded in greeting to each of them, calling their names.

"Lord Throg. Chief Nanzak. Father De'bias. Elder Ardin. Madame Sihla. Captain Korzan." Round the table he went, acknowledging each in turn—some two dozen or more—before he had finished. The assembly even included two Mock-Men chieftains and another inhuman creature about whose race even Blackthorn wasn't certain.

"I'd like to thank each of you for coming here," he said once he had completed the circuit. "I understand that you face the danger of severe repercussions, both from your own people and from the First Men, if your participation in this gathering should be discovered, and I don't take that lightly by any means."

The gathered village and tribal leaders glanced nervously at one another before returning their attention to the man in black.

"In the months since I first awoke on this world—your world, and now mine, too," Blackthorn continued, "I have met and spoken with each of you. My friends and I have assisted many of you in dealing with criminals, lunatics, warlords, and other threats to your people's safety if not to your very survival."

The assembled leaders, some of them reluctantly, nodded at this; though a number of those gathered here had reasons to dislike or distrust Blackthorn, none could dispute the fact that he and his companions had come to their aid in times of crisis and asked for little more than food and brief lodging in return—if that.

"During that time," the blond man continued, "we have demonstrated over and over that it is possible to stand up to the forces of tyranny and corruption that dominate this world. Indeed, it is not just possible—it is necessary. It is *vital*."

He paused then, gazing out at them, his eyes meeting each of theirs in turn, challenging them, measuring them. Some met his gaze; others looked down, or looked away. This he noted carefully.

"Beyond all the other forces of repression and tyranny on this world, however, we all know very well that four individuals stand alone as the major threats to our safety and security—as forces that deny us freedom and prosperity." He leaned forward, hands resting on the rough-hewn tabletop, his eyes narrowing. "The Black Sorcerer," he growled. "The Sorcerer of Fatal Laughter. Lord Ruin. The Sorcerer of Night." He inhaled deeply, exhaled, met their eyes again. "The First Men of Mars. *They* are the problem. *They* are the enemy—the enemy of *all* of us, human and mutant, Mock-Man and Mer-Man and Monstrosity alike. They are the enemy of *all* the people of Mars."

He halted again, straightening, his hands on his hips, blue eyes flashing.

"And they must be removed from power. Taken from their strongholds, stripped of their armies and their machines and their weapons of mass destruction, and cast out of our society forever."

He crossed his arms and looked at them—at all of them. He waited.

The room was utterly, deadly silent for several moments. Then a light murmur floated up as first one and then another of the tribal leaders whispered to his or her neighbor. Occasionally one of them would glance up at Blackthorn, only to be met by his look of steady, unflinching resolve. More whispering, growing louder, and finally a loud rumble as the voices grew full and strong.

"But how can we do this?" came the cry from a leader at the far end of the long table, silencing the discussion as suddenly as it had started. "How can we ever dream of challenging the First Men?"

"We challenge them already," Blackthorn responded. "Every time we fight their agents and their armies, their tax collectors and their kidnappers, we challenge their authority over the people of Mars."

"Beating back a rabble horde of reavers is one thing," muttered a regional elder. "Attacking the Black Sorcerer in his citadel—" He scoffed. "Well, that's something altogether different."

"Not different," Blackthorn argued, "just bigger. It's only a matter of scale. To do so, we simply need a bigger army of our own." He smiled at them then. "The time for meek acceptance of their dictatorship is over. Together, we are strong. We have already shown them in a hundred different ways in a hundred places that we will no longer yield to their domination. We've proven it is possible to stand up to the First Men. All that remains, my friends, is to challenge them directly." He brought his hands down hard onto the tabletop. "To confront them in their own lairs—and to defeat them!"

The room dissolved into near-chaos, with shouts and arguments and recriminations rampant. For a while Blackthorn tried to insert himself into the deliberations, but soon it became obvious his presence was not helping and was not desired.

Weary, frustrated and nearly despondent, the general exited the meeting hall and moved out into the cool evening air. A vague memory from his old life on Earth touched him then—somehow he suspected, for the first time since his awakening on Mars, that he had occasionally smoked cigarettes in his previous life. That was one change this new world had brought him that he couldn't complain about. And so he merely leaned back against the rough red adobe wall and stared up at the star-filled sky.

"You did the best you could," came a feminine voice from off to his right. "The best anyone could, given the circumstances. Given the collection of petty crooks and liars you were speaking with in there."

He tore his eyes away from the distant stars and met the gleaming eyes of Princess Aria. She smiled her wry half-smile, filled with all the arrogance and sarcasm he'd come to suspect from her. He found to no real surprise that he could no longer imagine his life without it.

"They don't want to listen," he said to her. "They're stubborn."

"They're afraid," she said. "They've spent their entire lives finding ways to avoid the attention of the First Men. That is, in large part, how they each came to be a leader of their people. And now here you come, saying—no, *demanding*—that they do the exact opposite. That they do everything in their power to make targets of themselves and their people." She laughed her cold laugh. "What in the name of all that's holy do you expect? That they'll throw you a parade? Build a statue of you?"

He sighed and shook his head.

"No. Just that they stand up for themselves."

"If they do, they do," Aria said after a moment. "And if they don't, they don't. Either way, you can't make them. If you try, you become just as much a dictator as the First Men themselves."

Blackthorn started at this. Eyes widening, he looked at her in surprise, then breathed out slowly and nodded.

"You're right," he admitted. "Why do you have to be right so often?"

"Because I'm not just beautiful but also quite brilliant," she replied instantly. Her smile now was not the half-sarcastic thing that drove him crazy but a warm and genuine one that reached all the way up to her dark eyes.

He was still searching for a worthy rejoinder to that when a sound like the cross between a dog barking and a goose honking echoed in the darkness.

"Yes," he said in the direction of the sound, "we do enjoy standing around in the dark."

"When the alternative is being inside there with those people," Aria added, motioning toward the meeting hall.

Oglok padded up and snorted again. He added a couple more barks and growls for good measure.

Blackthorn laughed. "You are very wise, my friend," he said to the Mock-Man.

"How so?" asked Aria, who spoke little of Oglok's language and had bothered to learn only the barest words and phrases in all her time traveling with him over the past few months.

"It's hard to translate directly," the general explained, "but it involves offering fine textile products to a nudist colony and expecting them to appreciate the craftsmanship."

"Ah. Pearls before swine," Aria replied, nodding.

Blackthorn's eyes widened. He'd forgotten that phrase, along with much of the rest of his life on Earth, but her saying it aloud brought it back to him with a bang.

"How—how could you *possibly* know that old saying?"

Her smile was halfway and sarcastic again. "There is still much you don't know about me, John."

"Much?" he said. "In all this time, I think I could jot down everything about you that I've discovered on the front of an envelope and have room left over for stamps."

She shrugged.

"I must admit I have enjoyed the time we have spent together thus far," she said. "So, no matter what those idiots in there decide, I will continue to travel with you."

Oglok barked his agreement.

"Whether you like it or not," she added. "Because you would be lost without me." She nodded toward the Mock-Man. "Without *us*, really."

Oglok agreed with this, too.

Blackthorn looked from one of them to the other and then smiled.

"Alright, then," he said at last. "I suppose I shouldn't be greedy, or impatient, with the people of this planet. They'll decide what they decide, and I'll respect that decision."

"And if they reject us?" she asked.

"Then we'll keep doing what we've been doing. We'll keep fighting to make a difference, one village and hamlet at a time."

Aria nodded. Oglok roared his approval.

A minute later, the door opened on the meeting hall and a slender young man emerged. His hair was brown and tousled and he wore a simple peasant's outfit of brown and tan. He looked around, his eyes adjusting to the growing darkness, and then approached the trio. He nodded respectfully to each of them, his manner somewhat nervous and agitated, and then turned to the man in black.

"General Blackthorn," he said. "The leaders have reached an agreement."

Blackthorn felt his heart speed up slightly. "Yes?"

"They will not attack the First Men directly—not now. But..." He looked at Aria and Oglok and his nervousness increased. "But they are willing to try to coordinate their actions. To exchange information—military intelligence, as you put it. To try to work together on some of the more limited operations you suggested."

Blackthorn absorbed this and then nodded.

"Alright. Alright." He smiled a tight smile at the young man. "Judan, isn't it?"

"Yes, sir."

"Thank you for the information, Judan. It's not quite what I hoped for, but it's certainly better than nothing."

The man nodded and then excused himself and hurried away into the night.

"That's it, then," Blackthorn said to his two companions. "Some limited cooperation. That's what we're getting."

"For now," Aria replied. "And it's a start."

Oglok barked agreement.

"Yes," Blackthorn said, nodding. "Yes, it's a start." He turned and moved toward the doorway, heading back into the meeting hall. "And a start is all we can reasonably ask for."

The other two entered behind him and he reached back to close the door.

"For now," he added. "For now."

In the hills above the village, a man clad all in red watched through ultra-sophisticated binoculars and listened via a tiny but incredibly powerful unidirectional microphone.

"Wonderful," whispered the man to no one but himself. "Absolutely wonderful."

He lowered the binoculars for a moment and laughed softly, then raised them again and watched as his former commanding general and the two Martians who had taken up with him disappeared back inside the building.

"You launch that rebellion, General," he said aloud. "You do everything in your power to sweep the First Men and their legions away." His smile was a crooked slash of white in the darkness of the forest. "And once you've done that, the way will be clear for me to take over the entire planet."

David Morningstar put away his binoculars and listening device and climbed into his flyer. Moments later he had lofted into the darkening sky and was sailing toward the horizon.

"Limited cooperation, you say?"

"For now, sire, yes," Judan answered, speaking into the communications box, nervously running a hand through his tousled brown hair all the while.

A pause. Silence; nothing but a low hum echoed across the audio channel for several seconds.

"I am most troubled by this development," came the voice on the other end at last. "Most troubled."

"Yes, sire."

"Action must be taken at once. Decisive action. *Severe* action." The voice hesitated for a moment. Then, "Perhaps I may even have to consult with the *others*, should this situation grow any further out of hand."

"Sire?"

"Never mind. Go back to the meeting. Gather up all the information you can. All the names, all the regions and tribes. What weapons they possess; what resources. Bring that to me at once."

"Of course, sire."

"That is all," the voice stated flatly, before the connection was closed. The communication box fell silent, even the hum vanishing.

Judan switched off the device and hid it away among his belongings before hurrying back across the village to the meeting hall.

He had more work to do before this night was over. After all, the Black Sorcerer had commanded it.

CONTRIBUTORS

Mark Bousquet is the author of the novels *Dreamer's Syndrome* (a speculative fantasy), *Adventures of the Five: The Coming of Frost* (a kid's adventure), and *Harpsichord and the Wormhole Witches* (a sci-fi actioner). He writes reviews of Doctor Who, science-fiction films, and whatever strikes his fancy at Atomic Anxiety (*http://atomicanxiety.wordpress.com/*). He recently earned his Ph.D. in American Studies from Purdue University and teaches at the University of Nevada, Reno.

James Burns is a graphic designer and illustrator who lives in Atlanta, Georgia. At age 45, he wrote and drew his first comic book, *Detached*, about his experiences with eye surgery. James' other comics include *Daemon Process* and *The Astral Crusader*. His other contributions include the first comic appearance of "Lance Star, Sky Ranger," as well as the 80-page anthology entitled *Real Magicalism*, which he also edited. His work has also appeared in the last several editions of *Not My Small Diary*. His weekly comic strip, *Grumbles*, ran for six and a half years in Atlanta's *Sunday Paper*. His comic work can be found online at *www.jamesburnsdesign.com/comics*.

Joe Crowe is lead writer and editor for *RevolutionSF.com*, a criticism, commentary, and comedy magazine about sci-fi and its related genres. Crowe is a copy editor and writer at the media company Birmingham News. He copy-edited and contributed stories for the comic-book commentary series *ASSEMBLED!* and edits sci-fi books and stories and hosts the game show "Stump the Geeks" at conventions. He lives in Birmingham, Alabama.

Comics, and the creation of such, have been an obsession for most of **Chris Kohler's** life. Many years had been spent trying to be the next John Byrne (or at least the next Sal Buscema) while floundering for some sort of direction and style to go along with the passion. Finally, at age thirty, there was a synergy between the discipline required in order to draw and the joy felt due to drawing. Since then Chris has worked on a variety of short comic stories while looking into larger projects. He's been producing illustrations for Van Allen Plexico's *Sentinels* novel series for the last four years, as well as the ongoing *Portland Underground* comic project for the last two.

When not making excuses to do anything and everything else, **Bobby Nash** writes. A multitasker, Bobby's certain that he does not suffer from ADD, but instead... ooh, shiny. When he finally manages to put fingers to the keyboard, Bobby writes novels, comic books, short prose, novellas, graphic novels, and even a little pulp fiction just for good measure. You can check out Bobby's work at www.bobbynash.com, www.facebook.com/bobbyenash, www.twitter.com/bobbynash, www.lance-star.com, and http://BEN-Books.blogspot.com among other places across the web.

James Palmer has written articles, interviews, and fiction for Airship 27 Productions, Pro Se Productions, and White Rocket Books. He lives in Georgia with his wife and daughter. For more examples of his fiction, please visit *www.jamespalmerbooks.com*.

Van Allen Plexico writes and edits for a variety of publishers. Best known for his "Sentinels" series of superhero novels and the *ASSEMBLED!* books of comics commentary that he created and edited, he also helped create and edit New Pulp anthologies such as *Gideon Cain: Demon Hunter* and *Mars McCoy: Space Ranger*, as well as contributing stories and novellas for numerous others. He lives near St. Louis and serves as an Assistant Professor at Southwestern Illinois College. See more of his work at *www.plexico.net* and follow him at *www.twitter.com/vanallenplexico*

Sean Taylor writes prose, graphic novels and comic books (yes, Virginia, there is a difference between comic books and graphic novels). In his writing life, he has directed the "lives" of zombies, super heroes, goddesses, dominatrices, Bad Girls, Pulp Heroes, and yes, even frogs.

He's the former managing editor of Campfire (formerly Elfin) graphic novels. He's also been a staff writer, managing editor and editorial vice president for iHero Entertainment's *Writer's Digest* Grand Prize Zine Award-winning *Cyber Age Adventures* magazine ("The very first zine award, as a matter of fact," he adds with great pride).

He's also the former editor-in-chief of Shooting Star Comics, and he has written and edited for the role-playing game industry, having contributed to the DCU Role Playing Game published by West End Games. He's the former editor for the *Baptist Men Edition of On Mission* magazine and the former associate editor of *On Mission* magazine. He has won several awards for his periodical and fiction work and has contributed articles and book and music reviews to many national periodicals.

For more information visit *www.taylorverse.com*.

I.A. Watson loves telling stories, especially the sort with heroes and villains that speak to the best parts of us about our own morals and beliefs. He's the author of *Robin Hood: King of Sherwood* and *Robin Hood: Arrow of Justice* and his work appears in anthologies like *Gideon Cain: Demon Hunter*, *Sentinels: Alternate Visions*, and the popular *Sherlock Holmes: Consulting Detective* volumes one to three. He received eleven nominations for awards in 2010 and won Best Short Story category in the Pulp Factory Awards. Most of his trophy made it across the Atlantic to his home in Yorkshire, England. When he's not writing, Ian charges people far too much to set up companies, deliver projects, and troubleshoot ailing corporations. That also includes stories, heroes, and villains.

Made in the USA
Charleston, SC
16 September 2015